Roger Meadows is also the author of *HANGMAN, A Deadly Game*, a suspense novel about the boundaries of personal honesty, and what happens when they are violated.

# ROGER MEADOWS

# A CHANCE ENCOUNTER

*For Sharon,*
*God's Blessings!*
*Roger Meadows*

This novel is a work of fiction. Any resemblance to actual events or persons, living or dead, is entirely coincidental and beyond the intent of either the author or publisher.

ISBN: 1502388537
ISBN 13: 9781502388537

*For my wife Wanda and my mother, Lorene, who read to me*

# PART I: THE SEA

# CHAPTER 1

*O* *ctober 1999:* I was alone in the vast Pacific Ocean. The late morning sun hovered over my wake and a flock of white cumulous grazed on the western horizon. A few had merged to create a rainsquall, its blue-purple rain churning the surface. It was beautiful. I filled my lungs with sea air and blessed my decision to be there.

Just to the left of the squall, a dark speck appeared. Binoculars turned it into a cigarette boat, probably sixty feet in length. It was making tracks, cutting a long wake, heading opposite to my course, toward the California coast. It was black, an unusual color. As it drew nearer, passing by a couple of miles away, the staccato roar of its engines interrupted the silence. What was a boat like that doing out here?

It was the closest contact of a human being for the three weeks since I'd sailed out of the Strait of Juan de Fuca in Washington. My quest for solitude caused a universal reaction from my acquaintances, "Gideon, you're nuts!"

The wind was swinging around, so I changed to a flatter headsail to get back on course. When I returned to the cockpit, another boat appeared in the distance, dead ahead. Without the course change, I might have missed it. The ocean was getting crowded; two boats in thirty minutes. The sun was nearing its zenith so I took a quick sun-sight and position plot, recording it in the log.

Wouldn't hurt to stay on course and see what they were up to. They didn't seem to be moving, but we weren't closing rapidly. My little boat is seaworthy; but swift, it isn't.

As distance decreased, it was apparent something wasn't right. Its sails weren't drawing properly. They were hoisted, but slack. The boat rounded up into the wind, then fell off with the sails flapping and the booms swinging back and forth. No one was visible, and something else was odd: the craft sat low in the water.

It was a fine-looking yacht, fifty feet or more, two masts, three sails, a ketch rig. All three sails began to draw for a few minutes, then got out of trim again since the helm was out of control. She was beautiful, dark green with cream-colored deck and house.

What the hell was wrong? There had to be a connection to the black boat.

What would I do now? It was obvious that whoever was on board might be in trouble. I couldn't sail on without checking it out. Why did this have to happen? I'd sworn off other peoples' problems. Now what could I do? Board her and see what the story is? There goes the solitude. I heard somewhere it's okay to whine if you're by yourself.

The wind had picked up and clouds started to congregate. As I drew nearer, the big boat went through another cycle, presenting her stern with the name *First Edition* lettered in gold. Her home port was San Francisco.

My boat was named *Chips* after the cedar and oak she was made of and the silicon chips in the computer industry that ground me down. Boarding wouldn't be easy. Even low in the water, *First Edition* had higher freeboard, and *Chips* had no engine.

As she came toward me and passed within fifty yards, I shouted as loud as possible, *"Hey! First Edition! Anybody aboard?"* Nothing happened. A repeated hail produced no result. We were close to her next stall into the wind. I blasted a canister-type signal horn several times. Still nothing stirred. As close as we were, the sound was loud enough to wake the dead. Whoops. Not a good thought.

Resigned to the decision, I scrambled to get everything ready while *First Edition* made another cycle: fenders out, boarding ladder in case of a miss, long tether to my harness, and lines to stern and bow of *Chips* to carry with me when I clambered aboard.

A worse possibility than falling overboard would be falling between the two hulls as wave action slammed them together. Here she came again. My knees were knocking.

I sheeted in my mainsail and accelerated to the point where she'd be when she slowed. Closer…closer…Now! I engaged the wheel brake and darted forward. We bounced against the fenders. I leaped for the railing.

Made it! Using both hands, I managed to clamber aboard with my lines to *Chips*. Would have been harder with a cutlass in my teeth.

After the boats were tied together, it was a matter of wrestling the big, stiff sails down and under control. I cinched in the little sail at the stern to act as a weather vane to keep the rafted boats into the wind.

With a sense of dread, I headed for the hatch and stuck my head into the gloom created by the clouds and the advance toward evening. The saloon was awash in seawater and flotsam of all description. I shouted again, *"Hello! Anybody here?"* No answer. *"Hello in the boat! Is anyone here?"* Again, no answer.

I didn't have much time. She was taking on water, and it looked deep enough to cause problems finding the source. I dashed back to the rail, leaped down to the deck of *Chips* and dropped the flogging mainsail. I hurried below for a waterproof flashlight.

Back on *First Edition,* surging water was knee deep over the cabin sole. A loud "Meeorow!" startled me and I shone the flashlight around the interior. A calico cat had taken refuge atop some books on a shelf on the front bulkhead. Its eyes glowed as it stared at me, mewling plaintively.

"Hang on, cat. We'll see if we can keep afloat." But where are your humans?

There was a gurgling of water running. It seemed to come from my left, behind the storage areas in the galley. I opened cabinet doors and hatches, reaching under water to clear away soggy cartons and packages. The problem wasn't visible, but a current streamed against my hand. Holding my breath, I stuck my head under water and crawled half into the cabinet. A hose had been disconnected from a through-hull fitting, and the ocean was pouring into the vessel. Closing a seacock stopped the flow.

Were there more? I splashed through the water and debris, opening hatches and feeling for hoses and water flow. In the engine compartment, everything seemed in order.

The navigation station was on the starboard side, by the ladder that descended into the mess in the saloon. Circuit breakers were all popped on the electrical panel. Something else caught my eye: The panels on the radios were shattered, but the other instruments looked okay. Hard to tell what had happened, but it looked deliberate.

Maybe it would be best to take the cat, open the valve, and get the hell out of there. The situation had a creepy feel about it. There hadn't been time to search the rest of the boat, though, and whoever had been on board deserved better than my running away. It looked like no choice but to pump the damn thing out.

I sloshed back through the water and up to the cockpit. The sea was running five-foot waves, and the boats were not dancing in sync. I found more fenders and heavy dock lines and stabilized them, then located a large manual bilge pump mounted in another hatch. I put the handle in place and started pumping. There was a satisfying resistance as the pump primed and started sucking water. The hundreds of gallons below would take me most of the approaching night.

Night fell, and with it an intensifying cloud cover. It began to rain. I took a quick break and jumped back aboard Chips, went below, and climbed into foul weather gear. I took a long drink of water and devoured a couple of energy bars, then remembered the cat. I grabbed a can of tuna and a can opener.

Back aboard the big yacht, I placed the opened can of tuna on a shelf the cat could reach. It had not moved from the perch atop the books. Maybe the water level *was* a little lower, but it was hard to tell.

I pumped on, exhausted, into the night. The rain stopped for a time, then resumed with more vigor. Lucky it wasn't a violent storm. I regretted making the course change that caused me to be here.

At three o'clock in the morning, the weather broke and skies began to clear. The water level was finally coming down. It was a little more than ankle deep above the sole, so I took a break, collapsing on a bunk back aboard *Chips.*

I awoke with a start. For a moment I couldn't remember where I was. Then it came back to me: there was a large problem tied to my boat. Concentrating on keeping it afloat, I'd pushed the real problem to the back of my mind. What would I do with it? It seemed to me that there was no choice but to get it into the hands of authorities, and let them figure it out. Then I could be on my way again. During my movement

about the boat, there were no signs of life—or death, for that matter—
except for the cat.

I started coffee brewing and went on deck. It was five in the
morning and stars were visible. I shot three favorites with the sextant
and plotted my position, recording it in the log. San Diego was the
nearest U. S. port, and it was just under three hundred miles away.
San Francisco, *First Edition's* homeport, was even farther. Maybe
something worked on the other boat that would allow summoning
help, but the looks of the instruments made it doubtful. All I'd
brought was a short-range handheld radio, another avoidance of modern technology.

I resumed pumping until the water receded below cabin sole level.
The sun made a spectacular appearance on the horizon as that milestone
was reached. We were still riding to the rolling waves, still weather-
vaned into the wind.

The tops of the battery boxes were above water, so I went below and
punched in all the breakers except the communications stuff. A few green
lights appeared in the gloom. The pumps in the bilges kicked on with a
welcome whine. The cat had moved from its perch.

I dragged across to my own home and fried a skillet of potatoes,
onions, and Spam. Thinking about food, I thought again about the cat
but didn't remember seeing the can of tuna on the shelf. Perhaps the cat
had knocked it off.

Back aboard *First Edition*, in the light of dawn, I contemplated what
to do next. There seemed to be only two options: If the radios worked,
summon help. If not, then try to deliver both boats back to the main-
land. The first step required descending into the saloon to check out the
boat's systems. The cat was crying from forward, so I went to investigate.

It was standing in the V-berth in the bow next to a jumbled blanket
I'd noticed when first looking through the boat. The cat's tail was standing straight up, the tip twitching, and it peered intently at the blanket.
It arched its back and stared at me, then retreated as I drew near. I moved
the edge of the blanket to disclose a tiny bare foot.

# CHAPTER 2

As I stared, dumbfounded, the toes spread, and curled again. I lifted the blanket to reveal a little girl, lying on her stomach with her knees drawn up, bottom in the air. She had her hands clamped over her eyes, and she lay still.

I was amazed. She'd been hiding here all the time I'd been working with the boats. I'd never paid much attention to little kids, but guessed she was three or four years old—past babyhood, but not by a great deal.

"Sweetheart, don't be afraid. I won't hurt you." It was all I could think of to say. She didn't stir, continuing to hide her eyes with her hands. The empty tuna can was next to her.

I picked her up and turned her to face me. Her body was rigid. Her eyes opened to a squint, then she squeezed them shut and began to cry a loud, wailing cry.

Ignoring her fear of me, I held her and murmured in her ear. "It's okay...I won't hurt you...Let me take care of you and we'll figure out what to do next...you'll have to tell me what happened to you."

It astounded me to think of this little person, alone and trapped in a sinking vessel, hiding in the darkness. What must have gone through her mind? What gave her the determination and discipline to hide from me? What strange circumstance left her here?

She was a pretty little creature. That brief glimpse revealed eyes of golden brown, and her hair was long and dark. It was now matted in tangles from hiding under the blanket. She had soiled herself, a forgivable lapse considering her circumstance.

Her sobs gradually began to subside as I continued murmuring to her and stroking her matted hair. Her body became less rigid against me.

I began a one-sided conversation, pausing between questions for reply, but she remained silent.

"My name is Gideon. What's yours?

"We have to become acquainted so we can take care of each other. Can you tell me your name?

"What is the name of your cat? I saw your cat before I saw you, then your cat led me to where you were. It wanted me to find you and help you. I think it likes me because I gave it some tuna. I think it likes you, because it shared with you."

I kept up the one-sided dialogue, hoping it would calm her. The situation had become more complicated: not only two boats to take care of, but a little girl and a cat. I didn't have a clue how to take care of a little girl. Driving two boats at the same time seemed the smaller of the problems.

It was easy to understand how she could be afraid of me, a stranger, in such circumstances. I'd been letting my hair and beard grow, and probably looked like a wild man. My hair is red and naturally curly, so it rose about my head in a wild tangle. My heavy beard concealed most of my face.

"Sweetheart, I'm going to put you down for a few minutes and see if I can start the engine on the boat. Then we can have hot water. We'll find clean clothes for you and something for you to eat. Will that be okay?" No response.

"I won't leave you. No matter what, I'll take care of you."

What the hell else could I do?

The cat came close when I put the girl down, no longer wary of me.

The pumps were still running. I opened the hatch to the engine and found the water level hadn't been high enough to reach any intakes. I hoped the batteries had enough juice. The damaged panels appeared related only to the communications and navigation gear. I'd need to go to the cockpit to start the engine.

The girl was still watching me, but covered her eyes again when I glanced in her direction.

"Little Girl, I have to climb outside a minute to start the engine. I'll be right back. You can listen and yell, 'Okay!' when it starts." I didn't expect anything, but it would keep her engaged.

The engine cranked flawlessly and came to life.

I went back below and checked out the head. The shower stall's base formed a small tub. The owners probably had set it up with their daughter in mind. She needed to be cleaned up, fed, and set right. I started the water running. The big question kept popping back into my mind: What in God's name had happened on the boat? Had they fallen overboard? Had they been kidnapped? Or worse?

The owner's stateroom was set up in the stern, so the girl's stuff must be forward where she was. "Babe, I'm going to find clean clothes for you, and we're going to have a bath and lunch. Is that okay with you?" No response.

"Where are your clothes?" This time, a little finger pointed at the bank of drawers next to a hanging locker. At last, a response.

The bottom drawer had been under water, but the others revealed her clothes, neatly folded. In one I found a tee shirt and underpants with pink flowers on them. Another gave up a pink sweat suit with a bear appliquéd on the chest.

Addressing my charge again, I said, "Babe, I may look strange to you because I have a lot of hair on my face, but behind it I'm a good guy. You'll see. Remember I told you my name is Gideon. Can you tell me your name? Otherwise, I'll have to call you Babe."

She looked down and said something.

"What did you say?"

"I'm notta pig," she said, speaking in a stronger voice.

"What?" Then I got it. "Oh, you're talking about the movie star pig, aren't you? I never thought of that. Sometimes when someone is really cute, or we like them a lot, we call them 'Baby' or 'Babe.' Do you understand?"

She nodded.

"I think the farmer in the movie felt that way about the pig. But I won't call you that anymore. It's obvious to me that you are a pretty girl, and I'd like to have your name."

She spoke again in a soft voice, "My Mama said not to talk to strangers."

"I understand, and you've been really good, hiding like you were told, and not talking to me. But now things are different. I'm sure your mother would agree that we have to work together to decide what to do next. It will help if we can talk with each other."

"When is Mama coming back?" She looked up at me with wide-open brown eyes. Her face began to contort again and she started to cry.

"I just don't know where she is or what happened. I have a little boat and was sailing by when I saw your boat. No one was here except you and the cat. We'll stick together until we know what to do next. You've been a brave girl. Please try not to cry."

She rubbed her face with the back of her fist. "I w-want my M-mama."

"I know, but for right now, you need to keep being brave. Come with me to take your bath."

She looked down at her feet. "I'm poopy," she said softly.

"It's okay. You've had a hard time. Do you want me to help you clean up?"

The thought seemed to change her focus, "People aren't s'posta see your bum."

"That's a good rule, but can you do it yourself?"

"I can do it."

"Well, just put your clothes outside the door and I'll take them away."

"The doctor has to see your bum, because she gives you a shot. Sometimes it hurts, but I don't cry."

"Well that's really good. And I suppose the doctor sees lots of bums, so one more doesn't make much difference."

"Yes," she agreed.

Thanks to bums, we had broken the ice

While she splashed in the bath, I rummaged in the bins and lockers. Seawater had done some damage, but the canned goods had all been lettered with permanent marker and the labels removed. Remembering my own childhood, I selected a can of Spaghetti-Os and started it heating.

I knocked on the door of the head. "Is it okay for me to come and help you finish? Are there still plenty of bubbles?"

"It's okay."

Her bum was safely hidden beneath the foam, but the better light revealed beautiful skin of mocha and cream. I shampooed her hair, which was dark brown, not black. I turned my head and held a towel for her to wrap herself. "While I dry your hair, will you tell me your name?"

"Ab-Abigail."

"Abigail. That's a pretty name. Does your mother call you Abby?"

"Sh-she calls me Abigail."

"Then I'll call you Abigail also." I wasn't used to conversation with someone so small, so I had to listen closely. She spoke softly, low in spirit, and continued to hang her head.

"Can you dress yourself, or do you want me to help?"

"I can do it," she said.

The cat followed me, rubbing against my leg, until I provided a dish of cat food from a locker.

While Abigail ate her Spagetti-Os, I checked the electronics. Nothing worked except the radar. At least it would be helpful in single-handed sailing. An alarm could be set to sound upon contact with a target.

Without long-range communication, I saw no choice but to set a course for California. I tried to control my frustration at the situation I found myself in. I couldn't blame the little girl, but here I was, finally doing something for *me* for a change, and it wasn't going to work. For more than ten years, my life has not been my own. Every moment of those years was committed to the clients I served. Of course I could have refused, but I have an overactive sense of obligation, without knowing how to apply it properly. It resulted in the loss of my marriage and a separation from people who were my friends.

"Why couldn't you have focused more of that dedication on us?" Regina had asked, after it was over. Good question. But for now, no looking back. Decision made; get on with it.

I made a quick mental list to accomplish in short order: Rig the boats and get underway; look at the boat's papers for clues to the owners and what happened to them; and start cleaning up the mess.

I found deck shoes and life jacket for Abigail and took her on deck with me for a noon position plot. The sun was shining, not a cloud visible. Seas were running about three feet.

I found a lanyard and clipped it on the harness built into her life jacket, then to one of the jacklines the previous skipper had rigged. These were strong webbing strips running the length of the yacht. "Abigail, I'm going to go aboard my little boat and get a couple of things I need. You're hooked to this line, so you can watch me. See, the hook will slide along so you can move about. I'll be right back. Okay?"

I went back aboard *Chips* and packed a bag with clothing and toiletries. *First Edition* would have to become the mother ship. Abigail said little as we sat in the cockpit and I scanned charts. It appeared best to head north to dodge the strong southerly California Current along the coast, then let the North Pacific current push us in to San Francisco. Wouldn't take more than a day or two longer than San Diego and we'd be in her home port.

I spent the next half hour rigging to tow *Chips* with heavy lines that would trail her about fifty yards astern. I closed the hatches, bent on a storm trysail, and lashed the boom amidship to make her trail properly. Back on board *First Edition*, I led the towlines through chocks in the stern and to her two primary winches normally used for adjusting the headsail. *Chips* was cast loose and we used the engine to pull away.

Abigail watched all of my scurrying back and forth with sad eyes, saying little in response to my explanations. She was a dejected soul, completely outside the world she knew, without the warmth and love of her parents, wherever they were.

I cleated off the towlines and hoisted the mainsail on *First Edition*, then the big, powerful genoa jib. The sails bit into the stiff breeze, the big yacht heeled, then began her charge through the waves. I killed the diesel, set the steering vane, and we were on our way to whatever the future held for our crew of three.

I retrieved a comb from below, and sat Abigail on my lap. "Let's see if we can comb out some of the tangles. Okay? Let me know if anything hurts."

She nodded. The sun and fresh air had dried her hair and it blew in soft curls about her face.

"What's your cat's name?"

"Her name is Jemima. We call her Jem. Mama said she can sing pretty."

We worked on the hair with an occasional "Ow!" from her and answering "Sorry" from me. I finished by braiding it in one long queue, tied with a ribbon.

"You can pretend you're a pirate. Pirates and sailors in the old days wore their hair in braids."

"I'm notta pie-rut!" Then a pause and cloudy expression. "My mama braids my hair. When is Mama comin' back?"

I had to give her my usual answer. "I don't know, Sweetheart. We'll go to your house, and see if we can find her." I knew in my heart that there wasn't much of a chance of a happy ending. There was little evidence of a struggle, no blood I could find, but how could everything be all right? How could I face this little person on my lap and explain to her the evil things that happen in the world?

I got my equipment and began the process of making myself more human. I sat across the cockpit from Abigail. "Watch this. I'm going to get rid of this beard and hair, so you can see that there is a man inside."

She watched intently as I used the scissors, letting handfuls of hair fly to the breeze. Eventually I got down to lather and a safety razor, shaving by feel, using a bucket of water at my feet.

She walked unsteadily across the cockpit sole to take a closer look.

I gave her a big smile. "What do you think? See, I told you there was a man in here."

She smiled back at me for the first time, and felt of my cheek. "You have a face! I didn't know you hadda face."


I was weary from being up most of the night pumping out the boat, getting rigged and underway, and worrying about how to get my unwelcome charges to port. Single-handed sailing under the best of conditions is tiring, and some criticize it as unsafe. Before the encounter, I had managed a reasonable schedule of catnaps and watches, albeit with some risk if I encountered a stray ship not alert to its own radar. With Abigail, I had to worry about her schedule and keeping her safe if she was awake while I slept. She had faithfully followed her mother's instructions. Hopefully, she would obey mine.

I kept avoiding the other two chores; cleaning up the boat below and doing some research in the owners' papers. I decided to put it off until next day. It was time for a meeting of the captain and crew. She had climbed on the seat next to me, and was lying on her back, hugging a stuffed bear.

"Abigail, let's talk about how we'll operate together."

She sat up and looked seriously at me, mouth open, the tip of her tongue pushing and twisting behind her lower teeth. Saliva ran out one corner of her mouth, so she slurped, then wiped her chin with her hand.

"I'm going to stay awake as much as I can, but sometimes I have to lie down and sleep. When I'm sleeping, you must promise me that you won't ever, ever, ever come up here by yourself. Okay? Do you understand?"

She fidgeted in the seat, and drummed her heels on the fiberglass. She nodded her head.

"Don't *ever* come up here unless I come with you. You could fall in the water and I couldn't find you. I don't want that to happen. You'll stay down below unless I say so, okay?"

"'Kay," she said softly.

"We're going to sail to San Francisco, where I think you live. It will take several days and nights for us to get there."

I made us our supper and tucked her in for the night. I went on deck and checked the horizon, then went below and read from *Snow White* until she dropped off to sleep.

I put myself on a schedule of two hours awake and one hour sleeping. It was a long night, that first one with the new direction my life had taken. Skies were partly overcast, with the wind steady and seas still running at three feet.

When it came time for my last nap before dawn, I tacked, setting a course as close to the wind as I could. I checked on Abigail and went to the quarter-berth to sleep.

# CHAPTER 3

In my dream, we were seated around a conference table, going through a merger agreement line by line. Tension was high, and the opposing counsel and I were debating a key clause in the negotiations. Suddenly she grabbed my nose and started shaking my head from side to side.

I awoke with a start, groggy from the night's watch. Abigail was standing beside me in her pajamas, grasping my nose and shaking me awake.

"Kitty-on! Kitty-on! My Barbies are all wet! They're icky!" She held a doll over my face, dripping seawater.

"Oh-h-h," I groaned, rubbing my eyes. "You're right. We'll see if we can fix that. Let me get out of bed. Do you want breakfast first?"

She shook her head. First things first. I yearned for coffee. I was amused by her fracturing my name, Gideon, into "Kitty-on," so let it be. Cute.

I stuck my head out of the main hatch. The horizon was clear, and *Chips* still followed in our wake.

Next to more important matters. Abigail had assembled a pile of wet Barbie dolls, in various states of elegant dress and undress. They were lying on the teak-and-holly sole in a widening pool of seawater. Fortunately our yacht was blessed with desalinization equipment and a large fresh water tank. I ran a bath and put Abigail and all of her retinue in it together. There were at least two guys in the group, but maybe no one would mind.

After the bath and breakfast, the crew assembled in the cockpit. The sun was up and we were blessed with a warm breeze, which drove us forward at five knots. It was about the best I could get out of the boat with the drag of *Chips*.

Abigail began to place the dolls in a row on the upwind seat. "They're takin' a break, so they can dry their clothes. When their hair gets dry, will you braid it like mine?"

"We can give it a try, but my fingers may be too big. Do you want me to braid that guy's hair?" I indicated a bronzed, handsome dude with razor cut blond hair.

She scoffed at me with a big smile. "Boys don't braid their hair, silly."

"It's not so silly. I've seen guys with braided hair, but you're right about him. It's too short. Who is that guy?"

"He's Tarzan. And this is Ariel. She's a mermaid." My question unleashed an introduction to the entire cast. There was Sleeping Beauty, Cruella De Vil, and Pocahontas; Prince Charming, Prunella, and Snow White; Deserella, Ursula, and Barbie-Q. The list went on, through more than twenty.

She waited until last to present a dark-haired beauty and a smaller companion. "This is Christie. She looks just like Mama." Christie had beautiful brown skin.

Then she held up the little one. "And this is Desiree. My Mama says she looks like me, but not as pretty." Desiree was a toddler copy of Christie.

"I agree with your mom. Desiree is cute, but not as pretty as you."

The resilience of the young amazed me. Abigail had managed to talk about the past without clouds gathering. Earlier, while she ate her breakfast cereal, she'd asked me that question I could not answer, "When are Mama and Daddy coming back?"

I'd put off looking at documents and cleaning up after the water incursion as long as I could. Taking care of Abigail and the boats took first priority, but that had all stabilized.

Abigail was working with her dolls, getting them in order after their bath. I took her below and got her settled with some books and crayons in the forward V-berth.

The boat had to be treated like a crime scene, basing any actions on movies and television. I got a supply of garbage bags and gathered all the stuff that had floated about in the water that filled the saloon. With a flashlight, I searched all the corners and crevices. Jem thought it was a new game, and stalked imaginary foes alongside me, chasing the flashlight spot. Near the electrical panels, there were a half-dozen 9-millimeter shell casings rolling about in the corners. I bagged them in a separate Ziploc bag, picking them up with a pencil just like the cops do it.

On the floor under the gimbel-mounted stove, there was a glint of metal. I raked it out with my pencil. It was a small gold ear stud, about the diameter of a pencil eraser. I picked it up by the shaft and held it in the bright beam. Looking back at me was the snarling face of a lion. Interesting. I bagged it and looked for the back clip, but didn't find it.

I got on my hands and knees and wiped the entire cockpit sole and all of the drains with damp paper towels, bagging and labeling each with a diagram of where it came from. The police might give me hell for disturbing everything, but there didn't seem to be a good way to avoid it. Living in the big boat would disturb things more than what I was doing. Fingerprints were another sticky question. I hadn't taken any precautions to avoid touching anything, but when I looked in the navigation station I put on gloves.

Abigail had been following my progress from her perch, and now came to me. "Kitty-on, look at this." She held up a picture she had colored in her book.

"Hey, that's pretty. I think blue turtles are the best kind. Now let me show you something I found." I held the earring in the beam of my light, turning the lion face to her.

"Is this your mother's earring?"

She touched the clear plastic with a finger. "I don't think so. She wears loopy ones."

"Thank you for showing me the picture. Will you color another one for me?"

She nodded and climbed back in the berth, steady on her sea legs against the continuing motion of the boat.

I stuck my head out of the hatch to check the horizon. All was well, so I went back to work. The navigation desk was full of the expected—pencils, parallel rules, dividers, protractors. Pads of paper had scribblings of numbers from position plots and others I could not decipher. There were instruction booklets for various instruments. What I did not see was the logbook. It would normally be right on top, ready for periodic entries. I dug deeper and found it jammed underneath all the other clutter, in the back corner of the desk.

I flipped it open and turned through several pages. The entries were mostly short, starting with a time entry for each watch, and a position plot. Weather conditions were concise and to the point. If they were keeping a diary of the events of each day, those writings had to be in another notebook. Her handwriting was loopy like her earrings, and back slanted, with circular dots over the i's. His entries were all in strong block printing, all capitals.

With my gloved hands, I flipped through the pages until I came to the last entries. The first one on the last page was similar to the previous pages, the time given as 0800 hours. The last one, in her hand, was of a different nature.

"1115 hours. Black powerboat following us for the last several miles, now gaining speed. I'm scared. Brad said he tried to contact by radio, but no answer. Oh God, don't let it be pirates. What will I do with my baby? They're almost on us. I'll hide her the best..."

The entry ended in a squiggly line. And that's all there was.

I put the log back in the corner where it came from. Among the other papers, there was a folder of specifications on the boat from the builder, including a bill of sale itemizing all of the options, like the sticker on a new car window, but much more detailed. In the heading, the owners' names were listed: Bradley R. Dickerson and Solene G. Dickerson. Abigail's parents.

It hit me with a punch in the gut. I knew who they were. The beautiful Solene was an Olympic gold medalist in both the 400 and 800 meters a few years ago from a small African country. Seems like she competed for someone in Europe...France? She'd met and married an American journalist shortly after she returned to her homeland. He was assigned to cover the civil strife in her country and helped her escape when the government fell.

Theirs was a storybook princess-and-knight drama that caught the country's fancy. It was covered for weeks on the talk shows and in the magazines and papers. They married and settled in California, and I had lost track of them since.

Couldn't think of anything else, but there was a knot in the pit of my stomach. I now had names and faces for Abigail's parents, and the chance that they were alive seemed more remote.

Wind and weather continued fair for the afternoon. Abigail and I sat in the cockpit as the sun descended in the west, over my left shoulder. The wind direction had shifted counter clockwise, so I eased the sheets and disengaged the steering vane for a while. With the more favorable wind, the boat heeled less and the motion became easier.

Abigail made a game of running against the limit of her tether and letting it spring her back into the center of the cockpit, like Muhammad Ali's rope-a-dope maneuver. Then she started fiddling with the Wichard hook that held it to the jackline.

"Hey! Don't mess with the hook," I scolded.

"Why not?"

"So you won't fall overboard. You must stay hooked up just like I do." I held up the end of my tether.

"Why?"

"Because the ocean is big, and I might not be able to find you. Promise me."

"But I don't wanna be tied up anymore."

"Doesn't make any difference. You still have to do it."

"Don't want to." Stamped her foot, testing me.

"Then you'll spend all your time down below. Not on deck."

"*No!*"

"That's enough. You're going below to think about being good, so we can stay safe."

I engaged self-steering, unhooked Abigail's safety line and carried her below. She put up a token struggle, but soon gave in. "You just as well have a bath and get your pajamas on before I fix your meal."

She kept an unhappy face as we went through the evening preparations. By the time I'd fixed her a little-person meal of pasta with Parmesan and butter flavoring, she had thawed out and was happy to sit on my lap while I read her a story about sea otters. I kissed her forehead and tucked her away for the night.

Being with her and caring for her was a new experience for me, but I couldn't help regretting the change in plans. Most of the time she was well-behaved and always bright, with a sense of humor in her play activities. She no longer asked about her parents, but I observed brief interludes of sadness and quiet time mingled with her bubbly personality. I wondered how much she knew about the events of the day her parents disappeared, but I decided to wait until some healing took place before asking her about it.

When the stars came out, I took an evening sighting. Calculations showed us on course, and seventy-five miles made good since yesterday evening. If everything held about the same, we'd be out three or four more days. I'd begun to fret about making a landfall, and facing the inquisition civilization would bring. In spite of some negative feelings, parting with Abigail had started to occupy my mind.

I checked out the lines to *Chips*, following faithfully in our wake. I'd left the navigation lights on, night and day, so I could track her better in the darkness. During the day, the solar panels were keeping the batteries up. Everything else was in order, so I went below for a short sleep. I set the radar alarm and turned in, soon falling asleep.

A sudden lurch of the yacht brought me instantly awake, alarmed by the change in motion. An inventory of disasters reeled through my sleep-fogged brain. Had we hit something? Was there a violent change in the weather? I yanked on my boots and sprang up the steps, now wide awake.

# CHAPTER 4

I t took me a few moments to figure out what it was. We seemed intact and still sailing forward. I looked astern, and solved the riddle. One of the towlines to *Chips* had parted, and the little yacht was yawing to our starboard. With the unbalanced connection she was skiing at an angle to the tow, like a water skier leaving the wake of the towboat.

The strong side-thrust overpowered the self-steering mechanism and we luffed into the wind, sails fluttering and crackling. I dropped the sails and went below for my safety harness and clipped on, then reeled in my errant *Chips* to re-rig. Bringing in the slack towline confirmed my worries about chafing. It had parted where it went through the bow chock on *Chips*. Getting re-rigged would take some thought. Maybe a piece of anchor chain would work.

Sliding my tether forward on the jackline, I used my light to peer into the chain locker in the bow. No anchor and no chain. Nothing there but nylon line.

Oh God.

Could it really mean that? Chain-wrapped bodies at the bottom of the ocean?

A shiver went down my spine. Oh Christ.

It was no longer possible to ignore the evidence.

I thought about opening the seacocks on *Chips* and letting her go. But when I remembered some of the happiest weeks of my life, sitting in that boatyard in Port Townsend, Washington, I just couldn't do it. For five months I sat by her side watching as she took shape: laying the keel, steam bending her oak frames, fitting her cedar planks, and finally the finishing and rigging. It was a therapy surpassing anything in the handbooks of psychiatry, and was exactly what I needed at the time.

Nothing could change what had happened on this yacht. Getting everything rigged and going again was the best thing I could do. Doubling the line where it went through the chocks should help, and we'd stop and inspect every day or so.

We were soon underway, all sails set and on course for that invisible point in the Pacific where we could make our turn for San Francisco. I went below to finish my short sleep. Even as weary as I was, sleep did not come immediately. Thoughts of the missing chain and anchors, and visions of where they might be now, kept intruding.

After a night of watches, on and off duty, I sat in the cockpit drinking coffee, waiting for the appearance of Abigail and Jem, my two companions. The sun was a half-disc of gold on the horizon, and another sail begin to eclipse it in the distance. We'd seen a boat or two, and could probably reach someone on my handheld radio. I decided the situation was too complex to explain ashore second-hand through a stranger's more powerful radio. I wanted to make the approach in person, with Abigail by my side.

Facing what most people call civilization was not something I relished. I needed those months in the South Seas before I wanted to go back. Having Abigail with me, depending on me, on the other hand, was seeping into my thoughts as an unexpected pleasure, in spite of my initial resentment. I had to accept that I'd begun to think of her as my family, and I'd be damned if I'd let any harm come to her. Those thoughts led to other questions about her real family. Nothing would make me happier than to find her parents alive. But if the worst had happened, what would become of her? Did she have other relatives? Could I find a way to take care of her?

My parents were lost to a car accident when I was about her age, barely able to comprehend the permanent nature of their departure. I went to live with my grandmother, my mother's mother, who is my only living relative that I know of. Life had gone on, and memories of my parents receded as I grew up. I knew I was different from most of the other kids, but I never lacked love and attention. Grandma Maureen O'Brien lives in Modesto, California, and I keep in touch as often as possible. She's middle seventies, and in fine fettle. Leaving her behind for an extended period was the only drawback to my escape plans. She said to call her from Fiji, or wherever, and she'd come for a visit.

My grandmother encouraged me throughout my schooling and career, so I made the most of it. I could certainly afford to provide whatever Abigail needed financially. I received my B.S. in Computer Engineering from Stanford, then went directly into Stanford Law School. I'd like to claim that brilliant foresight put me in the right industry at the right time. It was more a matter of luck, simply pursuing subjects that interested me.

I established myself as an expert in law related to computer technology, just as the fledgling Internet left the nest and began to fly. I joined a conventional law firm right out of law school, but went out on my own when they provided little support for what I enjoyed the most. Since money wasn't my major focus, I often took part of my fees in stock in the startup companies that couldn't afford to pay me. My classmates from computer engineering were salted in firms throughout Silicon Valley, several of them in management positions. Mergers and acquisitions stampeded through the industry. Demand for technology contracts soared. My straightforward legal language and trouble-free agreements created more demand than I could handle. I added lawyers to my firm as rapidly as I could find the right people, but twenty-four-hour days were not uncommon.

Along the way I lost Regina, and finally reached the breaking point in my grueling work schedule. I sold the firm and cashed in all my stock in the companies who'd been my clients. I was astounded when I totaled it all and stashed it away in blue chip mutual funds and certificates of deposit. Good luck prevailed again. Later I was to learn that my exodus from the industry took place precisely before it hit its peak and the bubble burst.

My reverie was broken by the sight of my companions. They appeared in the morning sunlight, Jem jumping over the lower hatch board onto the bridge deck, and Abigail standing on the top step inside. She held her bear in one arm and rubbed her eyes with the back her other hand.

She raised both arms, bear dangling, and looked at me, squinting in the light. "Kitty, will you hold me?" She'd now simplified my new name.

I engaged the steering vane. "Of course, Sweetheart."

I picked her up and sat on the upwind cockpit seat, cuddling her on my lap. Her bare feet peeked out of her flannel nightgown.

"Kitty, what if Mama can't find me? She doesn't know where I am."

"We'll go to the place you lived before you went away on the boat. That's where we're going now."

"Are we almost there?"

"It'll be a few more days. Try not to worry."

She sat up suddenly and pointed. "Look! Look!"

A school of porpoises surrounded us, leaping and frolicking in the waves, their sleek forms golden in the slanting rays of the morning sun.

"They're smiling at us," she said.

"I do believe they are."

There were dozens of them, and they soon pulled ahead of us and disappeared, taking her momentary sadness with them.

The appearance of the dolphin pod presaged good sailing days ahead. We settled into a routine togetherness approaching what I think families might have. Abigail was bright and sunny in disposition, only occasionally lapsing into moments of sadness. I delayed asking her the details of whatever happened on the yacht, instead letting time and routine heal her. For me it was an entirely new experience, giving love and attention to someone without the interference of outside pressures.

The watch schedule seemed to agree with me, and Abigail kept her word about staying below when I napped. We played games from her collection, I read to her, and she entertained me with song and dance. Abigail loved to sing, and invariably illustrated them with dance routines. She used the top of the cabin roof as her stage, adjusting nimbly to the motion of the big yacht as it charged through the waves. "YMCA" was one of her favorites. As she belted out the lyrics, she made each letter: Both arms up in a Y, then elbows up with fingertips at her chest, and so forth. Jem liked to sit on the foredeck, waiting for an errant flying fish to fall into her clutches. The two of them were constantly in sight of each other, Jem filling Abigail's need for a constant, a tie to the past.

One day, however, the fair weather we'd enjoyed began to change. In the afternoon, a cold front started to show itself with a dark bank of clouds in the west. Winds freshened, and seas began to build. A couple of hours before, my noon position plot had indicated that the time had come to turn toward San Francisco. The new heading, coupled with the freshening winds, gave us our best speed of the voyage, with a great, ballooning spinnaker pulling us along.

With the approach of the front, however, we were over-canvassed, and I had to ease off our heading and take it in, replacing it with a small jib.

Abigail and Jem played about on deck. I saw no harm in it, since Abigail wore her life vest and safety harness, latched into the jackline. Jem even had her own life vest, about the size of a beer koozy. I hadn't figured a way to tie her to anything, but cats are supposed to be more surefooted than the rest of us. Abigail was belting out a song, as usual.

"Abigail, you'd better climb down into the cockpit. It's starting to get rough," I said. The bow was occasionally dipping green water, and Jem had wisely retreated to the coach roof beside her.

"Pleeeeze," she said. "Can I finish my song?"

"*May* I finish my song. No, come down right now. You can finish in the cockpit." Geez, I sounded just like a parent.

She obeyed, Jem following.

"I think a storm is coming, so I want you both safe beside me," I explained, trying to soften my command. She looked at me and smiled, so it was okay.

As late afternoon approached, dark clouds obscured the last of the daylight as the front caught up with us. An eerie twilight settled in, with lightning punctuating the gloom. The seas had continued to build under what I judged to be Force Six winds. *Chapman's Piloting* described them for me: "2.5 to 4 meters; whitecaps everywhere; more spray." I'd reefed down as far as I could. Much worse, and we'd go bare poles. At least, I already had a sea anchor out—*Chips*.

I kept Abigail and the cat in the cockpit with me, both humans in bright yellow foul weather gear against the rain that now slanted into us in increasing amounts. Abigail protected Jem inside her parka. I could have put them below, but I wanted them close in case things got worse. We had a life raft in a rigid container on deck. The towlines to *Chips* were alternately going slack, then humming tight as bowstrings. Occasionally *First Edition*'s bow would drive into the backside of a wave, and the seawater would rush down the side decks and into the cockpit. It would quickly drain away with a sucking sound. Abigail showed no fear, sometimes laughing as though riding an amusement park ride.

After one particularly hard impact with a wave, I heard a loud crash from below. Something had come loose in the saloon. I knew I'd better investigate. I looked at Abigail and hesitated. She was hooked in with her tether, and seemed in no discomfort with the yacht's motion. I made a quick decision, a bad decision. I left her there and went below to check on the damage. One of the lockers had opened and canned goods had spilled onto the cabin sole. I quickly scooped them up and put them in the sink.

Brief moments later, I climbed back into the cockpit to find it empty. In panic, I looked forward. A flash of lightning lit a scene I will never forget. Jem scampered toward the foredeck with Abigail in pursuit, tether dangling. Just as she caught up with Jem, a wave crashed over the bow and swept them over the side.

# CHAPTER 5

I saw her in the crest of a wave as she swept past, a tumbling flash of yellow. For a second, her eyes met mine. They were wide with fright, conveying a wordless plea that gripped my heart. I sprang into action, trying to accomplish multiple tasks at the same time. I grabbed the man-overboard pole from its mount on the backstay, and threw it over the stern, into the dark water. Attached to it was a horseshoe-shaped life preserver, and more important, a water-activated strobe light. My watch said six-forty-six.

I whipped out my sheath knife, sharp as a razor, and slashed the towlines to *Chips*. The heading on the binnacle showed eighty-six degrees magnetic. I did the quick rule of thumb in my head: For reciprocal heading, "move a two," giving two-sixty-six. We were heading downwind, with the sails out. With one hand, I started bringing in the mainsheet, and with the other, spun the wheel to reverse course in a jibe. By the time I reached the proper heading, I had the reefed mainsail amidship, letting the jib flutter in the strong wind. I turned the key and punched the starter, bringing the diesel to life. Single-handed as I was, precise maneuvering under sail was almost impossible. I groped open a hatch and got out the boat hook and an electric spotlight.

The greatest obstacle to sea rescue confronted me. I swept the heaving sea in front of me and saw no sign of her through the rain and gathering darkness. In all the drills I'd been through in offshore school it was the duty of one person to do nothing but keep an eye on the "victim," usually a cushion tossed overboard. Now there was no other person, and I'd lost contact as I got the boat reversed and under control. In the middle of the Pacific there are no landmarks.

It was a good sign that *Chips* was directly ahead, but I didn't see the strobe, or the pole with its flag. *Chips* was closing with me, now weather-vaned into the wind, her navigation lights on. I reasoned that *Chips*, with the wind on her hull and masts, would drift faster than the rescue device that had a small drogue chute to reduce drift. Abigail, in her life preserver, would have a drift speed somewhere in between. I estimated that *Chips* would have caught up with Abigail by the time I got the boat turned around.

I pressed the electric furler for the jib and wound it in. Going into the wind under power, my main concern was overrunning her position. The ten to twelve foot waves made it impossible to see her or the strobe when they were in the troughs. There was scant hope she could swim to the horseshoe preserver attached to the pole. I'd never asked her if she could swim. Since the pole went into the water after she did, maybe she'd be lucky and drift into it.

I eased forward just above idle speed. *Chips* drifted by. I searched the surrounding waves in vain, trying to keep desperate thoughts out of my mind and think about the three drifting objects—Abigail, *Chips*, and the MOB pole. My only hope was to find the pole, then search the area between it and the drifting boat. Occasional flashes of lightning lit the surging sea in stroboscopic light, temporarily knocking out my night vision.

I forced myself to stay on my compass heading, searching the sea left and right. Still nothing. *Chips* was now astern two or three hundred yards. I looked at my watch. She'd been in the water nine minutes. Hypothermia was a concern. My only hope was that her personal flotation device kept her upright until I could find her. Foaming crests of waves flashed in the gloom, giving maddening false hope each time they caught my eye.

Please God, I breathed to myself. Let me have her back.

At last I saw it! Fifty yards to port, the strobe winked at me from the crest of the wave. I kept my eyes on the spot as it disappeared again into a trough. I turned the wheel to circle upwind of the spot. Now that it was located, I could see that each flash of the strobe lit the flag at the top of the pole with faint light. I resisted the urge to head straight for the pole, forcing myself to draw a circle around it from fifty yards. If I found her, I expected it to be on the line downwind toward *Chips,* whose lights grew fainter in the distance. As the pole rose again to the crest of a wave, a lightning flash dashed my hopes that she'd be clinging to the horseshoe collar.

As I completed the downwind half of the circle, I held my breath and searched the heaving waves, hoping for a miracle. I did not see her. She'd now been in the water fourteen minutes. I turned back upwind, making my turn inside the pole, trying to play the best odds that she had drifted past it. This time, I extended my track into a longer ellipse downwind toward the drifting *Chips*, about to disappear in the distance. It was becoming more difficult to keep track of the pole's position in the rain, as it grew darker. When I reached the imaginary drift line again, I turned into the wind and throttled back to idle, locking the wheel. Ignoring my own rules, I released my tether and left the cockpit, circling up the side deck and onto the bow, then back down the other side, clinging to the lifelines, searching the foaming crests.

Back in the cockpit, I unlocked the wheel and prepared to begin another circle. I started searching the immediate area one last time, now using the spotlight's beam. As I reached for the gear lever to start another circle, another flash of lightning lit the waves. There was something in the water, two boat-lengths away. I saw it briefly on the crest of a breaking wave, then it disappeared. I fixed the location in a beam of light, slammed the lever into reverse to make a turn in place, and eased forward to arrive downwind from the spot.

Then I saw her. Abigail was floating lifelessly on her back, her head elevated on the collar of the life vest, hair streaming in the water behind her. Jem clutched the front of her vest, and turned glowing eyes to look at me as I pulled even with them. Fishing them out would not be easy, with the turbulent waves tossing us up and down, out of rhythm. One moment they were far below me, the next above the rail on the crest of a wave. I ran to the rail and clipped my tether on the lifeline, using both hands on the boat hook to try for them as they rose on the next cycle.

I held my breath, hoping they were close enough. Up they came. The collar had a grab loop on top and there might be but one chance to catch it with the boat hook. Jem would have to hang on for herself. With a prayer in my heart, I made the thrust. Success! I tugged them firmly toward the boat, then lifted my baby aboard, hanging by the strap, cat attached. Jem dropped to the deck as soon as they cleared the rail. She mewled faintly and tried to rub against my leg.

Having Abigail back in my arms will remain a defining moment in my life, no matter what the future might bring. The sea had given her to me a second time.

She was limp and cold, not a breath or movement. I turned her over my arm, head down, and slapped her back. Seawater streamed from her and I couldn't tell whether any of it came from her lungs. I quickly laid her on the seat and removed her life vest. She had a faint pulse in her carotid artery. I put my mouth over her nose and mouth, exhaling gentle puffs into her little lungs, repeating, repeating, repeating. I allowed each breath to exhale between puffs. Other than that, there was no response.

The yacht wallowed out of control in the surging seas. As though dropping a curtain on the final act of a play, the storm released torrents of rain

Through my fingertip on her neck I could feel her thready pulse as I continued breathing into her. Time stood still. At last her body twitched and she made a low gurgling sound. Then she struggled to sit up, breathing on her own. She coughed violently. Then I was thrilled to hear her begin to cry—the same thrill a new mother must feel after giving birth.

"Kitty! Kitty!" she said between sobs.

"It's okay, Sweetheart. You're safe now. Everything is all right," I crooned to her as I held her to me and staggered down the companionway steps, Jem underfoot, into the saloon, closing the hatch behind us.

I plopped her on a settee. "Lie there, Sweetie, while I get some stuff to get you dry."

We were both soaked to the skin and dripping seawater. Jem looked as miserable as a cat can look, but began to groom herself. I got Abigail's clothes off and toweled her dry, then wrapped her in a blanket and put her in the quarterberth and hooked up the lee cloth. Her body shook with shivers and her teeth chattered.

After she quit shivering, I dressed her in a sweat suit and wrapped her in the blanket again.

She clutched my sleeve. "Don't leave me!"

"I'll be right here. I won't ever leave you." I toweled Jem dry, and thought about what I had promised. Was it a promise I could keep?

# CHAPTER 6

hat would we do about *Chips?* I pictured her drifting backward with the storm and current, her saucy stem pointed into the turbulent waves. If I chose to let her go, she'd be a hazard to other boats. More than that, my mind went back to those happy hours as she was being built; sitting among the fragrant cedar shavings, watching the steam-bending of her frames, reveling in the beauty of her interior brightwork. Now there was no plan for the future, no way to tell what would lie ahead. I hated to relinquish the object of those therapeutic days.

The best way to find her after the storm would be to duplicate her drift as nearly as possible. "Abigail, I have to go on deck for just a minute. Will you be okay?"

"No, no, please!" She grabbed at my sleeve.

"You can watch me from the hatch. I don't want you to get wet again." She set her face in a worried frown. "We'll put your coat on, and you can stand on the top step and hold to the rail."

After a long pause, she nodded.

The storm was still at full strength, the wind howling through the rigging and rain falling in sheets. I put up a tiny storm sail in place of the main, tensioned the boom amidships, and centered the rudder. Then I trailed a pair of long three-quarter inch lines off the bow. Gradually she vaned into the wind to begin our drift. The two boats were now in convoy, drifting backward, perhaps fifteen or twenty miles apart.

Below again, I put on dry clothes, wrapped a blanket about us and held Abigail cradled in my arms until she slept. The radar was operating, and the screen was visible from the settee. The yacht still pitched with the waves, but in a regular motion now that we were stabilized with the wind direction. With the hatches all closed, the shriek of the wind was mollified, but the rain hammered against the coach roof with a steady roar.

I awoke with a start, my subconscious mind picking up the change in the pattern of the sea. Our motion was easy, and the noise of the storm had ceased. Sunlight shone through the portlights, casting bright spots that danced about the interior of the saloon. Jemima ran back and forth on the opposing settee, trying to stay in a patch of light.

Abigail was still fast asleep, making faint snoring sounds, her beautiful features changing as she dreamed. Suddenly she stiffened and began coughing. It shook her awake and she squinted at me in the light. She coughed again, covering her mouth with her hand.

"I have a terrible cough," she said.

"It's terrible, is it?"

"That's what my mama says, when I cough."

"Mamas hate for their children to cough, and I don't like it either. I think you still have some seawater in your lungs. Do you want some breakfast?"

"Yes. Can I have a Pop Tart?"

"Kid, you can have anything on the boat."

While she went to the head, I slid back the hatch and stuck my head out. It was a beautiful clear morning, and we were drifting with our stern pointed at the sun, now well above the horizon. There was no sign of *Chips*. I knew it was too much to hope for. We'd take our time getting the nightmare of the night behind us, then get a position fix and plot our drift since yesterday. It should give us a line pointing toward the drifting boat, then with luck I could get some sails up and chase her down.

Abigail ate her breakfast with gusto, while I had coffee. She asked to sit on my lap while she ate.

"Let's go sit in the cockpit, and maybe we can see my little boat out there somewhere."

"Where did it go?"

"I cut it loose, Sweetheart, when you fell overboard."

"Don't you want it anymore?"

"I wanted only you, and to have you back aboard the boat."

I made a point of putting harnesses on both of us, and latching us to the jackline while we sat in the cockpit.

"I thought you weren't gonna' come back," she mumbled, looking at me with her face set in pain.

I hugged her to me. "I was so afraid I couldn't find you in the dark. But I would never give up."

"I was afraid. It was dark and the water was cold."

"I know."

"And the lightning scared me."

"But it may have helped me find you."

She smiled and reached up to wipe a tear from my cheek. "Don't cry, Kitty."

"I can't help it. I love you, Babe, and I don't know what I'd do without you."

"You called me a pig again."

I laughed. "I guess I did. Excuse me for that, unless you want to be a pig."

"Kitty, do you have a Mama?"

"Not any more, Sweetie. My mother and father were both killed in a car accident long ago, when I was not much older than you are."

"No, no, no. I mean a mama who lives with you, like my mama lives with Daddy."

"Oh, you mean a wife. No, I don't. I don't have anybody except my grandma, who raised me and took care of me."

"You don't have a little girl, either?"

"No, no little girl."

"Oh."

Then it was my turn. "Abigail, do you have a grandmother or grandfather?"

She looked puzzled. "No-o."

"Any aunts, uncles, or cousins?"

"What are cuzzins?"

"They're people who are part of your family, like if your father had a brother and he had a child."

"Oh. I don't think so. I have a friend Margie who plays with me sometimes."

I decided it best not to ask what led to her questions. She had avoided mentioning her parents for several days now, but I figured she must think of them, and wonder where they were. I didn't know how much children her age thought about the future.

For me, it consumed my thoughts. I dreaded landfall, and the anticipated hassle with the authorities. Most of all, I dreaded being separated from her. I had wild thoughts of sailing into the sunset; me, my little girl, and the cat whose name came from Andrew Lloyd Weber's original version of *Cats*. But it would never work. It wouldn't be right with the outside chance her parents were still alive.

I plotted my best estimate of a course, dragged in the trailing warps, and set sail toward *Chips* and the California coast beyond. A steady breeze blew from the starboard quarter, and the Pacific settled into moderate rollers worthy of its name.

Jem and Abigail had both received a shampoo, so Abigail sat in the cockpit and combed the tangles from her wet hair in the morning sunlight. Jem gradually assumed the appearance of a real cat as her fur dried, far different from the scrawny apparition that came aboard the night before. Abigail was securely clipped to the jackline, and Jem never got more than two inches away from her; two lost, now redeemed.

I stood on the coach roof at frequent intervals, scanning the horizon for signs of my missing consort. Twice I picked up sails in the distance, and once a freighter headed in the direction of ports in the Far East. I kept my handheld set on, listening for radio chatter, but I picked up no signals with its limited range. The radar was on, and had picked up blips confirming my visual sightings.

Lunchtime came, with all hands agreeing on canned tuna. Two of us had fruit cocktail. Abigail seemed to put the terrible night behind her, demonstrating a resilience I envied. While I cleared the dishes, she skated about the cabin sole with each foot on a paper towel. Jem chased after her.

Back in the cockpit, she promptly resumed her vocal drama, belting out "Itsy Bitsy Spider," with all the proper hand motions.

In mid-afternoon, I picked up a minor disturbance on the horizon; sea birds circling in a tight spiral. It could be over a school of feeding fish. I kept the glasses focused on it as we charged forward. The stick of a mast came into focus. It had to be *Chips*. In a few moments she was hull up, confirming my hopes and my logic in plotting a course.

The birds were not there just for the boat. As often happens in the open ocean, *Chips* provided a floating reef, which attracted first the small fish, then the rest of the food chain. The birds were batting cleanup.

I circled around her downwind, furling the genoa as we luffed up, and started the engine to ease alongside. Bumpers kept us apart, and I secured us with lines fore and aft.

"We found it!" Abigail said.

"We certainly did."

Abigail kept herself glued to her seat in the cockpit, now on her best behavior, while I maneuvered the boats into position.

We were soon underway in our old arrangement, after I fished out the long lines off her bow. They were already covered with tiny barnacles, and frayed where I'd slashed them with my knife. Otherwise, all settled in just as before, our speed reduced by the drag of *Chips*.

I decided it would be a good time to talk to her about the events surrounding the disappearance of her parents.

"Abigail, will you come and talk to me?"

I sat on the windward cockpit seat, bracing my feet against the binnacle. She climbed uphill and held up her arms for me to take her on my lap. "She's little, and she wants to be held," she said.

"That's fine with me. Sweetheart, I want to talk to you about the day when your parents went away. Okay?"

"'Kay," she whispered.

"I don't want to make you sad, but I want to know what happened."

"'Kay."

"Did you see another boat?"

"Yes."

"What did it look like?"

"It was blaaack, and it didn't have sails."

"Did you see it up close?"

"No, 'cause Daddy told Mama to take me downstairs."

"Did she do that?"

"Yes."

"What happened next?"

"I don't remember."

"Did she say anything?"

"She said, 'Be good and hide. Don't come out 'til I tell you.'"

"Did you hear anything?"

"Rilly, rilly loud noises. I was scared."

"I know you were, Sweetheart. You've been a really big girl. We don't have to talk about it anymore right now."

Everything she said confirmed what I had guessed, but added no clues to the fate of her parents. I recorded my questions and her answers in my logbook with the time and date. I decided not to trouble her with it again.

My noon sight allowed me to estimate our position and calculate a landfall in San Francisco. If the wind held, we should make port in the late afternoon tomorrow. A month away would not make me unhappy, but I had to be realistic. Only one more night on the water remained for us.

Abigail blossomed like a spring flower in the warm sun. She resumed her song and dance routines on the coach roof, now careful to remain shackled to the boat. This time she belted out lyrics from a medley of Jimmy Buffet songs. It was delightful to hear some of the lines emerging from the gyrating little body: "It's my own damn fault..." "Just another bluddy mary..." and "Drunk on the couch..." She even gave the Eagles a nod, "Just another ta-kee-la sunrise...."

Evening fell with a clear sky and continuing fair winds. I let Abigail stay in the cockpit with me after her dinner and bath. I knew time was growing short for us. She sat on my lap wrapped in a blanket as we rode the gentle swell.

There was no moon and the sky was uncontaminated with the lights of civilization. As the sun's influence receded, the night became a velvet black, lit by the faint brush of the Milky Way and millions of stars, so close we felt that we were floating among them. The phosphorescence of our wake drew a die-straight line across the surface of the ocean.

"Abigail, tomorrow we may reach land."

"Will I see my Mama and Daddy?"

"I don't know what will happen, Sweetheart." I had little hope for her, but I couldn't bear to destroy hers.

"Will you sing to me?"

"I haven't sung for a long time, Sweetie, but I'll try." Singing was a joy for me before I left a normal life behind. Grandma Maureen gave me piano and voice lessons when I was a child, and I sang in the church choir before I went away to college. I was able to dredge up the words of a song she sang to me, *Brahms's Lullaby*, words appropriate for the circumstances:

*Lullaby, and good night,*
*In the sky stars are bright...*

In a moment, she was asleep. I continued to hold her and sing to her, not for her, but for me. I blinked at the tears filling my eyes and wondered what had happened to me. I never disliked little kids; I just never thought about them, one way or the other. Abigail had totally captured my heart, and I would never be the same again.

# CHAPTER 7

I t was a night of little sleep. A watch schedule of two hours awake, one hour sleeping, doesn't provide much rest. This night, facing the coming landfall, was even worse. At five o'clock, I gave it up and sat in the cockpit to watch the sky turn pink with the rising sun.

The wind was gradually clocking around toward the bow, so I cranked in the genoa a few clicks on the starboard winch, and trimmed the main and mizzen. If my plot into San Francisco was accurate and the wind held, we should pick up a visual on the Farrallon Islands before noon. I cranked the diesel to warm it up and started the generator set to top out the batteries.

What would it be like to face the authorities when we landed? Who would they be? I could imagine we would create a stir with various agencies fighting over us. Protecting Abigail would be my first objective, now and forever into the future.

Below decks, the coffee was ready. I checked my little charge, sleeping peacefully in her bunk. She was lying on her back, arms above her head, with the face of an angel. Jem was an early riser, and rubbed against my legs aggressively, asking for her breakfast. She followed me back to the cockpit while I had my coffee and she scarfed up the canned cat food.

Jem took up her post on the foredeck to wait for fish dessert. I got out the cleaning supplies and scrubbed the decks with dishwashing soap, a stiff brush, and saltwater. After a final rinse with fresh water, I flemished all the line tails and wiped down the brightwork and metal surfaces. No point in arriving in civilization not looking your best. I'd tend to my personal appearance later. There wasn't much I could do for *Chips*, following faithfully in our wake.

I scanned the ocean at the right moment. Was it luck or instinct? Something disturbed the surface in front of us. I spun the wheel to bear away to starboard, off the wind. The disturbance was a large shipping container, afloat just beneath the surface. It staggered us as it scraped down the side of the big yacht, but the glancing blow was not enough to penetrate the hull. I grabbed a winch handle and tensioned the port towline to *Chips*, veering her out of danger.

I'd heard of these wandering hazards and hoped I never encountered one. With no radio and GPS on board, there was no way to report it. Unfortunately, we were about to enter the most crowded shipping lanes, the broad ocean highways from the West Coast to the Far East.

A tousled head appeared at the hatch. "I woked up," she said, rubbing her eyes.

"Who's a sleepy-head?"

"I'm notta sleepy-head. I just don't wanna wake up."

"Oh, I see. How about breakfast? Jem had hers already."

"Uh-huh."

"Do you want what Jem had?"

"No, silly. I want Pop Tarts."

"Pop Tarts it shall be."

After I fixed her breakfast, I went back to the cockpit to shave from a bucket while I kept watch. The closer we got to the coast, the more traffic I expected. A container ship appeared on the horizon, headed southwest. It would pass well south of our course. I hoped they had their containers locked down.

Jem's patience was rewarded. A fat little fish made a fatal mistake and the cat pounced, devouring it on the spot. The spot was on the deck I just scrubbed, but I had a bucket of hot water at my feet. No problem.

Abigail came back on deck, Barbie Christie clutched in her hand. She came to me with hands held high, to be lifted on my lap. She stroked Christie's long dark tresses. She asked the usual question. "Kitty, will Mama come back soon?"

I gave my usual answer, "I just don't know, Sweetheart."

"Is she with Daddy?"

"I imagine she probably is." Painful though it was, it was my best guess. She saw what I'd been doing, and touched my face.

"You're sm-o-o-o-th."

I tweaked her cheek. "So are you."

She rewarded me with a dazzling smile.

I picked up a sail in the distance, off the port bow. As we rode the gentle swell, there wasn't a lot to do after I got Abigail dressed and in her safety harness. The sail gradually rose out of the horizon, revealing a yacht much like our own. We were converging at our combined speeds, and soon it became evident that we would pass close to each other. I retrieved the handheld radio, and guessed what frequency to use. I picked channel 68, but heard no communication. It wasn't surprising, considering its range.

The other boat was on a starboard tack and had the right of way except for our boat in tow. I hoped he knew the rules, but one could never depend on it. I watched closely and hoped he was doing the same. We must present a puzzling sight.

I disengaged the autopilot and prepared to yield right-of-way. Just as I did, the large sloop-rigged sailboat veered off, to pass to our port. My radio crackled. I'd guessed right.

"Green ketch with the tow. Are you okay?"

"Affirmative. All's okay. Just have a big dinghy."

"I guess! Headed for San Francisco?"

"Right. Thanks for asking."

"Rog. Have a good day."

Two men in the cockpit stared at us from a distance of a hundred meters, and we both waved as we passed. If I'd been in their Top-Siders, I would have been hard-pressed to figure us out.

The closer we got to the coast, the more traffic we saw, a mix of commercial and recreational craft. We were dressed in foul weather gear for warmth, riding in on the mass of cold ocean water that cools the San Francisco area. Occasionally someone was close enough to gawk at us, but we got no more radio calls.

The smudge of coastline finally rose out of the horizon, out of focus in the parallax of bent atmosphere. In spite of my bold plan to escape the world and its problems, I did not have a great deal of sailing experience, and hadn't entered San Francisco Bay before. Nor did I have a clue who to contact about our situation. The Coast Guard sounded like a good bet, but they probably had some overlap with San Francisco police. At least I expected that the police would have jurisdiction as soon as the boats were tied up at a dock.

What would they do with me? What would they do with Abigail? Did she have relatives? She didn't seem to know about any.

In a few hours, the Farallon Islands came into focus. I'd made a good landfall. We would skirt them to the south and see if my radio would reach anyone as we drew abreast.

Abigail sat in the cockpit drawing pictures with her crayons. She'd drawn a figure with a scribble of red hair that I took to be me. I had a big smile on my face. Holding hands with me was a little figure, also with a smile. She had a triangular skirt to make sure we knew it was a girl, although she never actually wore one. A scruffy little figure depicted Jemima beside her. Even the cat had a crescent smile. The sun shone over our shoulders. Psychologists are supposed to be able to judge the state of mind of children by the pictures they draw. Unless I missed my guess, it was a happy picture. In my gut, I felt it was all about to change.

It was time to prepare her for what we might face.

"Abigail, we need to talk about what may happen when we get to land."

"Are we almost home?"

"We should get there before night."

"Will Mama and Daddy be there?"

"I don't think so, Sweetheart. Nobody knows exactly where we are."

"Why?"

"Because we have no radio so we could tell them. Why don't you come and sit on my lap, so we can talk."

"'Kay." She put aside her paper box and crayons and came to me again with arms held high. Jem moved over on the seat and rubbed against me; my temporary family...together.

"Abigail, when we get to the dock, the police will come, so they can help you find out where your parents are."

"Why don't you help me?"

"I will if I can, but they will know what to do."

"Will you come with us?"

"If they'll let me. You see, they will want me to help them with your boat."

"What if they can't find them?"

"Then they'll take care of you while they look."

"Why can't I stay with you?" My greatest concern, expressed by a child.

"We'll just have to wait and see." I held her close to me. "I want you to remember that even if we can't be together all the time, I love you with all my heart. Even if you can't see me, I'm always thinking of you, and watching out for you. Will you remember?"

"Yes." She looked down at the deck, and picked at the hem of her jacket.

"Kitty?"

"Yes, Sweetheart."

"I love you."


The sun was low in the west when the time came to make my call. The familiar city came into view from an unfamiliar angle. The bright spear of the Transamerica building dominated the skyline in the distance, and Golden Gate Bridge was in sight. I checked my *Chapman's* again and turned my handheld to channel 16.

"Coast Guard, this is *First Edition*, over."

Nothing.

"Coast Guard, this is *First Edition*, over."

Again, nothing.

"*First Edition*, this is *Mauna Loa*. Do you need help?"

"Negative, *Mauna Loa*, thanks. I have a tow, and need to see authorities. All I have is a handheld."

"Roger. I have you in sight. I'll call it in. Want 'em to intercept you?"

"That would be good. I'm going to raft up. Thanks again, *Mauna Loa*."

"You got it."

I cranked the diesel at idle and turned into the wind, then released the sheets on the genoa and began cranking it in with the electric furler.

The lines went slack to *Chips* as I released the mainsheet and let the big sail drop into its lazyjacks.

Abigail sat staring, hardly watching the activity around her. Gone was the ebullience of the future Broadway star that I had learned to love.

"*First Edition, Mauna Loa.* The Guard will meet you a couple of miles outside the Gate."

"Roger, thanks."

"Need anything else?"

"Negative, *Mauna Loa.* Many thanks."

"Roger, good luck. Out."

It took me a half hour to get out all the fenders, spring lines, and other gear, and raft up. I felt like throwing the slimy towlines overboard, but coiled them in the cockpit of *Chips* after she was fast to our starboard rail. My poor little boat looked neglected. She'd need a refit before my voyage could continue. But would that ever happen? Would I want to go, now that my life had changed?

We cruised under diesel power, crabbing slightly because of *Chips* bulging from the side like a misshapen pregnancy. With the autopilot engaged, I set about putting the deck in order. I also had time to duck below at intervals to pack a bag for each of us. It was unlikely we'd remain aboard after landfall. What came after that, I could only guess. I put in my logbook. It contained all my position plots, as well as word-for-word conversations with Abigail about the day her parents disappeared.

After nearly an hour more, we approached the Golden Gate itself. Lights were coming on all over the city, providing a spectacular welcome if not for the uncertainty of what would come.

A coast guard launch was idling on station to greet us.

"*First Edition,* this is Coast Guard. Do you read?"

"Roger, Coast Guard. I have you in sight."

"Good. We'll bring you in to the station on Yerba Buena Island. You know where that is?"

"Yes, Sir, I do."

"It'll take a while, but probably best. Understand you want to contact civil authorities?"

"Correct. Probably should have a female officer. Got a little girl here. And would you like to put someone aboard to help with docking?"

"Roger. We'll come alongside."

The boat accelerated into a turn, came down our starboard side, pulled around our stern, and up against the port side fenders I'd put out in anticipation of docking. A Chief Petty Officer scrambled aboard.

"How do you do, Sir? My name is Hyatt."

We shook hands. "I'm Gideon Grant, Chief. Thanks for your help. This is Abigail."

Abigail had come to stand behind me, and grasped my belt in the back.

Hyatt peeped around me, "Hi, Abigail. You don't have to be afraid of me. I'm just going to help your dad dock the boat."

A brief explanation was in order. "Actually, she's not mine. I found her alone on this big boat out in the ocean, when I was sailing by in my little one."

"Wow! That's strange."

"It certainly is. That's the reason I asked for the police to be contacted. And I'm sure we shouldn't say anything until they sort it out."

"Mum's the word, Sir."

I gave the controls to Chief Hyatt and we followed his shipmates under the beautiful span of the Golden Gate, with a river of headlights and taillights flowing over it. Darkness had fallen. We cruised on toward Alcrataz and passed by it. Abigail was tired, so I sat on a cockpit seat and held her on my lap.

Coast Guard contacted me again. "*First Edition*, police are on the way from Central. They'll meet us at the Station."

"Thanks, Coast Guard. Out."

At our slow pace, it seemed forever before we passed under the Bay Bridge, with its heavy stream of car lights, to approach the Coast Guard Station docks. I felt weary from the tension, and dread of the uncertainty that was sure to come.

The Chief expertly eased us in to a dock. I became a deck hand, readying mooring lines and boathook, making us fast to some cleats. A couple of uniformed police stood on the dock, along with a man and a woman in plainclothes. Abigail gripped my hand. Our lives were about to change.

# PART II: THE LAND

# CHAPTER 8

Abigail held one hand in the air for me, the other clutching Jemima. I picked them up and stepped onto the dock. The firm surface felt funny under me after several weeks at sea. I had trouble walking a straight line.

The man and woman proved to be as I suspected, plainclothes detectives. The man rumbled forward first. He was over six feet tall, and overweight, heavy of jowl, wearing a permanent scowl. His bulbous nose was blue-veined, and a gray bristle of mustache made me think he should have a pair of tusks.

"I'm Lieutenant Haney, and this is my partner, Detective Alvarez. And you are?"

"Gideon Grant, and this is Abigail Dickerson."

"What the hell's going on?"

So much for pleasantries. Alvarez nodded to me and smiled at Abigail. She couldn't be more opposite. She presented a size and perfection that could grace the cover of *Vogue*.

"I'll tell you what I know. Should we find some place to talk?" We were beginning to gather a small crowd of Coast Guardsmen.

"So you're in charge here?" Haney demanded. But he shrugged and looked at a lieutenant j.g., apparently the launch commander. The lieutenant indicated a small building on the dock. "There's an office in there you can borrow."

"Conchita, take the kid and send in one of the uniforms. I'll get a preliminary statement."

As the woman approached and reached for Abigail, she clung to me. "Kitty!" she said in distress, "I want to stay with you!"

"You can stay just outside while I talk to the policeman, Sweetie. I'll just be a little while. Correct, Detective Alvarez?"

"Yes, of course. We will stay right here, Leetle One." Then, "I'm confused. What did she mean, 'Kitty'? She has the cat."

"When we first met," I said softly, "I gave my name as Gideon. She heard it as 'Kitty-on' and has shortened it to 'Kitty.' I couldn't bear to correct her."

Alvarez smiled; Haney's scowl increased. "C'mon. Let's get on with it."

Haney took a chair behind the desk, got out his notebook, and I began. The uniformed cop stood by the door. I took him briefly through the sighting, the boarding, the pumping, and the discovery of the little girl. I mentioned the black cigarette boat I'd seen before encountering the yacht. Haney stared at me with his usual expression, scribbling brief notes. When I described the damaged radio panels and told him about the cartridge casings, he held up his palm.

"Officer, get on the horn and get a lab wagon down here," he barked. "Oh, and have Alvarez come here a minute."

Alvarez stepped into the hall outside, holding Abigail's hand, and looked in. "Yes?"

"Better call the DA and get rolling on some search warrants for both boats. We have us a crime scene. Oh, and get the Child Protection Center."

"Why the Child Protection Center?" I asked.

"It's routine."

"I guess I have to take your word for that."

"You're right. You do."

"By the way, you don't need a warrant for my boat, the little one. Feel free. I guess you do need one for the big one."

"Just let us take care of it, okay?" Haney said.

Alvarez withdrew with a pained expression on her face.

"Trying to be helpful," I said. "And while I'm on the subject, your lab people need to understand that I had to clear up the mess in the big boat from the flooding. I diagrammed and bagged everything the best I could."

"You *what?*" he shouted.

"I believed something bad might have taken place. I had to get the mess out of the way in order to bring both boats in."

"You had no business messing with a possible crime scene!"

"You expected me to park at a curb out there and call you? Maybe tie the boat to a telephone pole?"

"Don't be a wise ass." He glared at me. "I think we're done for now."

We went back out on the dock. Abigail and Jem ran to me, and the two detectives huddled, speaking in low voices, glancing from time to time in my direction. All of the Coast Guardsmen were gone except the lieutenant and the chief. Abigail wanted me to hold her, and she put her arms around my neck when I picked her up.

In a matter of minutes a van drove out on the dock; lights flashing, but no siren. A couple of technicians in lab coats got out and proceeded to get their gear out of the back. Haney and Alvarez went to meet them, and so did I.

"Back off," Haney said.

"I need to explain to them what I did and where I put the stuff."

"We'll take care of it."

Alvarez spoke, "Marty, may I speak with you a moment?"

They retreated a short distance and I could see Alvarez gesticulating and speaking in an intense whisper. Haney had his jaw set, but finally nodded.

"Is okay," she said to me when she returned. "I will watch the leetle one and the *other* Kitty, while you go aboard with them." There was a hint of a smile on her face. Now I knew what "bad cop" and "good cop" was all about.

I went below on *First Edition* and gave them a brief description of my first time aboard, about closing the seacock and pumping all night. I pointed out the damaged panels, and told them what I'd seen in the log. Haney observed without comment for a change.

"I had no way to get both boats back unless we used the big one as a mother ship. I drew a rough diagram of the saloon, sketched in sections, and wiped up the floor with paper towels. I put them in separated numbered plastic bags."

The older of the two, a man of Oriental extraction, nodded.

"I'd prefer to have been there, but obviously you had to do something."

"That's what I thought. In addition to the panel damage and what's in the log, I found two other items that might help." I brought out all of the stuff I'd collected.

"Here's a bag of cartridge casings. Looks like 9 millimeter to me. There's a sketch in there where they came from, near the panels. And here's a strange one. Might mean nothing, but you can be the judge of that." I handed him the plastic bag with the ear stud. "The little girl said it wasn't her mother's, for whatever that's worth."

"Thank you, sir. We'll take it from here."

"Okay. I may have removed some prints or something."

They shrugged and turned to begin their search. I followed Haney back onto the dock.

The rest of the evening started out okay, but began to change. We loaded into an unmarked Ford, Haney and I in the front and Alvarez in the back with Abigail and Jemima. Abigail was subdued, saying little as she looked out at the city flashing by as Haney sped through the downtown traffic.

Eventually, we drove up Vallejo Street and turned a corner around Central Station, a multi-story building, down a narrow alley, and Haney parked at the curb behind a couple of other cruisers. They led us in through a metal door with a security keypad and up a hallway to a booking desk. Behind me I could see a high marble counter with plate glass windows for walk-ins off the street. The redheaded sergeant also boasted a mustache. If this was a standard feature, thankfully it did not include Alvarez.

I dropped our bags on the floor in front of the desk. The sergeant grinned. "Checkin' in?"

"I would hope not."

"We'll be doing some questioning," said Haney.

A large mountain of a woman of African lineage rose from a chair in the corner and approached us. She flashed a big smile at Abigail. "So this is the little girl?"

Abigail moved behind me and clutched my belt, Jem draped over her arm.

"We'll get to you in a minute, Bernice," said Haney. She looked at him for a couple of beats and went back to her corner.

He turned to me. "We'll enter both of you in the desk log, get your prints for the lab, and take an I.D. photo."

"I'll help any way I can, but first can you have someone make a hotel reservation for us, so we'll have a place to stay when we're through?"

He glanced at Alvarez. "We can't do that. You're not related and we don't know what's going on yet."

I turned to Alvarez, "Please. She's been through untold trauma and I'm all she has right now. Help her make the transition, at least. That's all I ask."

She frowned. "I am sorry, but he is right. It is the procedure."

"Get connecting rooms or a suite. I'll pay for all of it. You can stay with her—with me in the next room."

"No can do," Haney said. "And you're gonna be here for a while."

"What does that mean? Am I being charged with anything?"

"Not yet. We just need some information."

I didn't like the way this was going but I could see their point. They didn't know me, and they couldn't understand how much I cared about Abigail; and that she trusted me and had adopted me. I decided to give in to the inevitable.

Through all of our hushed conversation, Abigail remained behind me, clutching my belt.

"At least let me explain it to her."

"We will," said Alvarez, looking relieved.

They took our fingerprints and our pictures. At least they weren't the post office poster variety, with number clutched below; just a quick shot as in the license bureau. Abigail made a face at the black ink on her fingers.

The time had come. I picked Abigail up in my arms, "Sweetheart, we have to go different ways for a little while." She clutched at my shirt. "Ms. Alvarez will want to ask you some questions, then you will go with that lady over in the corner and spend the night at her place." My other shipmate, Jemima, rubbed against my leg.

"*No-o-o!* I want to go with you! Where is my Mama? Will my Mama come?"

"They haven't had a chance to find her yet, Sweetie. I have to work with the police so we can find her. You be brave, and always remember what I told you on the boat: no matter where you are, I will be thinking about you, and I won't let anyone hurt you."

Alvarez looked on, and I thought I saw a tear glisten in her eye. She stepped forward and I gave Abigail to her, having to use gentle force to get her to turn loose.

"Com' with me, Sweetheart. Let us go see Mrs. Johnson. She will be good to you."

Abigail began to cry. "I don't wanta go!" she sobbed.

"Have the shelter come and get the cat," Haney said to the desk sergeant.

"Not that, too! Can't she keep the cat?"

"Rules again."

I gave up. I went to where Abigail and the two women were. "Abigail, Jemima will get to go stay in a cat hotel until we can get back together again. I'm sorry. I'm sure they'll take good care of her."

I followed Haney to a door leading into the bowels of the station, through a metal detector. As we exited the receiving room, I heard Abigail screaming, *"Kittteeee! Kittteee!"*

# CHAPTER 9

I preceded Haney into a large room full of desks in rows, only some of them occupied. Glassed-in offices lined the sidewall and the rear. Since it was early in the evening, business was not as active as I expected it would be after midnight when nocturnal creatures roamed the streets. As it was, however, it was difficult to identify some of the humanoid forms of life being questioned. I saw a lot of hair, dirty hair, and there were piercings in surprising places. I realized I'd lived a sheltered life. Some of them stared at me like I had stepped off a Martian space vehicle. I was shaved, clean, had a self-administered haircut, and wore clothes not reduced to rags.

"Lt. Haney, I need to make a phone call."

"Who to?"

"A friend."

"There'll be time for that later."

"No. Now."

He glared at me, and pointed at an empty office. "Make it fast, and no long distance. Dial 8 for outside."

"I need a phone book."

He yanked open a drawer and pointed.

Since it was near eight o'clock, I hoped Mangini was home, and I hoped home was still in San Francisco. I looked her up in the white pages and dialed.

A strong voice answered.

"Julie, thank God I caught you at home!"

"Gid? Is that you? Where the hell did you think I'd be on a Tuesday night?"

"Out with some tall, handsome fellow I suppose."

She snorted, "Yeah, right. I'd settle for tall. Where the hell are you? I thought you flew the coop."

"I did but I'm back in the coop, literally. I'm here in a police station for questioning. Can you tear yourself away and come down? Lieutenant Haney is about to blow a fuse, and we need to talk."

"Sure. Give me twenty minutes."

"We're at Central—"

"Since you mentioned Haney, I know where you are."

"Let's get on with it," said Haney. He tried again, "What was that about?"

"Just called a friend to come down. Julia Mangini."

He came close to a jaw drop. "You called *Mangini?*"

"You know her?"

"Yeah, I know her all right." He didn't look happy, but then he hadn't looked happy all evening.

He led the way to an interview room just like the ones you see on television, if you watch television: a sturdy metal table and four sturdy, uncomfortable metal chairs. A one-way glass was set in one wall, so an audience could observe the perp being questioned. For all I knew, they could set up video out there also.

A young man followed us into the room. Haney mumbled an introduction, "This is detective Peak."

Not taking his cue, the man smiled and shook hands, "Hi, I'm Greg Peak."

"Gideon Grant," I responded. He had a firm handshake, and was a handsome, blocky, blond-headed man with the build of a tight end. No mustache. Maybe it was a rank symbol. He carried a notepad. He and Haney sat with their backs to the one-way glass.

"Let's go through all of the details again," began Haney.

"Why don't we wait for Mangini? That way, I won't have to repeat."

"You got something to hide?"

"No, of course not. I already gave you the general outline of what happened."

"Mangini will have to take care of herself." Haney's veined nose began to glow

"No she won't. Let's get a few things on the table. In the first place, whatever happened on the boat out there is not in your jurisdiction. It would be FBI. And second, you know who the girl's parents are, so it seems to me that the first priority would be to see if you can find any trace of them here, and whether she has other relatives—"

Haney turned beet red, rose from his chair, and stabbed a blunt finger in my face, "You're not running this investigation! I am! And I'll damn well—"

He was interrupted by the door opening, and Mangini walking in. "Hi, guys. Sounds like everyone's having fun already."

Haney sat back in his chair. Peak leaped to his feet and retrieved a chair out of the corner and set it next to mine, at the same time casting an admiring glance at Mangini.

She ignored them and strode across the room to me. I rose and we embraced in a warm hug. "Gid, it's great to see you!"

"You too, Julie!"

Haney made a pained face, "Yeah, yeah, yeah."

Peak and Mangini introduced themselves.

"Well, shall we?" Julia said, seating herself. She flashed big brown eyes and a wide smile, brightening the drab room. She was taller than I, over six feet. Her thick black hair was cut in a no-nonsense short bob. She also looked in good shape, and could probably whip me if I got out of line. Not that I intended to. She'd played power forward in basketball for Stanford on a full scholarship. She and I were in law school together, but had gone in different directions.

"Well, what's the deal here?" she began.

Haney answered, "Your friend sailed in here under suspicious circumstances with a little girl in his possession."

She looked at me.

"I was sailing for the South Pacific when I found a yacht filling with water. I first thought it was deserted but found a cat and a little girl on board. I pumped it out and brought both boats back here. The little girl is the daughter of the Dickersons. You know, the reporter and the Olympian. Apparently, they're missing."

"Hm-m-m. I'd like a word with my client, please."

Without a word, Haney got up and left, jerking his head to Peak to follow him.

Julia led the way to a corner away from the one-way glass. Facing inward, she asked, *sotto voce*, "Anything I need to know?"

"No, absolutely not."

"No problem laying it all out for them?"

"Not a bit. The only problem I have is wasting time screwing around here, when they should be doing everything they can to see if the little girl has relatives...her name's Abigail, by the way."

"I see."

"Absent any relatives, I'm the nearest thing to a guardian for her, and she's been through a lot. The Child Protection Center has her now. I'd like to become her legal guardian, or apply for adoption if she has no one."

She gave me a strange look. "First things first. Let's bring them in." She walked over and tapped the glass.

Haney entered with a different man in tow—a slender young man with moussed, curly black hair. This one was not introduced, and meekly took a seat.

I went through the entire story, mainly for Julia's benefit. Haney watched eagerly for any discrepancies, and the other man took notes.

Few questions were asked until the end of my narrative. Then Haney began his "bad cop" routine.

"So now you can apply for possession of the yacht, under maritime laws, huh?"

"Well, no. As far as I'm concerned, it belongs to Abigail and her family. And I hope you have someone searching for them."

"I told you before, that's our business. Tell me, when did you start liking little girls?"

I jumped to my feet, upsetting my chair. "We're done!"

Haney rose also, "We're done when I say so!"

Julia followed suit. "No, my client and I are leaving, unless you can trump up some spurious charge."

Haney could only glare at us as we gathered our belongings and walked out of the room.

A half-hour later we were seated in a cozy booth in an Italian restaurant, where the proprietor knew Julia by her first name. Tony Bennett crooned, *"Just in time, I found you just in time..."* softly in the background.

"Julie, I don't know where to begin. Do you have time to help me?"

"Sure. I've got a couple of cases that are pretty heavy, but I have a great paralegal, and we can handle it. Remember the schedule in law school? Well, this is easier."

"Wonderful! We've been friends for a long time, but your work for me is business. The only way I'll let you do it is full billing, just like any other client. You can't cheat yourself; all involvement including tonight is billable hours. Okay?"

She shrugged. "Okay, but if you hadn't been in my study group, I might not have made it through."

"We all helped each other. Now, mind if I rattle off a few things?"

"Go ahead." She refilled our wine glasses.

"Abigail comes first. I want to find out where she is, and how she's faring. I worry that both her parents were murdered. Whoever did it might even come after her. We need to keep this out of the papers if we can."

She nodded.

"I'll need to establish a base here. I need an apartment, cell phone, car, computer, and all the other crap that comes with modern living."

"Yep."

"And third, I want to hire a private investigator. I don't want to wait for the authorities to get around at some bureaucratic pace to find out what happened. You know somebody?"

"I do. And I think there may be a condo for sale in my building. From what I know about your career, you can buy it and sell it later. Would that work?"

"Sounds great. Probably easier than renting. And I haven't called my grandmother yet to let her know I'm back."

The waiter brought steaming plates of ravioli in a white sauce, served them with a flourish, then cranked Parmesan shavings over them.

Julia's cell phone rang, and she fished it out of her purse. "Hello... yes...yeah, maybe, if it's okay with Haney...he isn't? Could have fooled me...sure...maybe tomorrow?" She snapped her phone shut, and gave me a sheepish look.

"That was Detective Peak. Wants to meet for a drink."

"So...true love blossoms."

She made a weird noise. "Yeah, right. I think he wants to pump me for information. Well, it goes both ways."

"You probably have the 'pump' part right."

She slapped my wrist and held out the phone. "Here, call Grandma."

After a half-dozen rings, I heard the familiar "Hello."

"Gran, it's Gideon—"

"Gideon! It almost sounds like you're right here!"

"I *am* almost right here. I'm in San Francisco. I cut the trip short. It's too complicated for the telephone, but I'd love to see you. Can you come over?"

"Sure. I'll cancel a couple of things and be there tomorrow before dinner. Tell me where and when."

"Let me give you a temporary phone number, and give me your cell number if you have one. I'll call shortly after noon." I looked at Julia and she shoved a business card across the table. We exchanged numbers and rang off. The team was coming together.

Just as the waiter brought plates of *veal piccata*, her phone rang again. She answered, listened for a moment, said "okay," and snapped it shut.

"We have a date with the FBI tomorrow at nine."

"Can you make it?"

"For you, sure."


I spent the night in Mangini's condo over in the South Beach District. The condo was small by middle-America standards, but classy and modern. It had only one bedroom, but the couch beckoned my weary frame after my weeks of short watches on the boat. Rather than going to sleep, I died. In spite of the fact that I was worried about my little friend, I knew nothing until Julia shook me awake and handed me a mug of coffee.

"Time to get up and face the music."

"Oh...thanks, Julie. I wonder how Abigail is doing."

"Already called. She had a little trouble falling asleep, but she was still sleeping when I called. She had them going last night because she

kept crying and asking for 'Kitty.' Took them a long time to get it...
that she meant you."

"It's my new name. Stands for 'Kitty-on'."

"Cute. Think I'll use it."

# CHAPTER 10

We shot across town in Mangini's BMW and arrived at the FBI offices on Golden Gate Avenue. For this encounter, we were shown into a room more like a conference room than the grim compartment in the police station. An agent seated in the middle of one side of the table displayed the demeanor of a bald eagle, hooked beak included. He gestured toward the two chairs across from him. To his left sat a large young man with shaven head.

"I'm Special Agent Scott," he began, "and this is Special Agent Liggett. And you are the man who brought the yacht in yesterday?"

"Gideon Grant," I said, partly rising from my chair and extending my hand. He did not see it. I let it drop. "This is Julia Mangi—"

"Yes, I know. Thank you for coming, Counselor. Let us begin—"

The door burst open and Lieutenant Haney rushed in, his trench coat flapping.

Scott glanced at his watch and pointed at the end of the table. "You may sit there, Detective."

"It's Lieutenant."

"Right, *Lieutenant*. Now, where were we? Is your client prepared to give us a complete statement, Ms. Mangini?"

"Of course," I said. "Above all, I want to find out what happened and protect the little girl, Abigail."

"Why?" The eagle eyes bored in.

"What kind of question is that?'

"A simple one. What's your stake in this?"

I slapped both hands on the table and gave him my own eagle stare. "I'm not playing silly games. We can work together to solve this, or I'll do the best I can on my own."

"You needn't be touchy, and I wouldn't advise interference in the case." He snapped a remote over his shoulder to start the video recorder, and droned his name and the date. "Now, please state your full name and place of residence."

"Gideon Paul Grant. I have no place of residence, except my boat."

Scott raised his grizzled eyebrows, "No place of residence?"

"I sold my practice—"

"Practice?"

"Law practice. It was Grant & Associates in San Jose, until a few months ago."

Scott glanced at Julia, then stared at Haney. "You didn't tell me we had another lawyer on our hands."

Liggett took his eyes off Julia long enough to look at me for the first time. Julia rested her hands on the table, doing a Mona Lisa impersonation.

Special Agent Scott turned back to me. "Okay, let's get on with it."

I laid it all out for them, beginning with the decision to leave my career. There were few interruptions through most of it. Haney looked at his notebook, seeking discrepancies. When I got to the first sighting of the yacht, Scott interrupted.

"Do you know the approximate location?"

"We can get pretty close. I have my logbook—"

"You have your logbook?" Haney shouted from the end of the table.

Scott held up his hand, "Please, Detective, I mean Lieutenant."

"Yes, I have it. We didn't get to that point, Lieutenant Haney. You were too intent on accusing me of pedophilia." I turned back to Scott. "I took a position plot not long before I boarded the boat and again after I pumped it out."

Julia took the log out of her briefcase and handed it to me.

"You're welcome to copy it or read it. I'll help with any interpretation."

There were no interruptions as I detailed finding Abigail, and my observations on the condition of the boat. Scott seemed to understand my dilemma and the efforts I made at preserving evidence.

We took a short break before I disclosed losing Abigail over the side. That bit of news caused startled looks. Julia turned to me.

"You didn't tell me about that."

"Not until now. I'm ashamed of the fact that I allowed it to happen, and it terrifies me still to think about it."

"Wow! Were you lucky!" Her knuckles turned white as she gripped the table edge.

"I know. It scares the hell out of me." I turned back to Scott, "Perhaps now I can answer your question. Here's this brave, helpless little girl, left to die. She came to depend on me, and I found her to be one of the brightest spots in my lifetime. Then I almost lost her, but the sea gave her back to me for a second chance....I'll do anything in my power to see that nothing bad ever happens to her again."

Scott's fierce look softened, "I think I can understand."

We finished by noon with Scott's promise to apply all the resources of the FBI. He shook hands as we parted.

As the meeting broke up, I caught up with Haney, "What happens to the boats?"

With some effort, he looked me in the eyes, "They're impounded until all the evidence is collected."

"Okay, but I want to know as soon as mine's released, so I can have it refitted."

He turned and walked away. "You will."

Julia had to get to her office, so she gave me a key and entrance card. We agreed to meet at her place at five o'clock. I wanted to go spring Abigail, but knew they were unlikely to talk to me. I used Julia's cell to call Gran again to give her the address. Then we parted ways and I grabbed a cab. As he looked at me for an address, I couldn't help myself. I gave him the address of the Child Protection Center.

In a few moments, I pushed my way through a revolving door into a large waiting area half-filled with unhappy people. Innocent or guilty, they all had something in common. They wanted their child or children back and chances are they would be turned away. I joined the mood as I approached a small window available to supplicants.

Expecting to be confronted by Bernice Johnson or her clone, I was dazzled by a beautiful young woman with emerald eyes. "Yes, may I help you?"

"My name is Gideon Grant. I'd like to see Abigail Dickerson, if I may." Might as well go for it.

"I'm sorry, Mr. Grant. We don't do walk-in visits, unless you have custodial paperwork." She continued to rub lotion into her hands and looked back at her desk top, dismissing me.

"Uh, excuse me, I don't know the procedures but I have to see if she's okay." I gave her a sad puppy look.

"I'm afraid I can't help you." Then she paused, made her lips a rose-bud, and turned her head. "Sandy, can you take over for a minute? Mr. Grant, go to that door to your left."

She beckoned me into a nearby office and waved me into a guest chair, taking a seat behind a scarred oak desk. She had fine hair to her shoulders, perhaps called blonde by some but it was blessed with a hint of red, giving it the color of twenty-four-karat gold. Her voice was kind.

"I normally wouldn't do this, but I heard there was a story behind Abigail. I'd like to hear it. By the way, my name is Grace O'Quinn."

I took her hand, scented with lavender. "Call me Gideon, Miss... Mrs...Miz—"

"And you may call me Grace." The smile sparkled again. "I'm single, if you must know."

"You caught me. I'm single—divorced, actually—and I'm also Irish."

"Is that a good thing?"

"Can't hurt. Seriously, about Abigail...first, I'm concerned for her safety because we don't know what happened to her parents."

"And?"

"And second, I've grown to love her as I would my own daughter... or I assume it's how parents feel."

Now she was the one with the puppy look, and a sigh caused the rise and fall of her blue cashmere bosom...not that it was the first time I'd looked. I gave her the short version of finding Abigail and how I came to care for her.

She frowned and shook her head. "They really won't allow you to visit her. I'm sure you can understand that seeing you, then saying good-bye again..."

"Yeah, I guess so. But is there any way I can take a peek from a distance?"

She glanced at a slim gold watch. "They would be through with lunch by now, so maybe she's in the playroom. There's a one-way glass. This is irregular, but come with me."

"I'm grateful." I followed her down a stairs and along a hall, receiving a couple of questioning stares from staff. Watching the movement of her tweed skirt and long slender legs, I realized how long it had been since I'd encountered the thoughts that came to me now. I inhaled the scent of my hand where she had touched me.

We arrived at the glass, and could see several kids scattered in the disarray of a large room. Two or three little urchins were climbing about on an indoor plastic gym. It took a while for me to find her. She sat by herself, half hidden by a dollhouse, staring at the floor. She clutched a small stuffed cat. I pointed her out to Grace.

"She's a sweetheart," Grace said softly. "She looks so sad."

"Of course she is. She's lost her parents, she's lost her cat, and she's lost me."

"I'm truly sorry. I wish there was something I could do."

"There is. Tell her that you saw Kitty, and he loves her and is trying his best to get to see her. Will you do that?"

"Kitty?"

"It's what she calls me. For Kitty-on."

Her lips trembled, and she nodded, a tear starting down her face.

"What will happen to her?"

"She'll be placed." She whisked away the teardrop with a swipe of a finger, under control again.

"Placed?"

"With a foster family."

"Why not me?"

"You can try, but they'll never do it, not to a single man in these circumstances."

"Will you marry me?"

She gave me a stern look, "Don't be flippant."

"I'm not. I'm desperate."

"How romantic."

"I didn't mean it that way. I'm serious. All you'd have to do is go through the motions..." Unexpected images formed in my mind and I felt my ears turning red.

She smirked at me.

"Wh-what I'm trying to say is, you wouldn't have to do anything except on paper, and help serve as her guardian until we sort this out, find her parents if they're still alive."

"I understand what you mean in spite of how you say it, but I won't help in any kind of subterfuge."

"If all goes well, you could get an annulment. You'd get a nice settlement."

"Be still my heart. Give it up. I'll do my best to monitor her, and I'll give her your message...*Kitty*."

# CHAPTER 11

I spent the afternoon cranking up my life ashore. The real estate firm that had the condo was located a few blocks away. An agent was sent immediately. I waited at the door of the for-sale condo.

A chunky blond woman in business attire came clicking down the hall at the appointed time. Half glasses hanging on a beaded chain swung to and fro. She raised her hand high, thumb up, for a quick handshake, flashing a smile. "Hi, I'm Cindy."

She produced a key for the lock box on the door and let us inside. The place was sparkling and clean much like Julia's, but with a second bedroom and a city view rather than the bay on Julia's side. Realtor Cindy followed me at a quick pace through all the rooms, still smiling and pointing out various features, such as the remote-operated gas fireplace, and the various appliances in the kitchen. It had the same piano-finished blond hardwood cabinets and black granite countertops. After a few minutes, we paused in the dining area.

"How fast can possession take place?"

"Oh, it could close quickly; say within a couple of weeks."

"That isn't quickly."

The smile disappeared, "Well, uh, what did you have in mind?"

"Tomorrow."

"That would be, uh, unusual. I-I could see what I could do. Are you ready to move from your present home?"

"You could say that. I don't have time to mess with offers and counter-offers. One offer only. The place is listed for a million-two. Offer your client a million-one, take it or leave it, and immediate closing applies."

Her plucked eyebrows formed tiny arches. "H-how did you plan to finance?"

"I'll have a cashier's check in hand tomorrow for the full amount. Can you get back to me later today, including closing costs? I'm not trying to be difficult; just don't have time to waste."

She promised to track down her client, and would call me at Julia's before bedtime. Money talks. I gave her Julia's cell number also. Not found wanting, she whipped out an offer sheet and filled it out for me to sign and I wrote a check for five thousand earnest money. We parted with another pump-handle shake. She looked bewildered.

That freed up the rest of the afternoon for me to further entrench myself back into modern society. I called a Toyota dealer and insisted on speaking to the sales manager. It was similarly comical to get him to fast-forward to the deal. He met my terms on a Land Cruiser, and agreed to have someone meet me with the car, paperwork, keys, and temporary license at a nearby Bank of America branch the next morning at ten.

Timing was a little tight for my next shopping expedition, but I found an electronics mega-store within walking distance. It was a bit strange reentering the world I left behind. I was surrounded by reminders of those all-night sessions and endless negotiations that made me wealthy, but ground me into the dirt. I bought a high-end laptop and signed up for a cell phone.

That was about all I could do until the condo was settled. There was a wine shop on my way back to Julia's, so I arranged for a case to be delivered within the hour.

I was in the midst of unpacking my toys when Julia came breezing in, followed by a young man carrying the wine. I gave him a tip and carried it into the kitchen.

"Let's get right into that," she said. "It's been that kind of day."

We'd just settled into the leather furniture and clinked our glasses, when the intercom spoke to us. "Ms. Mangini, there's a lady here for Mr. Grant."

"Oh, send her up."

In a few moments, the door chimes sounded, and I opened the door. A red-haired stranger stood before me.

"Well, don't just stand there! Give me a hug."

"Gran?"

"Of course, dear boy."

She swept into the foyer and embraced me, pecking me on the cheek and whispering in my ear. *"Well, what do you think?"*

"You look great, but the hair, and—"

"You need go no farther."

"But—"

"No buts...well, speaking of that, plastic surgery, my boy. It's called a *Brazilian Butt Fill.*" The last three words were spoken in a strong whisper.

"You look ten years younger...at least."

"Correct. And don't ask what he did with the extra skin."

"Agreed. Gran, it's so good to see you!"

*"I think it's time we used 'Maureen',"* she whispered.

I led her into the living area. "Julia, this is my...this is *Maureen*, the woman who devoted her life to raising me."

They shook hands, "It's great to meet you. Gid has often spoken of you," Gran said.

"And the same. I think you must be very proud of him."

"All right, you two. Gr...Maureen, a glass of wine?"

I sensed disappointment, a hesitation..."or something else?"

"Martini, if you have the ingredients," she said before I had finished the question.

Julia pointed. "The bar's over there, Gid. Vermouth's in the fridge.'

"Good girl!" said Gran. She watched my every movement while I placed a generous mix and cracked ice in a shaker.

Gran had just settled back and taken a long, grateful drag on her drink when the intercom spoke again.

"A Mr. Tolliver to see you, Ma'am."

"Send him up, please, Jorge."

Julia brought in a small but muscular man with a shaved head and a blue beard shadow. "Mrs. O'Brien and Gideon Grant, this is Gulliver Tolliver."

"Gully," he said. He came up to my shoulder, and I'm not tall. When he grabbed my hand with a firm grip and a fierce look, I wasn't sure whether I should hire him or send him down a tunnel after a badger.

"Nice to meet you, Gully. Call me Gideon. Drink?"

"Scotch, neat," said Gulliver Tolliver.

When we were all settled, with Gran a fresh drink, I began. "We're all here about a little girl named Abigail Dickerson.

She's in Child Protective Services. I managed to see her there today through a one-way glass, but they wouldn't let me talk to her. I'll lay out the story, then we can discuss it."

I told the whole story again, with some background about me for Tolliver's benefit. They let me tell it with few interruptions. Tolliver took notes, and seemed particularly interested in the description of my evidence collection, and my quotes from memory of the log of *First Edition*.

"Here's how I see it. First priority is to protect Abigail from harm. Then we've got to find out if her parents are alive and where they are; or if not, who did them in and why. After that, we'll have to see where we go. If Abigail's parents are not in the picture, does she have any other family? If she doesn't, I want to apply for adoption...but I'm getting ahead of myself, I guess. Anything else?"

Julia spoke first, "if there are any lingering suspicions about you, we've got to knock that out."

"Right. Gully, if you come on board, how would you approach this? Also, do you have time to work for me?"

"Yes, sir, I do have time. Assuming my main focus would be the Dickersons, off the top of my head, I'd dig into his professional life and their personal life. He wasn't popular with the people he screwed... excuse me, ladies...in the press. I'd go over his stories for the last five years. I'd look into friends and acquaintances. As they say, most murders are by people you know."

I wrote a check and ripped it out. "Here's a retainer. Let me know when you need more. That enough?"

"Yes, sir! You want weekly reports? Monthly financials?"

"Fine, but I'd like to talk every day about this time, unless you have something sooner, even if by phone. And call me Gideon."

"Yes, Sir!" then he smiled for the first time. "By the way, I think I know who did the deed...or at least took part."

"You *do*?"

"The earring. Buddy Lyon, L-y-o-n, a small-time hood. You know, *Lion?*" He made a silent snarl and made a claw with his hand. "But he'd just be a hired hand. I'll ask around."

"Good. Now, Julie, is your date set up?"

"I'm meeting him for a drink at nine. He's not free until then."

Gran perked up, "What's this all about?"

"Our Julia has caught the eye of the handsome Detective Peak of the Central Station."

Gran pumped a fist, "Yes!"

"Julie, do you think you can feel him up...I mean *out*...about my case? Also, I want to know what kind of surveillance they have on Abigail."

She gave me a withering look, "Just keep that up, buster. Yes, I'll do it for little Abigail's sake."

"Now, Gran, I mean Maureen, that leaves you and me. Can you stay a few days?"

"You bet."

"What about your house and cat?"

"Reggie is looking out for them as long as I wish."

"Reggie?"

Gran blushed beneath her newly unwrinkled cheeks. "Reginald Thurston, former member of the Coldstream Guard, now living near his daughter in Modesto."

"The plot thickens. I look forward to hearing more about Reggie. Meanwhile, I really need your help in setting up home base. I made an offer today on a condo in this building. They're to let me know tonight and close tomorrow if it goes through. I'll want you to go on a shopping spree and stock it with furniture and everything else to make it livable."

"Charge! And I mean that both ways! Out of my way out there!" Gran shouted, rubbing her hands together.

"But before that, I want to send you on a rescue mission. Abigail's cat, Jemima, is being held prisoner. Do you think you could pose as a grandmother, armed with a cat carrier, and spring her?"

"I'm pretty good at pretending."

We concluded our first team meeting, agreeing to meet at the same time next day. Tolliver departed with a handshake and a determined set to his blue jaw. Cindy the Realtor called with a promise to close in her firm's offices the next day at two, provided I brought a certified check for the amount offered plus the closing costs, which she'd itemize for me by ten tomorrow. She spoke with a note of wonder in her voice, no doubt stunned at her good fortune. Julia promised to send her paralegal, Salvador Torres, to the closing.

Gran and I booked into a hotel a couple of blocks away, where Julia promised to meet us for breakfast the next morning.

"Now, you behave yourself, tonight," I admonished.

"You haven't had much fun lately, have you?" she shot back.

# CHAPTER 12

Gran and I met for breakfast in the hotel dining room, after a fit-ful night on my part. Julia called and said she couldn't make it. I replayed my time with Abigail and came close to regretting the decision to bring her to San Francisco. In the end, however, I knew it had to be. I hated being outside any chance to look after her, but regret-tably could see the other side.

I pointed at Gran's oatmeal. "That looks delicious."

"You behave yourself. It's the price I pay to protect my investment." She glanced downward. "Or I should say *your* investment. Thanks for your generous allowance. I first thought of hoarding it, but then decided to enjoy life."

"You should. Times must have been hard for you, doing all you did to take care of me."

"It was my pleasure. Another thought I had: you're the only one I'd leave it to, and you don't need it."

"Exactly. Back to breakfast, the way this day is shaping up, I don't think we have to worry about calories. I have to pick up a car I bought, close on the condo, and make a few calls to get started on this situation. I'm going to see if the police or the FBI know anything, if they'll talk to me."

"If they have any sense, they will. You know, Gid, this has surprised me a bit."

"Why's that?"

"Well, you never seemed interested in children much. I'd hoped that you and Regina..." She stopped, and looked down at her fruit cup.

"I know, and I'm sorry it didn't work out that way. It was my focus on the wrong things, I guess."

My vibrating cell phone changed the subject. "Excuse me, Gran. Hello?"

"It's Julia."

"Oh, how was it?"

"Fine. I hate to disappoint you but he was a real gentleman. I didn't find out much but I do know why Haney acted like a bear with hemorrhoids." She told me.

"Oh, now I guess it makes sense. Thanks." I told her my schedule and repeated I'd see her at five o'clock.

"Disappointed you, right?" She hung up.

"Well, Gran, I think it's safe for you to buy the stuff to stock a kitchen, and have them hold it for delivery. Also, you might look at furniture, but maybe we will actually look at the place after I close at 2:00."

"I'll do the cat mission first."

"Right. I'm going to call about Abigail, then get the car at ten. Good luck."

"You too."


After getting her a cab, I called The Child Protection Center and asked for Ms. O'Quinn. I didn't realize what a nice voice she had until I heard her soft hello.

"Hi, this is Gideon—"

"Oh, my future husband! I wondered when you'd call."

"Please. Let me apologize again. It was really stupid of me—"

"I'll quit teasing you about it. Actually, I was touched. I spent a little time with Abigail after you left and it's evident that she's attached to you."

"That's why I called. Is she okay?"

"She's just okay. She asked about you first. She said, 'When is Kitty going to come and get me?' I had to tell her you couldn't come just now, as you were trying to find her parents. Only then did she ask about her mother."

"Oh, my. I don't mean to replace her parents but I'm touched by that. I'm just the most recent in her memory, I guess."

"Well, it's apparent she really cares for you. But she does miss her mother and she wonders what will become of her cat. By the way, the police came by to interview her late yesterday."

"What happened?"

"It went fine. The actual talk with her was done by one of our specialists while we watched through a one-way glass. I got to be there by elbowing a few people out of the way. A cute little detective named Alvarez was here, also an FBI agent with a shaved head."

"Probably Liggett."

"Abigail had nothing but glowing words for you and she told what little she knew about her parents' disappearance. It was just as I heard it from you, without the detail, of course."

"So Abigail did okay?"

"You'd have been proud of her. They wanted to focus on when she first saw you, whether you were there in the beginning. After a repeat or two, she got pretty impatient, and said, 'I *told* you already!' I got a kick out of that."

"Good. I'm going to see if the police will talk to me about it."

"I got the impression Alvarez would cooperate in anything you ask. You know, a certain sparkle in the eyes when your name came up."

"Oh, please. I'd better deal with Haney, her boss. Will you not hang up on me if I ask you a question?"

"Depends on the question."

"Will you forget the clumsy past and meet me somewhere after work? I want to fill you in on our plans for finding out what happened to Abigail's parents. Also, I want to know you better."

There was a long pause.

"Are you there?"

"Yes. I'm trying to decide what I should say."

"A simple 'yes' will do. If it would make you feel better, you could come to a task force meeting at my lawyer's condo. We meet around five. You could meet her, my private eye, and even my grandmother."

"I'll do it. It's not something I'd do if it weren't for the approval of a certain little girl. You can skip the 'getting to know you better' part."

"We'll keep it strictly business." I gave her the address, then jumped up and clicked my heels, drawing a glance or two from passersby.

A cab dropped me at a State Farm office to fill out paperwork, then I went to the Bank of America branch I'd selected. The first order of business was securing a large certified bank draft made out to the escrow account Realtor Cindy had given me when she called with the numbers. The clerk looked a bit startled, but handled it in the back, taking my identification with her.

A few moments later, a man about my age, dressed in a suit, came in off the street and looked about, spotting me. "Mr. Grant?"

"That's me." We spent a quarter hour filling out paperwork, exchanging keys, checks, and handshakes, and the car was mine. I called the insurance company with all the final numbers. Geez, no wonder I decided to leave this world behind. Just a couple more annoying chores, then I could get on with the main objective.

I found my new white Land Cruiser parked on the street. I dialed Central and asked for Lt. Haney.

"He won't be in 'til three."

"How about Detective Alvarez?"

"And you are?"

"Gideon Grant. She'll know what it's about."

I paced the sidewalk with the phone in my ear, on hold. The Bay sent a swirl of cold air up the street, causing me to shiver. After days of characteristic clear weather, there was a bank of fog along the Sausalito side of the Bay and low clouds hid the sun. I climbed into the Toyota, greeted by the odor of vinyl plasticizer oils, better known as "new car smell."

Finally, "Mr. Grant?"

"Yes. I understand you questioned Abigail. Can you share anything with me? Is she okay?"

I heard a sigh before she answered. "I wish we could talk about it. I understan', I really do. But Marty, he would have my scalp."

"Marty?"

"Haney."

So much for my animal magnetism. Rules are rules. I'd try "Marty" later.

Still sitting in the car, I dialed Gran's cell. "Do I have Special Agent Maureen?"

"I got the cat!"

"Wow! Any trouble?"

"I handled it. Had to act like a poor, broken old lady. Had to shed a tear or two. No problem. They wanted paperwork."

"Are you ready for Hollywood?"

"Wouldn't waste my time."

"Where are you?"

"In a cab, almost to Julia's. Jem's a little cagey in her cage, but we'll get along. I got a bed, a litter box, all the cat stuff. I'll leave her at Julia's...then *shopping!*"

"Good for you. See you at five, if not sooner."

I pulled out into traffic, a strange feeling after being car-less so long. I made my way to the vicinity of the real estate office, then decided to go to the condo since it was not far away. I found Gran still there, getting Jem's new stuff laid out. She was surprised to see me until I explained.

"Also, I wanted to see this girl." Cats don't exactly come charging to humans; licking, barking, and wagging, like dogs do. Still, she knew me and marched sedately to me, arched her back and rubbed against my leg, about as demonstrative as cats get. I scooped her up and held her in my arms. No rules against humans displaying a little affection.

Julia's Salvador Torres met me at the entrance to the real estate office. He had a gleaming smile below a pencil mustache, moussed hair combed straight back, and an Italian cut to his pinstripe suit. He looked like a movie-role Latin lover.

"Call me Sal," he said. "Julia speaks very highly of you."

"Thanks, and the same about you. Are we ready?"

We went inside and met the realtor and the owners' lawyer. Coffee was served while Sal dived into the paperwork. We practiced thumb-twiddling. Sal worked. The other lawyer glanced repeatedly at his watch.

"I think we need to check the plot call-out," said Sal. "I researched Ms. Mangini's condo in the same building, and this is different."

After a few phone calls and data base searches, his concern was found correct, a couple of numbers reversed, and we closed.

Back in the car, I tried Haney again and was told to try again later. I left my cell number but had little hope he'd call. I dialed Special Agent Scott, of the eagle countenance. Better luck this time; they put me through.

"Scott."

"Gideon Grant here. I was wondering if you can share any progress on Abigail Dickerson."

"I'm sure you appreciate that we can't talk about an investigation in process."

"I guess I can understand, if not appreciate. Can you tell me *anything* about the search for her family?"

"I will say this much. We have located paternal grandparents. Any on the other side are outside the country, with whereabouts unknown."

Selfishly, I felt disappointment. "Are they coming for her?"

"Sorry—"

"Yes, I know, you can't talk about it. Thanks anyway. While I think of it, I have one little piece of information. My investigator suggests the earring might belong to a local hoodlum named Buddy Lyon. That's L-y-o-n."

"And who is your investigator?"

"A private investigator named Tolliver."

"Thanks. Just don't get in our way."

# CHAPTER 13

I got back to Julia's before the task force meeting and found a note that Gran was out shopping. Jemima was there, and acknowledged my presence by actually trotting across the floor to rub against my leg again. I poured a glass of wine and sat on the couch to think, Jem purring by my side with her head on my lap.

Abigail seemed to know nothing about her grandparents when I asked about family. Yet, now they were there, hovering in the backdrop of the case. If they were devoted to her, then so it would be. But I felt the same feelings as before: *You'd better not mistreat my kid!*

Julia was first to arrive, followed soon by Tolliver. We made small talk over our drinks, waiting for Gran to show up. Grace expected to be late, so I decided to let her appearance be a surprise to the team.

Gran came waltzing in at ten after, arms loaded with shopping bags. "Hi, everybody! I've been shopping, shopping, shopping, spending Gid's money."

"Good for you. Grab a drink, and we'll get started."

After a few noises of ringing glass, tinkling ice cubes, and a refrigerator door closing, she came in and seated herself by Julia on the other couch.

"Wow, that's a martini! Is there a homeless goldfish lurking about?"

"You behave. I'm celebrating a good day."

"Great. Why don't you go first?"

"Well, as you can see, I rescued the cat—"

Julia applauded and I joined her.

"I bought a whole bunch of kitchenware, dishes, and such. It's to be delivered tonight if I call them."

"You can do that now. Here's your key to the condo."

"Thanks. I've also ordered a few basic groceries and looked at furniture, but thought I'd better look at the place before I pull the trigger on it. Probably can't get that done until tomorrow. Reggie's coming over to help, if that's okay."

"Good. Look forward to meeting him. Why don't you go have a look, get the stuff on the way, then come back by. There's someone coming I want you to meet. I'll fill you in on whatever else we say here."

"Someone coming? Who?"

"A lady I met at the Child Protection Center."

"Hm-m." She gulped the last of her martini and left in a whirlwind of packages.

"Okay," I began, "I found out from the FBI that they've located Abigail's father's parents, but I don't know more about them than that."

"I can add to that, Sir," Gully said. "The grandparents are in Atlanta, and have more money than God. My contacts say that the Fibbies had their local agent check them out and they seem to have nothing to do with their son and his family."

"That confirms what I heard," Julia added. "My source tells me that the grandparents don't want their granddaughter—won't come for her or anything."

"That's really weird," I said. "What's wrong with them? Rhetorical question; but I have to say with all selfishness that I didn't want to see her swept away by people I don't know. We need to find her parents if they're alive, but if not I want to adopt her."

As though on cue, the intercom buzzed. "Miz Julia, there's a lady for Mr. Grant."

"Thanks. Send her up." Then turning to me, "I assume that's your mystery guest."

"Right. She's joining the team, I hope."

"Your team or our team?" said Julia.

"Getting back at me, huh? We'll wait and see."

I anticipated her arrival and went to the door to open it right after it rang. I wanted to give her a friendly hug but shook hands instead. After my premature proposal, I decided on a slower approach. She smelled of soap and all things fresh and clean. How does one do that after a day's work?

"Come in, Grace. Meet our host, Julia Mangini, and this is our investigator, Gulliver Tolliver."

They made appropriate noises and shook hands.

"Gran's left for a little while, but will be coming back, and this is one of the characters in our boat drama, Jemima. Why don't you sit with us on the couch? Oh, pardon me. A drink?"

Grace glanced about. "I'll have wine, if that's okay."

Julia fetched a glass and poured. As she did so, she raised her eyebrows at me.

"Grace is a counselor at the Child Protection Center. I'm hoping to learn more about foster parenting and adoption if it comes to that. Also, she has access to Abigail and I'm hoping she can keep an eye on her for me."

"Good," Julia said. Gully nodded agreement, rubbing his chin with the sound of sandpaper on oak.

"Grace, to bring—" I stopped with my mouth open. Grace had raised the wine glass to her lips and there was a great, fiery diamond on her left ring finger.

She stared at me. "Yes? Is something wrong?"

"Uh, no," I mumbled. "To bring you up to date, my grandmother is busy getting my condo up to speed after rescuing Abigail's cat from the shelter—"

"You bought a condo? And how did she get the cat?"

"First question, 'yes,' and second, when you meet her, you'll know. To continue, we've all had feedback that Abigail has grandparents on her father's side but they don't seem interested or involved in their son's family."

"The police relayed that information to us at the Center. Therefore, she's been placed with a family. I'm sorry." She reached over Jem and patted my hand.

"Oh, gee. I want her to be safe somewhere but I'd hoped it could be with me."

"I know. It really is a temporary placement to get her out of the institutional environment, so there's still hope."

"Is she safe? Is the location secret?"

"We certainly hope so. And the police say they will keep an eye on her."

"Well, not much we can do about it now, so let's continue. Other than that little tidbit about grandparents, I've spent most of my time becoming a land creature again. Julie, what do you have?"

"The same about the grandparents, of course. Also, my source tells me that you are no longer under suspicion of any wrongdoing, although Haney gave up reluctantly. The FBI people are going through the stuff you gave them from the boat. I fed them Gully's supposition about Buddy Lyon of the earring."

"I did that, too. Are they looking for him? What about the big black boat?"

"Yes, he's definitely on the wires all over the state. And there's a hint that the boat may be one that was impounded in San Diego for drug running, then stolen."

"You're kidding!"

"Nope."

I reached down to pet Jem, but she wasn't there. She'd moved to the other end of the couch and was sitting in Grace's lap. "Hey, what's going on with my cat?"

Grace gave me a smug smile and tossed her hair in triumph.

"Gully, I guess you're next."

Gully sat as tall as his genetic code allowed, rubbed his chin and began. "Sir, as I proposed, I've been concentrating primarily on Mr. Dickerson. First, there's the family situation we discussed. Seems strange to me, Sir."

"Me, too. Do you think it would be worth talking to them?"

"Yes, Sir, and better you than me, if you can do it. They're way above my level."

I knew he meant socially and financially. "I'd like to confirm that business about no interest in Abigail, and see if I can find out why."

Grace said, "Though one might think otherwise, grandparents have no automatic claim to a child."

"Really? I'd still like to get it pinned down. I have serious doubts they'll talk to me, either. What's next, Gully?"

"I'm digging into news stories that Mr. Dickerson broke to see which ones resulted in criminal prosecution. There are several and I'm not sure yet which ones are worth more digging. There's a good one about state hiring practices, one involving embezzlement, and another about public works contracts."

"Sounds like a good collection. Do you need more time on those?"

"Yes, Sir. But there's another lead I'm following." He cleared his throat, looked at the women present, and colored slightly.

"Go on. It's okay."

"Well, uh, I checked out some of the help at the club the Dickersons belong to, and, uh, there seems to be some sports other than tennis and handball, if you get my drift."

"Involving the Dickersons?"

"Well, you know how they are—the hired help. They look over their shoulders, roll their eyes and won't come out and say things plain, even when they aren't at work."

"But you think they were saying, 'yes'?"

"Yes, Sir. And Dickerson's boss belongs to the same club. They seemed to get really nervous when I asked about their relationship."

"Who is he?"

"Name is Bart Richie. He's one of two managing editors, or some such. It's a funny setup. He seems to be responsible for all the business and politics, the area where they dig dirt. Dickerson is, or was, the star reporter. Dickerson'ud write only when he had something juicy. Rest of the time he's digging in sh—uh, dirt."

"What's Richie like?"

"Big, rawboned guy, movie-star looks, trophy ex-wife, sort of like me." Gully chuckled at himself and glanced at his staring audience. "Just a little joke, there, Sir. Uh, he seems to be in the social whirl."

"Maybe I can talk to him, also."

"Good idea, Sir. He wouldn't even notice me. But that's giving you a lot to do, what with the Dickersons."

"That's okay. Just keep doing what you're doing. Okay, any questions?"

"Anything else for me, other than listening to the progress of the police and FBI?" Julia asked.

"Just give my thanks to Sal. Great job on the real estate. And I may want you and Grace to look at a paper I'll draw up for the grandparents." Both nodded.

I collected email addresses from everyone, just in case.

Gran came breezing back in as we were rising. "Oh, I stayed too long," she said, "The meeting's breaking—"

She stopped in mid-sentence, her mouth hanging open, when she saw Grace. She regained her senses, and extended her hand. "I'm Maureen," she said, with her brightest smile.

"I'm Grace O'Quinn."

I knew what was coming. Gran looked at me with her eyebrows raised. "'Lady-I-met-at-the-Child-Protection-Center,' huh? You didn't tell me she was young and beautiful."

"I figured anyone could see for themselves."

Grace blushed.

Julia watched with a smug grin on her face.

Gully ignored the little scene we were playing and excused himself with a firm handshake, scurrying out the front door.

Gran jabbed me gently on the shoulder, "Well, you rascal, what's next?"

"I thought the four of us might go to dinner, if Grace can make it. She and I have some talking to do about foster parenting, and so forth."

Gran looked at each of us in turn, "Thanks, but I have far too much to do. I have deliveries coming—"

"Me either," Julia said. "Thanks anyway, but I have a business meeting."

Grace turned those beautiful green eyes in my direction, "Perhaps we can make it another time." Then turning to them, "It was a pleasure meeting both of you."

"You, too, dear," Gran said. "Come back soon and I'll show you what I'm doing with the condo."

"Grace, won't you reconsider? We have to talk, and we have to eat. You'll be safe with me."

"It's not that. I just…well, okay, I'm sure it will be all right."

Julia punched me in the ribs when Grace's back was turned. I shook my head and frowned.

# CHAPTER 14

The hostess, who was also the owner, greeted us as we entered. "Gideon! It's good to see you. I had heard that you were gone away." She clasped me in a warm embrace.

"Thank you, Marta. It's good to see you, too. I'm back, for a while, at least."

"And who is this?" Marta turned to appraise Grace, a gleam in her eye.

"May I present Grace O'Quinn?"

"I'm charmed," Marta said, grasping Grace's hand in that strange fingertip handshake women often use. "Come with me. Franco will be right with you. Enjoy your dinner."

Franco appeared in an instant with a bottle of '89 *Barbaresco*. "Welcome back, Mr. Grant. Compliments of the house. I hope this will be suitable?"

"Of course. Thank you." After the opening ceremony, he presented the leather bound menus and retreated.

We sat in a quiet, candle-lit booth, the murmur of conversation, the soft music, and the tinkling of glassware emphasizing our cozy separation from the outside world. We were seated in Marta's restaurant, "Chelsey's," which was on the second story overlooking the Ferry Building and the Bay, a classy place in the Financial District not well known to the general tourist trade.

I lifted my wine glass. "Thanks for coming, Grace."

"I'm not sure this is such a good idea," she responded. "I really shouldn't be in a place like this."

"It doesn't suit you?"

"Too well. If your intention is to impress me, it's working, but that's not why we should be here."

"I intend no harm. I truly meant for Gran and Julia to come too. But if I intended to impress you, there is no way I could compete with that enormous rock you're wearing, even though you concealed it when we first met."

"Concealed it?" she said, then lowered her voice. *"I didn't conceal anything."* She whispered fiercely. *"I happened to be putting on lotion when you came to my window."* She reached for her purse.

"Wait. Please wait, Grace. I apologize. I confess to having thoughts I shouldn't have. But Abigail's situation must come first. I beg you to stay."

"Well—"

"I promise to treat you exactly as I would Bernice Johnson, if she were here."

"Yeah, right." A small smile told me I was forgiven.

She changed the subject. "Why is it called 'Chelsey's'?"

"For her daughter, sadly lost to the drug culture."

"Oh, I didn't intend to bring up sadness. You can see it in her eyes." She abruptly changed the subject. "I enjoyed meeting your team, though I didn't get a chance to talk to your grandmother much."

"You did see the gleam in her eye when she saw you, I guess?"

She laughed, "Typical. I have two grandmothers so I know how they are. You'd get the same kind of attention, believe me."

"You flatter me. But this is strictly business isn't it?"

"Of course. That's why you brought me here, I'm sure." She waved her hand at our surroundings. "You didn't instruct Julia and your grandmother ahead of time, did you?"

"You have a suspicious mind ever since I proposed to you."

"No kidding. As you and I know, this isn't a 'date' and there won't be one. Besides my personal situation, it would not be professional of me and I take my work seriously."

"I'm sure you do. I respect that." I hoped she didn't sense my disappointment. Who was the guy? I could hope that he was some two-timing creep that she'd reject as soon as she'd been around me for a while. To use her phrase, "Yeah, right." Maybe time would help, like the Colorado River made the Grand Canyon. But I didn't have that much time.

Franco took our orders, topped our glasses with a flourish, and departed.

"Before we talk about Abigail, Grace, at least tell me how you came to be working there."

"We really should be talking about you but in a few words I'm a crusader, I guess. My parents live in Beverly Hills. Dad's a movie producer and Mom used to have a few minor roles until she gave it up to raise me and my little sister."

"Is he *that* O'Quinn?"

"Yes, he's that one. He's *Oscar* famous. Mom wanted me to follow in her footsteps but they both allowed me to leave that world behind. It never appealed to me to spend my life pretending to be other people. I want to be me and I want to feel that I'm doing something that helps others. I hope that doesn't sound sanctimonious."

"Not at all. I'm glad you chose what you did, but you left someone out."

She glanced at her ring, sparkling in the candlelight. "We've been engaged for two years now. He's doing residency in Cedars-Sinai. Wants to get into plastic surgery, keep the world safe from ugliness."

"A noble cause. Set a date yet?"

"No."

She sipped her wine and looked at me over the rim of her glass, "I'm happy I chose my profession also...now tell me why you are here. I know about your discovery, but not what came before."

"I'd rather hear more about you, but I suppose it will serve another purpose. Your organization will need to know about me—"

She held up her hand, "Please, I want to know who I'm dealing with. They'll get a shot at you later."

"You implied we weren't here to get acquainted, but I'm willing. Let's go with the short version." I told her about my parents, and Gran's sacrifices to put me through college and law school.

"Right after law school, I married a classmate from college. She trained to be a teacher and I guess that's what she's doing now. The breakup was my fault. I rode the dot-com rocket into endless days and nights of work. I wasn't able to balance my business obligations with the rest of my life."

"I'm sorry," she said. "It happens too much, I fear. Makes one worry about finding the right person."

In the silence that followed, she gazed out over the Bay and at the lights of the Oakland Bay Bridge. The bridge suffered damage in October exactly ten years ago in the Loma Prieta quake. It was in operation but there were plans underway to replace it, at least in part.

"Like I said, my problems were my fault. However, it's in the past and will stay there. Anyway, after a few years of that I ditched it all—sold the law firm, had the boat built, and sailed away."

"Only to get right back in the mix."

"Right. The break served its purpose, though. I didn't realize what kind of person I want to be until I encountered Abigail. That changed everything."

"So now you know?"

"I'm getting there, I think."

"I can see that," she said, gazing again at the Bay Bridge, its stream of lights sparkling against the night sky. "I didn't think about anything but school and work myself, but reached a bit of burnout, perhaps not like yours. I was on track for a doctorate but dropped out to work awhile, see if it's really what I want."

"Well?"

"I'm learning more every day, such as today."

"What did you learn today?"

She looked away. "Well, it's about people and families and relationships that aren't always of a conventional kind."

Franco returned with a silver domed tray in his white-gloved hands. He placed our steaks in front of us, beautiful Kobe filets, fare a few steps above the Spam onboard *Chips*. He refilled our glasses, lifted the empty bottle, and glanced at me. I nodded. "I'm happy to pay for this one."

Grace observed the exchange and whispered to me, "I'd better not have any more."

"About to lose control?"

"Of course not. I have to work tomorrow."

"I'm kidding. We'll see that you get home safely."

We looked at each other for a long moment, then lapsed into silence, concentrating on our food.

I spoke first. "You talked about focus. I thought I had it, then lost it when Abigail came into my life like she did...and now I'm losing focus again."

She looked at me in the flickering light. "Don't go there. We've already covered that. The subject is closed. We came to talk about Abigail and I think we must. Remember what I said earlier."

"I know. I allowed myself to become distracted. Tell me about foster care."

"To begin, it isn't true that they won't consider single men or women for foster care. It's just considered a lot better in a balanced family—father, mother, and even other children. These days it's becoming politically incorrect to say so, but I'll always believe in the sanctity of conventional marriage."

"A little out of place living here, aren't you?"

She smiled. "Not as much as you might think, among the large majority of less vocal citizens. Now, don't take this as a proposal of marriage, but it is easier for couples. I was thinking...what is your grandmother's situation?"

"Not going to let me forget it, are you? Gran has her own house in Modesto, and just this week I found out she has a boyfriend."

"Serious?"

"How should I know? I can talk to her. You mean it might be easier if she and I formed a family?"

"I believe it would."

"What else is involved?"

"Just what you might expect. The application and investigation can all be done at the same time for adoption, pre-adoption, foster care. After all, it's all about the same issues—safety and security of the child, seeing to their education, health, and welfare."

"I can certainly do all of that."

"It's a matter of convincing *them*. You would fill out a lot of paperwork and an investigator will be assigned to your case. They'll want to go all the way back in your past. Of course, before adoption could take place there would have to be closure on the fate of her parents. I'm not totally familiar with how it takes place, but I'd assume they'd have to be declared dead and notices would be posted looking for close relatives, and so forth. We know about the one set of grandparents, of course."

"Any chance they'd look for the other grandparents?"

"From what I hear, I doubt it."

"Who would the investigator be? You?"

"I don't think that would be fair. It could be the lady you met the first night, Mrs. Johnson, or someone else."

"Financially, I have no problems."

"I gathered that. But the state is responsible for her up until adoption, so if foster care worked out they'd pay her way."

"I'd waive it, or give it back. With no apologies, I'm filthy rich."

"Congratulations. That's not supposed to affect anything but might be viewed as an awkward attempt to buy favors."

"Okay. I'll be subtle like I've been with you."

"Right. Bringing me here was not very subtle, but thanks. Dinner was fantastic."

"You're welcome."

"Is this where you brought all your lady friends?"

"No lady friends. Remember I was married. I never even brought her here. It was always business, business, business."

"Too bad."

We lingered over coffee and dessert, lapsing into silence at times, a comfortable silence rare for a first non-date. Regardless of what she said, it was a date for me. Being with an intelligent, beautiful woman in a setting like this was something I hadn't experienced in a long time. Maybe nothing in my experience could compare. Despite what she said, I could still hope.

She refused my offer to drive her home...part of that accursed professionalism. Instead, I got her a cab, paid him well, and sent her into the night after a businesslike handshake.

# CHAPTER 15

The telephone awakened me from a deep sleep. When I spoke a groggy hello, a blunt voice responded, "This is Lieutenant Haney, SFPD. I need you at Central as soon as you can get here."

"And good morning to you, also. What is this all about?"

"You'll find out when you get here." He hung up.

I hate it when people plead and beg, and grovel at my feet. Why didn't he just come out and say what he wanted? I got ready with reasonable speed, mainly out of curiosity. I slipped a note under Gran's door on my way out, grabbed a foam cup of coffee in the hotel lobby, and headed to the station in my Land Cruiser.

When I checked in with the desk and they called a number, I expected Haney, but it was his partner who came through the swinging door to lead me back to the interior.

"Com' with me." Alvarez crooked a finger. "Marty will be free in a moment. Meanwhile I will entertain you."

She filled two cups with coffee at a station and led the way into one of the drab interview rooms. "Sit, please."

I took what I assumed was the perp chair, the one facing the one-way glass.

She gave me a crooked smile, "Well, here we are. I am Conchita. We met at the docks. What would you like to do to amuse ourselves while we are alone together? Eh?"

She was a different person when Haney wasn't around. Her manner caught me off guard.

"Nothing I can think of in a police station, I can assure you."

"Perhaps someplace else, huh? You know I have special training. I could subdue and handcuff you, do anything with you that I wanted."

"If I get your drift, your suggestion is rather shocking."

"No, no, not shocking. That is the tazer and the stun gun—not fun for most people."

"Still, I'm surprised. I bet you're not recording this."

"No, no. But maybe another time. I can wear a uniform, if that is what you like."

"What if I report you for harassment?"

"Nobody will believe you. And besides, you like it, don't you? Admit that something is stirring at the thought."

She was right. It was.

Haney barged into the room, breaking the mood, if that's what it was.

"Alvarez, you got something else to do?"

She frowned, "You don' want me here?"

"Not now."

She got up and left, her chair screeching as she shoved it under the table.

Haney slapped a file on the table and sat down to face me. "I'll get right to the point. You're stickin' your nose in where it doesn't belong. That's a good way to get hurt."

"Is that a threat?"

"No, this is a threat. You screw up this investigation, I'll cut your nuts off and feed them to you."

"My, my, you're right. That does sound like a threat. Did you learn that from television?"

He leaned over the table and turned purple, "Listen you little shit. Don't get wise with me."

I wiped flecks of spittle from my face. "You listen to me, Lieutenant. We're both on the same side here. And I'm growing weary of your attitude. I have every right to look into this situation, and I intend to continue. And I know about you."

"What the hell does that mean?"

"I don't mean to open old wounds, but I want you to treat me with more respect. Twenty years ago, you lost your daughter to a miserable creep. You have never recovered and I understand that. But I am not the bad guy here."

Haney sank back in his chair, his shoulders slumped, and turned his face away from me. He swallowed a couple of times, then cleared his throat, speaking in a near-whisper. "And I shot the son of a bitch. I was lucky. He pulled a piece on me. I would have killed him anyway. They cleared me on it. I wish I could have killed him more than once..."

"I'm sorry for your loss. But it doesn't help to give me a hard time."

He sighed, "You're right. But you'd be advised to butt out. You could get your ass killed, and not by me. We don't know who did this."

Back in my Toyota, I scanned the street for some place to quiet my growling stomach, try to figure out what had just happened and decide what to do the rest of the day. Nearby was a brightly lit diner with parking around back. I pulled in next to a patrol car, one of many, and walked around front. In a newspaper vend box I saw it: screaming headlines on the front page of *The San Francisco Clarion*, "**CLARION STAR REPORTER MISSING.**" Oh, geez, just what we didn't need. I bought a copy and went inside, scanning the article as I was led to a booth. I got the expected once-over from a diner full of cops, coming off and going on shift. Was I a serial killer? Plainclothes detective from Internal Affairs? Just a regular geek? Unable to solve the problem they went back to their plates.

After a grateful drag from my mug of coffee, and getting my breakfast order on the way, I read the dreaded article. It featured file photos of the couple, followed by a sub-heading:

BRADLEY AND SOLENE DICKERSON MISSING,
DAUGHTER FOUND

A reliable source reports that a yacht belonging to the Dickersons was found adrift in the Pacific west of San Diego with no one on board except the couple's 3-year old daughter. The yacht, named *First Edition*, was reported to be filling with water from an open valve. The discovery was made by Mr. Gideon Grant, former principal of Grant and Associates, a law firm specializing in computer and Internet law.

The Dickersons left on an extended vacation aboard their boat two weeks ago, planning to sail to Australia, according to friends. Dickerson is considered one of the paper's most enterprising investigative reporters, having exposed numerous cases of fraud and criminal activity.

Mrs. Dickerson is an Olympic gold medalist in track and field, and is well known in the Bay Area for her charity work and for her acting and modeling career.

The Federal Bureau of Investigation, the Coast Guard, and San Francisco Police have been contacted, but will not comment on details of the investigation.

The daughter, Abigail, rescued from the sinking yacht, has been placed with Child Protective Services, pending location of the parents or other relatives...

"Son of a bitch!" Four cops at the nearest table looked up from their plates. "Sorry," I said, shaking my head and staring at the paper.

...It is customary to place such children with foster families until a proper conclusion of a case involving missing parents, according to an unnamed contact at CPS.

Bradley Dickerson is the son of Abigail and Joseph Gaines Dickerson of Atlanta, Georgia. The senior Mr. Dickerson is well known in real estate and banking circles. He also refused comment when contacted by *The Clarion*...

The piece went on with more details about their social and business activities around the city, but nothing specific. Apparently someone in law enforcement or Child Protective Services leaked the story, someone like a little Hispanic cop I'd just encountered or a loose-lipped CPS employee. I couldn't believe a pro like Haney would do it. But what about Haney? Why had he called me on the carpet? Was he getting inside stuff from somewhere? He didn't seem to have specifics, so I decided he was just doing a cop-thing.

After scarfing down my bacon and eggs, I threw some money on the table and dashed out on the sidewalk. I dialed Child Protective Services. I worked my way through their electronic menu, and finally got a human. "This is Gideon Grant. May I speak with Grace O'Quinn, please?"

"She doesn't come in until 9:00. Can someone else help you?"

"Not really. Please ask her to call me. It's urgent." I gave her my cell number.

I dialed Central Station and asked for Haney, hoping he was still there.

"Haney."

"Why in the hell didn't you tell me somebody leaked to the paper?"

"What are you talkin' about?"

"The paper has blown the story about the Dickersons. I hope you know what this has done to that little girl!"

"Hey don't rag my ass! I haven't seen it, but believe me, I'll find out who the hell did it."

"Sure!" I switched off my phone. Just as I did, it rang.

"Gideon."

"Good morning. It's Grace. Thanks for—"

"Have you seen the paper? Somebody blew the cover on the Dickerson story!"

"Well, good morning to you, too."

"Look, I apologize, but I'm really upset. Now Abigail may be in more danger. Who do you think did it?"

"I have no idea, but it was bound to come out—"

"Yeah, but that doesn't help. Look, I want to hire some private security for her. How do we do that?"

"I'm sure the police will see to it."

"I'm not. Back to my question. How do we get it done?"

"Well, you know we can't disclose her location, and if we told you where to send them, that wouldn't work."

"How about if I provide the money and you hire them? I wouldn't even have to know who they are, but you'd be responsible for finding the right people."

She sighed, "I've never done this kind of thing."

"Let me know how much to send to you and when."

"I'll look into it."

"Please do more than that. If anything happens to that little girl, I will not be happy."

"A threat?"

"If you like."

"Just let me do my job!" She hung up.

What next? Maybe Dickerson's club. And I wanted to try again for a chance at seeing Abigail. Also, a visit to Atlanta should be scheduled soon to scope out this Grandma and Grandpa. I didn't know enough yet about the graft issues Gully was working on.

I called Gully from my car, still parked in the lot.

He answered with a military, "Tolliver speaking, Sir."

"Gully, Gideon here. Have you seen the paper?"

"Yes, Sir."

"I'm trying to get Child Protective to hire extra security and let me pay for it. They sound wishy-washy. Do you have a way to find out where Abigail is?"

"I'll look into it, Sir."

"Good. Meanwhile, do you suggest I try a visit to Dickerson's club?"

"Yes Sir. I have a starting point worked out for you. Already talked to her."

"Her?"

"Yes Sir. A broad...er, woman...named DeeDee Marshall. Been around awhile, likes to gossip, I hear."

"Just what I need. What is this place?"

He gave me the name, North Beach Tennis and Health Club, and the address and phone number.

"Do I need an appointment?"

"I don't think so, Sir. She said to ask for her at the gate."

# CHAPTER 16

The guard on the gate wasn't a good example of the benefits of a sports club. His girth challenged the confines of his booth beside the ornate, wrought iron gates. They and the fence were glossy black, the fence palings topped with golden spear points, and the gates emblazoned with gold heraldic crests. He was middle-aged, crew cut, muscle turned to fat.

He squinted his beady eyes when I gave him DeeDee's name, but triggered the gates and waved me through. I followed the circular drive past the entrance columns and parked in a visitor slot. The receptionist behind a standup counter was a short blonde with muscles and a deep tan. I signed in as a visiting non-member and filled in the name of my contact.

"Ms. Marshall is expecting me. Can you tell me where to find her?"

She looked at a clipboard on a hook behind her. "She's just finishing up an exercise class. I'll take you back there."

She stuck her head in an office behind her and said, "Troy, can you watch the front for a minute?"

Troy, also muscular and tanned, came out and asked, "You looking for membership? We have a waiting list."

"No, just here to see a member of the staff."

"Who?"

"Ms. Marshall. She's expecting me."

"Be careful."

I didn't ask him what he meant, but followed my escort down a couple of corridors until we arrived outside a glassed-in exercise room. Leotard-clad bodies inside gyrated to the beat of hard rock, which penetrated the walls.

"Mr. Grant, if you will wait right here she'll see you and come out after the class is over."

At that moment, the music stopped and the dancers with it, breaking formation to say a few words to their comrades. They all began to move toward an archway to my right, but the leader strode gracefully in my direction. She was tall, with her height coming from long legs clad in shimmering green tights. She had bright red hair, cut short, and an angularity from too much exercise, in my view.

I opened the door, and as she stepped through, I said, "Ms. Marshall? I'm Gideon Grant. Mr. Tolliver—"

"Yes, Gully said you might stop by." She stuck out her hand. "What can DeeDee do for you?" She fixed me with her gray-green eyes, staring straight into my own at exactly my height. I sensed a double edge to her question.

Ignoring anything other than my mission, I spoke softly, trying to set a confidential atmosphere. "I'm worried about the Dickersons, so I want to talk to people who know them." I looked over my shoulder, down the empty hall. "Is there someplace we can talk?"

She looked about her in the same way, then leaned toward me speaking almost in a whisper, "I saw the paper this morning. You're the one who found the boat."

"Yes, but I'd rather not discuss it here."

"Right. This sounds interesting but I have a full schedule and can't leave until five. Can you come to my place about 5:30?"

"Well…"

"Don't worry. I won't hurt you." She flashed a wide smile full of white teeth.

Even that statement could have a double meaning. "Oh, it's not that. I'll have to reschedule a meeting but I'll be there."

I followed her to a small office down the hall and she wrote her address and telephone number on a sticky note. "See you then," she said, fluttering her eyelids.

Now here I was at mid-morning needing to wait until 5:30, no plan, and a thousand things to do. While I thought about it, I drove back to the condo to check on Gran. I found her in the middle of the great room directing traffic. Two or three pairs of delivery people were scurrying about the condo with boxes and pieces of furniture.

"Hi, Gid. How are things with you? No, no, not over there! Turn it at an angle. That's it. Don't scratch the floor!"

"Okay, Gran. Looks like you're into it."

"Right...That goes in the back bedroom...Where was I? Oh, are you having any luck?"

"Not much. I have an appointment at 5:30 today, so I guess we'll skip the task force meeting. I'll phone everyone and send a group email. If anyone has anything of importance they can let us all know."

"Well, I'm fine here. We'll be able to move in for tonight. Reggie's coming by around five, so he and I will have cocktails here and wait for you for dinner. You won't be long, will you?"

"Shouldn't be, but I'll call if it takes longer than an hour or so. Can I hide in a bedroom and make my calls?"

"Sure. Use the guest room, which will be my room."

"No, you're going in the master bedroom. You deserve it. I insist."

"Well...I shouldn't. But I do like the idea of that Jacuzzi. Reggie... uh...never mind." Her newly-smooth cheeks colored slightly.

"It's settled." I went to my room and left phone messages for Julia and Grace. Gully answered. "Gully, what do you think of my talking to Bart Richie at the newspaper?"

"I think that would be fine, Sir, as long as you don't give him any details of the evidence on the boat. Now that it's in the paper he'll want to talk. Be a good chance to see what he knows about that couple. How'd it go with the health club broad?"

"Didn't get to talk much. I have an appointment at her place at 5:30. That's the reason I had to cancel our task force."

"I see. Un-huh."

Why did he say that? I plugged my computer modem into a phone line and sent my group email. Gran had it connected already. Amazing. I called Special Agent Scott, ostensibly in charge of the investigation. Didn't get him this time but left a callback.

Fighting frustration at my lack of control, I called the *Clarion*. When I gave them my name, the reason for my call, and asked for Bart Richie, they put me through immediately.

"Mr. Grant! So good of you to call. Can you come into the office or meet me somewhere?"

"Sure. But I'd just as soon meet away from the office. Are you on a deadline?"

"Actually, yes. Can you meet around two? Do you know a place called 'Clancy's'?"

"No, but I'll find it."

As I left the condo I met a delivery boy in the hall pushing a handcart loaded with bar supplies and a case of Bombay Sapphire Gin. Gran has good taste.

I found Clancy's Bar, a true Irish pub, well in advance of our appointment so I could enjoy a corned beef sandwich and a pint of Guiness. The threat to precious Abigail weighed on my mind, and I felt guilty that I had found no way to see her and comfort her. I could see the logic of what CPS was trying to do but that didn't help much. The only way I could see hastening contact with her was to find out what happened, and failing that, fill out the paperwork and try to adopt her.

As I was finishing lunch, my cell rang. It was Scott, with a terse, "You called, Mr. Grant?"

"Yes, Mr. Scott. Thanks for calling back. I'm concerned about the newspaper article and also wondered if you have any news."

"I understand. There is nothing specific to report but I can tell you we have agents all up and down the coast, trying to locate the boat involved. Also, the investigation is continuing in other directions."

"I assume you're looking into Dickerson's background?"

"Well, you understand I can't comment on specifics."

"I guess I do. I also wanted to let you know I'm going to talk to Bart Richie at the *Clarion*."

"I don't think that's a good idea."

"I wasn't asking permission. He is or was Dickerson's boss. I want to see what he knows. I assure you I won't release any inside information on the evidence collected. I may trade the general outline of my encounter for whatever he can tell me."

"Let me warn you again that he's a pushy journalist."

"I can be pushy, too."

Bart Richie walked in right on schedule, and there was no doubt who it was. Gully had him pegged. I waved from my booth and he strode purposefully to greet me, hand extended for a crushing handshake. He was over six feet tall, with wavy black hair and neat mustache to match. He had a movie-star smile as Gully had suggested, square jaw, and a firm, dimpled chin. He wore a smartly cut navy pinstripe suit, pink shirt with white collar and cuffs, and a pink silk tie with tiny white whales spouting on it. Not exactly the picture of the disheveled newspaper guy.

"Mr. Grant, I assume. Pleasure to meet you."

"The pleasure is mine. Call me Gideon, or Gid, if you like."

"I'm Bart. Some of my friends call me Blackie. Looks like you're out. Want another?" He waved to a barmaid, who was dressed in a frilly white dress and green apron.

As she bent over the table to pick up my mug and wipe up the moisture, I thought the white globes of her breasts might leap out of the bounds of her elastic bodice. She looked directly into Richie's eyes with a predatory smile.

He smiled back, of course. "I need to have some lunch."

"I had the corned beef and a Guinness, but I'll go for coffee this time."

"Bring me what he had," he said. The waitress left, almost running into a table as she looked back over her shoulder.

"Well, here we are," he said. "I presume you had some reason for calling me? Of course, I was in the process of trying to get in touch with you."

"Good. My main reason is my concern for the safety of the daughter. We don't know what happened on the boat or why, and whatever it is might put Abigail in jeopardy. The story was not supposed to hit the papers yet. Maybe you can tell my how that happened."

"I understand your concern. They were friends of mine, also—"

"You said 'were.' Are you assuming they're dead?"

"No, not at all. I just meant they were friends when they lived here, but they left for faraway places. Back to your question: the tip came in anonymously about the yacht being found. Even if I knew who called us, I couldn't disclose who it was. I'm sure you know that."

"I suppose. But that doesn't help Abigail's safety. I understand you were friends of theirs socially. I would appreciate it if you could tell me a little more about them. I've hired a private investigator to supplement the efforts of the police and FBI, and I want to do all I can for Abigail's sake."

"What kind of reaction are you getting from the police and FBI about your efforts?"

"As you'd expect, they don't like it much, but if it motivates them to try harder, so much the better."

He took a slim tape recorder out of his breast pocket. "May I tape our conversation? Helps accuracy."

"No problem. I'll tell you about finding the yacht but there are boundaries I can't cross about some of the details. I'm sure you understand."

"Perhaps a few questions off the record, just for background?"

"Can't do it that way. Once something is said, I always assume it is public knowledge."

"Well, okay. Let's see where this leads."

The waitress brought his lunch and my coffee. She aimed her mammaries at his face all the while she was serving us, so all I saw was her rear end.

"While I eat my sandwich, can you fill me in on your personal background, why you were out in the ocean, and so forth, plus anything you can tell me about the encounter with the yacht." He switched on the recorder and placed it between us.

I started my narrative with the buildup and the sale of my law firm and continued with my plans to sail to the South Pacific. I gave him a sanitized version of finding the yacht, leaving out the black boat I saw coming from the scene. I made it more of an adventure story about bringing back the two boats, and my concern for helping Abigail in any way I could. He let me talk without interruption, but I could see that he was fidgeting with questions when I paused.

"Was there any evidence of violence on the boat? Anything bad, like bloodstains?"

"Not that I saw, or could talk about."

"Which is it? Nothing, or won't talk about it?"

"I saw no bloodstains."

"Did Abigail see anything or say anything?"

"You'll have to talk to the authorities about anything that specific. They interviewed her."

"Gideon, you tell an interesting story, but I'm sure you realize that it answers no questions. Do you think they're dead?"

"I won't speculate. I don't know where they are, or what happened to them. The answers aren't out in the Pacific. They're here. Something in their background or relationships will tell us what happened. That brings us to you and others who knew them."

"The FBI and police have talked to me, but there wasn't much I could tell them. Being in the kind of profession he was, Brad did make some enemies. Some of it naturally spilled over to me. We had threats. Some of that might have led to his decision to take a sabbatical."

"You think one of these threats led to his disappearance?"

"Who knows? One would think it would be simpler to carry out a threat here in the city. And the threats often didn't seem tied to a particular story, if you understand what I'm saying. They would just come in randomly with a phone message, such as, 'you've got your nose in something that's none of your business, and I'm gonna chop it off.' That kind of thing."

"Would you be willing to give me your five biggest stories where someone really got wiped out?"

"Let me give it some thought. Yes, I think I can come up with some possibles. The FBI wanted the same information so I already have a head start."

"Tell me about the Dickersons. Did they have a good relationship? Any personal problems?"

There was the tiniest flicker of hesitation before he answered. "Oh, no, nothing that I know of. They seemed to be fine."

"Can you tell me a little more about them? She was an Olympian, wasn't she?"

"Yes. She won medals in the '92 Games in Barcelona. Liberia was in a mess, as usual, so she got permission to compete for France. She'd been going to school there for some years, and her home country had no team. There were some complaints after she did as well as she did, but she kept her medals."

"I thought Liberia changed leaders in 1990."

"It did, but then the rebels splintered and began fighting each other and the Liberian army and the so-called peace-keepers. She'd gone back home in the middle of that mess after the Barcelona Games. Her father worked for Doe, trying to help set up a stable government, and Doe was assassinated. He was a descendent of American slaves, an *Americo-Liberian*. Brad was over there in '93 covering the fighting as a free-lance correspondent. He helped her get out, they came here, and got married. Their daughter was born about a year or two later, I think."

Richie waved at the waitress, holding his glass in the air.

"What about her mother?" Selfishly, I wondered if Abigail really might have another grandmother.

"I think she died sometime in Solene's childhood. I don't know for sure."

"Does Solene have enemies? Could she have been the target?"

Black Bart creased his forehead in thought. "I can't imagine such a thing. She blossomed like a spring flower after she got settled in this community. I'm sure you must have heard of her, being in this area."

The waitress brought him a frosted glass of Guiness, and plopped another coffee in front of me without looking in my direction.

"Yeah, something about modeling, I think. You have to understand I didn't have time to follow much about local society."

"Well, she got into modeling, and made some magazine covers. She was...there I go again...*is* quite striking. A natural beauty, inside and out. She gave of herself in many organizations and charities."

Sounds like she had one committed fan. I wondered how far "gave of herself" went. "So how did Brad take it?"

"What do you mean?"

"Did he get out-shone by her?"

"I don't think I saw anything like that."

"Did you see them socially, or just business?"

Again that little flicker at the back of his eyes before he answered. "My wife and I went out with them on occasion, and we were members of the same tennis club, so we'd see them there now and then."

"That would be the North Beach Club."

He stared. "You've been doing some homework?"

"I told you about my private investigator. Speaking of that, I'm getting input that Bradley's parents weren't too keen on having Solene in the family."

Bart sighed and took a long pull of his drink. "Yeah, I didn't know much about that, but I think it caused some problems. I think he was disappointed they didn't come out for the baby's birth, or anything."

"Where did the Dickersons live? Did they keep the place?"

"They were in an upscale townhouse, but they sold everything, put some stuff in storage, and took off."

"Did it surprise you?"

"Yeah, I guess it did. I didn't get the impression Solene was keen on the idea."

"How do you know?"

He shrugged and took a look at his gold Rolex. I got the hint.

"I guess we're about done?"

"Yes. I'll listen to the tape. May I call you with any questions?"

"Of course. I'd like to think this over and talk again." We exchanged cell numbers, shook hands again and left. He detoured to say goodbye to the waitress. It looked like she slipped him a card.

Back in my Toyota, I thought about "Blackie" Bart. Did I learn anything? Hard to tell, but maybe it would give me something to play against whatever DeeDee had to say. I put in a call to Grace and got through to her this time.

"It's Gideon. Look, I'm sorry if I came on too strong about Abigail."

"Well, you did. I'll forgive you... once again. But you need to understand that she is one of many we have to deal with, and maybe you don't think so, but if we ranked our most critical cases, she wouldn't be very near the top. I have a little boy with cigarette burns on his arms for bed-wetting. I have a little girl who's been locked in a closet for most of a year, and nearly starved—"

"Please. I get the point. You're right, of course, but it doesn't help me much. Have you found a security firm?"

"I've made a call or two, but I think employing one would be highly irregular."

"Well, do what you have to do. I'll start from another angle."

"What angle?"

"It's best you don't know."

"Look, Gideon, if you want my help we need to be honest with each other."

"How about if I tell you before I actually do anything?" A suggestion I knew I couldn't keep.

She sighed. "What choice do I have?"

I cranked the engine and pulled out into traffic. As I did so, I glanced into the rearview mirror and noticed a black Camaro or Firebird pull out also, about a half-block down the street. Might be my imagination, but it seemed to me that I'd noticed it before.

# CHAPTER 17

I found Marshall's address over near Alamo Square Park. After circling several blocks I found a parking spot. Typical of San Francisco residential areas, three- or four-story apartment houses stand shoulder to shoulder, most having garages on the ground floor. The trick is to find a section of curb between the "driveways" crossing the sidewalks long enough to squeeze in a car. I pressed her call button and was buzzed into the front entrance, then climbed flights of stairs to the third floor.

She heard me coming and opened the door with a flourish, flashing her impressive collection of white teeth. She was dressed in a black silk kimono that reached only to mid-thigh, displaying those long, well-toned legs down to bare feet and painted nails. She'd spent some quality time on herself since I saw her in the health club costume, then glistening with perspiration. Now she was fully made-up, effectively enlarging her gray-green eyes, extending her lashes, and accentuating her wide mouth with lip gloss. "Gideon! May I call you Gideon? Please come in. Right on time. I like that."

"Thank you for seeing me," I said. Her demeanor and appearance made me nervous. "Your place is really striking. Did you do it yourself?"

"I had a little help, but the theme is mine. I spent some time in Japan. They said I could decorate to my taste if I paid for it, even the carpeting and tile. "

In contrast to a fairly normal-looking building, her apartment décor surprised me. The whole place was mostly black and white, and done in a Japanese theme of spare elegance. A black glass crane stood four feet high in the black marble entry. Walls and carpeting were white and furniture was all glass, white leather, and chrome. To provide contrast, the walls were hung with silk tapestries in striking colors of Oriental design: cherry trees, storks, pagodas, and the like. I kicked off my shoes immediately before I followed her inside. Oriental vases, lacquer bowls and other knickknacks graced a wall unit, also of black lacquer finish. I knew the things were there, but had difficulty taking my eyes off the swaying silk in front of me.

She led the way to a leather couch, and motioned for me to sit. "I fixed us a little refreshment," she said. "I hope you like martinis."

"Th-that's fine," I said, my tongue refusing to function since so many brain impulses were going elsewhere in my body. As she seated herself sideways, the kimono gapped, exposing most of her inner thighs, leaving little uncharted territory to my imagination.

She poured us generous drinks from the frosty pitcher and raised her glass. "Here's to getting better acquainted."

This wasn't the way I expected or wanted the meeting to go, but I touched her glass with mine and drank. Then she bounced up and went into the kitchen area and brought out a glass tray of sushi. My anxiety increased. Maybe the martini would help restore calm. God knows they are good at wiping out inhibitions, which is not always for the best.

"Well, my intent was to see if we can discover anything that might help us find the Dickersons."

She fluttered her hand, now terminated in glossy red artificial nails. "Oh, sure. I know. But it doesn't hurt to get to know each other does it?"

"No, of course not."

"So you've been at sea for a few weeks, sailor?" She gave me a quirky grin.

"True. Right now, though, all of my focus is on that family, particularly the little girl. I'm really concerned about her."

"All of your focus? But whatever you wish. We have plenty of time, don't we? Tell me about your adventure."

I gave her the short, sanitary version. By now, I'd told the story so many times that it rolled easily off my tongue, now beginning to limber up with the martini, which she had already refilled.

"Was there any blood?"

"I can't get into any details."

"Was the boat sinking?"

"As I said—"

"I know, no details. But I won't tell anyone. I just want to know if Bradley was...uh, and Solene, were okay."

"I just don't know any more than I've told you.

"So you've become enchanted with the little girl?"

"I don't know if that's the right term. She's all alone right now, and has gone through a lot of stress. She became attached to me and I guess I felt the same way. I'd never been around little kids before, and she's really something."

"You sound like a softie." She moved closer and put her hand on my arm.

"I don't know about that. Did you know the family?"

"Yeah, they were members at the club. Solene took some of my classes. She played tennis. Brad played handball and tennis. Probably saw the little one, since they have a nursery there. Yeah, they were pretty active."

"Did they have enemies?"

"Doesn't everybody? Oh, I don't mean bitter enemies, but in a club there are currents—you know, somebody drinks too much, ogles the wrong person, beats the crap out of somebody at handball. We're all children in many ways." She refilled our glasses, then bounced up and went to mix another batch.

"Any games other than handball and tennis?" She'd come back and seated herself with her silk shoulder touching mine. She nudged me and smiled.

"Well, d-u-h! What do you think? All those healthy bodies, dressed in skimpy clothes? Competition. Lots of parties..."

"Anybody I know?"

"Here's where we have a problem. I shouldn't—"

"I know, but it will go nowhere besides me. If there's *anything* that might help find them, please tell me."

She downed the rest of her drink and reached to set it on the coffee table. When she slid back, she turned to face me and in one swift motion, straddled my lap, facing me.

With her face almost touching mine, she whispered, "Oh, what should I do? Will you help me decide?"

Before I could answer, she put both arms around my neck and crushed my lips with a kiss, her tongue darting between my teeth. She smelled and tasted wonderful. She moaned and held the kiss, while she released her grip around my neck to reach for the sash of her kimono. All of those nagging questions about what lay beneath were answered: Absolutely nothing.

The kimono slithered off her shoulders as she stood to face me. She was slender and superbly toned, with small firm breasts, her nipples standing erect. She was a natural redhead, based on the evidence presented to me at eye level. She reached for my hand.

"Come with me."

Starting to stand, I experienced that bashful feeling from adolescence when a boy's body reacts in an uncontrollable response when others might be looking. After months alone, I felt like all of the blood in my body was concentrated below my belt line.

She looked down. "That's *good*. It looks uncomfortable, though. Let's see what we can do about it."

"I have to make a telephone call."

"*Now?*"

"Yes. It'll be quick." I speed-dialed Gran on the way to the bedroom. "Gran? Don't wait for me. Looks like I'm going to be tied up for a while."

DeeDee bumped me with her shoulder. "How did you know what I had in mind?"

She handed me a couple of foil packets out of the nightstand. "You might want these later, but there are a couple of things I might show you first."

She didn't tie me up, but I was treated to a demonstration of some things I hadn't experienced before. At times I thought *I didn't know you could do that!* Must be my sheltered life. She certainly was flexible. Also, I hadn't been to a gym for some time, and now I lay on my back exhausted and depleted, with a silly smile on my face, feeling like I'd done a set on all the equipment in North Beach Club.

She crawled on top of me again. "Well, what do you think?"

"I can't. My brain isn't working."

"Well, tiger, everything else seems to."

"Not anymore. Will you remind me who I am and why I'm here?"

"You were about to tell me all about what you saw on the boat. I really do want to know."

"No, I wasn't. I do remember that much."

"Well, you'll come around. Let's take a shower and get dressed. DeeDee gets what she wants."

"Not this time. I will buy you dinner somewhere. I'm hungry."

We wound up in a small Mexican restaurant a half block from her building. We started on big frosty margaritas, and I ordered Number Eleven off the menu, with an indifferent curiosity about what it would be.

"You asked me to help you decide what to tell me about the club members. Was I successful in doing that?"

She made a face. "That wasn't what it was. I was horny. Nothing good has come along lately. I suppose it wouldn't hurt for me to repeat some of the gossip. That's what it's for isn't it?"

"By all means. Gossip spoils if it isn't kept moving."

She delayed by dipping another nacho into some salsa. "Well, to start with, Solene was the toast of the club, and everyone liked her in the beginning. When all of the men started going out of their way to drool over her and vie for her attention, the wives started getting weary of it. Catty remarks, you know."

"Did Solene take part?"

"She ignored it, mostly."

"Mostly?"

"Well, she had to know about it. Eventually it settled out into people she associated with, those she didn't."

"Any of it rise to the level of revenge against her?"

"Sure wouldn't think so. But some people are nuts, you know."

"How about Bradley?"

"He didn't like it. But he was someone to talk."

The waiter interrupted her, placing my hot Number Eleven and whatever she ordered in front of us.

"He a player?"

"Maybe I shouldn't have said that."

"You had a reason." She wanted me to pry it out of her.

"Brad had a reputation."

"Was it true?"

She looked a little flustered, "Yeah, I think it probably was. In any setting, Brad always went after the good-looking women."

"With success?" Considering what happened to me, it wasn't hard to add two and two.

"Sometimes, but not like his boss."

"Black Bart?"

"You know him?"

"We met."

"Then you can guess how it was with him."

"Solene?"

"Look, I've probably said too much already."

"Did it have anything to do with Bradley's decision to sail away?"

"I don't have any way of knowing why he went. We weren't that close...by then. He did sell his townhouse to pay for the yacht. Also, Bart Richie and his wife split last year and she went back to Chicago with their kid. I'm not saying there was a connection. People do that all the time nowadays. In fact, I think Bart bought Brad's place from him, since *his* wife got their house and sold it."

"Cool. Sounds like your everyday soap opera. What did you mean, 'by then'?"

"Oh, come on! That didn't mean anything."

Not a lot to go on, but time would tell. I paid the check, bid her an awkward goodbye at her building entrance and retrieved my Toyota. It was now pushing ten o'clock, and the side street was dark. As I pulled out of my parking space, another car did the same. I couldn't see what it was, but a dark car with a higher profile than the Camaro/Firebird.

In fifteen minutes, I pulled into my own parking garage for the first time and found my parking spot, next to Gran's car. I'd bought two to go with my human space. As I rode up in the elevator, I began to feel guilty and wondered how I should explain myself, just like being back in my high school days when I was late. I needn't have worried.

I entered the living room, now completely furnished, lamps softly aglow, artwork on the walls, a thick Persian carpet on the floor. Jemima bounded out of a chair and ran to me, rubbing against my leg. Gran and a distinguished elder gentleman sat on the couch, both feet on the floor, their hands in their laps, trying not to look guilty. The gentleman shot to his feet, braced to attention. All he lacked was the click of heels and the quivering, palm-forward salute. Gran rose also.

"Gideon, may I present Sergeant-Major Reginald Thurston. Reggie, this is Gideon."

The Sergeant-Major took two swift strides across the room to meet me and extended his hand, grasping mine in a firm handshake. "Pleasure to meet you, sir!" he barked.

"The pleasure is mine, sir. Gran has spoken so highly of you."

"She's very kind," he said in his strong bass voice.

"Please take your seat. I'm sorry. I meant to get here in time for dinner with you—"

We're fine, aren't we, Reggie?" She took his hand.

Sergeant Thurston was a half-head taller than I, with close-cropped white hair and a bristling white mustache that turned up at the wings. His complexion was ruddy, and he was slightly overweight, a muscular body gone a bit soft with age. I saw regimental tie, brass buttons, and starch in the shirt and in the spine. What a figure he would be in his bearskin hat.

He placed his other hand over hers and they looked at each other. There was a moment of awkward silence, then he cleared his throat, and looked at me, a slight flush of color lighting his face. "Maureen and I...Well, I say...I wonder if I might have a private word with you, Mr. Grant."

"Of course. And please call me Gideon, or Gid, as Gran does. What shall I call you, sir?"

"Reggie is fine. We Yanks don't stand on ceremony, what? In the old days, in the Coldstream, some of the chaps called me 'Thursty,' if you get my drift."

"Reggie just got his citizenship, Gid."

"Congratulations!"

"Yes, well, it seemed a good plan."

Gran jumped up and headed for her bedroom. "I'll leave the two of you to talk."

"Would you like a brandy? Or a whiskey? I'm assuming we have it all." He seemed a bit nervous about something.

"Splendid. Whatever you're having."

I found a bottle of Famous Grouse and splashed a couple of fingers into crystal glasses. I sat in the chair to his right and we clashed the glasses in salute. "Now, what is it you'd like to discuss?" I knew the answer, of course.

"Well, I hardly know how to begin. One lives what one considers a fine and full life as the decades go by. There is love, there are children to nurture, there are times of trial and of happiness..." He paused and looked into space, sipped his drink. Then he turned back to look at me and there was a shine of tears in his eyes. His lip trembled and he spoke in a soft rumble. "We lost our son many years ago, then my dear wife passed away some ten years ago. I emigrated here to live with my daughter, my only surviving family. I was prepared to be content to let the rest of my days slip by. Then I met your grandmother Maureen—"

"She's happy that you did." I interrupted him to let him regain his composure, but it didn't work.

"I love her very much, you see," he said, almost with a sob, "and I want to ask for your permission for us to marry..."

"You needn't have asked, but I'm flattered that you did. You have my blessing, of course."

He leaped to his feet and said with his parade-ground voice. "Maureen, Dear, can you come? We need you."

Gran must have been listening at the door, for she was embracing Reggie in mere seconds, then me, then both Reggie and me.

"I can't imagine that there isn't champagne in the refrigerator? I'll get it."

Gran held up her left hand, which sparkled with a diamond. "I knew you'd approve, but Reggie is an old-fashioned gentleman."

We drank champagne to the betrothed, who looked happy as two people can look as they sat together on the couch holding hands. Thoughts began to form in my mind and I wondered whether to broach them and interrupt the celebration. I made a decision.

"Gran, may I have word with you? It'll take only a minute, if you'll excuse us, Reggie."

He shot to his feet as we set down our glasses and stood, "Of course, of course."

Gran followed me into the master bedroom with a question arching her brows.

I took her hands in mine. "Gran, I love you and I don't want to embarrass you, since you raised me with the highest of principles. But I think there is a time for grown people to make some decisions that are in the best interests of everyone."

"Yes?"

"What I want to ask, would you like for Reggie to stay with us? It's up to you. In my view, it makes sense—"

"Oh, Gid, you wonderful straight arrow! I wouldn't have asked but I would love it. Now, I will have to convince Reggie. He has very high standards."

"I knew that. He loves you, doesn't he?"


We retrieved Reggie's luggage and mine from our hotels and I moved into the guest room. Our temporary family settled in after midnight, a happy couple embarking on a new life together, and me—physically sated, emotionally at a low level. I didn't like what happened with DeeDee and it wasn't clear what I'd learned. I believe she was in the middle of whatever games took place, but who knows whether it went beyond games? Her apartment décor went beyond the grade level of her occupation. Was there a sugar daddy involved? A former rich husband?

I was happy for Gran and Reggie. They truly seemed a great match. But for me, there was an emptiness in my heart. Somewhere out there was a little girl who needed me, and a lovely woman who didn't.

# CHAPTER 18

I awoke to the heavenly smells of bacon and coffee, and faint sounds of activity in the kitchen. I rushed through my shave and shower and went in to find Reggie filling the space between the island and the stove. He wore a great white apron and his face was pink from a fresh shave. He turned to greet me, "Good morning, sir!"

"Good morning to you, Reginald. And please, no 'sir'."

"Sorry. Force of habit. Because of your intelligence and success, I think of you as the commanding officer. How do you like your eggs? I have popovers coming out in ten minutes and the bacon is done."

"You're going to spoil me. Over medium is fine."

"Jolly good. Here's coffee. Maureen's having hers whilst she reads the morning paper and does her puzzles, but you probably know that."

Reggie and I were new to each other but settled in to have our breakfast. "Has Gran told you of my troubles?"

"We share everything now."

"What do you think?"

"Look first to the family. You shall usually find yourself correct."

"This guy made a lot of enemies."

"The kind who would murder?"

"Won't know until we check them out."

Gran swept into the dining area, all robed and fresh, her bare feet making kissing noises on the polished floor. "Well, how are the men in my life?"

Reggie shot to his feet, and headed for the stove.

I said, "Just plotting a course but I feel a bit rudderless."

"Well I hope we don't add to your troubles, but we do have a few things to discuss. After breakfast?"

What was this about?

After Gran finished eating we took our coffee to the living room. I thought we'd already discussed everything.

Gran began, "Gideon, I know you are trying to develop plans, but I'm afraid we didn't discuss everything last night."

The devil in me wanted to say something clever, like, "You're not in a family way, are you?" But I couldn't do it to her and Reggie, with their worried expressions.

She glanced up at Thurston, sitting beside her. "We'd started planning before your return, you see. It's selfish of me, but we want to marry right away and begin an extended honeymoon. Reggie wants to show me some of the many places in the world where he has been..." The words tumbled out in a rush.

I was disappointed, of course, but determined not to show it. I went and knelt by the couch and took her hand. "Don't worry about a thing. I'll figure it out. You deserve all that life can give you."

Tears coursed down her cheeks. "Oh, thank you, my dear son." We rose together and she gave me a fierce hug. Then even Reggie, despite his natural reserve, joined in a three-way.

In the awkward silence that followed, my cell phone rang, allowing me to disengage myself from the betrothed. I answered as I drifted toward my bedroom.

"Sir," said Gully, "I've found her."

"Abigail?"

"Yes, Sir. We've found the preschool where she's enrolled. Would you like to go there?"

"By all means."

"I'll be by your place in fifteen, if that suits."


I was waiting eagerly at the curb, when a small silver Dodge pickup pulled up. It had a cap on the back and the little second seat, which was filled with boxes of papers and electronic equipment. I jumped in before it reached a full stop.

"I haven't been there yet, Sir, but I know where it is. It's a church out in the area between Pacific Heights and Knob Hill that has a pre-school and kindergarten."

"How did you do such a thing?"

Gully looked embarrassed, "Uh..."

"Ignore that. Maybe I'm not supposed to ask."

"You're paying for it Sir, but I don't want to get anyone in trouble. Would it satisfy to say that it's a matter of...well, these places have to be licensed to establish schools. Through a related route, it's possible to get a student roster."

"How clever."

"Well, we got lucky. Computers help, and of course someone on the inside. There will be a little extra on my statement for it, which I hope—"

"No problem. Results are good."

As we drew closer, Gully put on a battered baseball cap and sunglasses. "Sir, it might be good to hunch down a bit, and there's another cap or two in back. We don't know if the police are actually watching her."

I followed his instructions. The church was a very large gray stone structure looking somewhat like a castle. It was on a corner and we turned down the flanking street, trying to look disinterested. Both the facing street and side street were clogged with traffic, all in line to disgorge little people. A short bus was doing the same in front. Teachers were on duty to usher their charges, some babes in carriers, into a side door. As we crept slowly by, I strained to catch sight of her to no avail.

It appeared that the church depended on street parking plus a mix of parishioners using public transportation. What little precious extra land they had was used for a playground in back, which was enclosed by a tall chain link fence topped with an angled barbed-wire projection. It contained all sorts of playground equipment surrounded by deep shredded wood mulch.

We failed to see evidence of police presence, meaning that they were either absent or good at what they do. We found a rare parking spot up the street, from which we could observe the playground and the side entrance. Gully produced two vacuum bottles of coffee and a box of donut holes. I poured myself a cup, but declined the holes.

"I don't know yet where she lives, but either I or my man will follow her at the end of the day," said Gully. "I've lined up a security firm who will start today, taking over when we leave."

"Great! I'm impressed."

Gully looked embarrassed. "It's what we do, Sir. And on another front, we've been looking into some of the people he investigated."

"Anything interesting?"

"Don't know yet. But give me a moment if you will, and I'll explain."

He got out of the truck and went about four doors up the street to an apartment house. I could see from a distance that he examined the cluster of mailboxes and buzzers. He made notes on a pocket notebook and returned, climbing into the driver's seat.

"Might need a name," he mumbled. "On the other thing, remember a few years ago, a city manager named Emmit Dilbeck?"

"Sounds familiar. What did he do?"

"Just about anything he thought he could get by with. If it hadn't been for your friend Bradley, he might have made it. For starters, he managed to get a salary nearly twice his predecessor's. Then he set up several phantom employees and funneled their salaries to bank accounts he controlled. What really brought him down was...."

Gully interrupted himself, staring into his rear-view mirror. "There's a coupl'a cops coming."

One approached Gully's window, which Gully rolled down. The other came up my side, stopping behind the cab corner where he could keep an eye on me.

"Let me have your license and registration," demanded the uniform on Gully's side.

Gully complied, handing over his documents, including his concealed weapons permit.

"Where's the piece?"

"Under my seat."

"Just keep your hands on the wheel. What are you guys doing here by this school and who's he?" jerking his thumb in my direction.

"Didn't notice a school. Got the place up the street staked out. Guy named Gonzalez has a wife who wonders what he's doing while she's at work. My friend here is just keeping me company."

The cop sneered. "Well, good luck in the sleaze hunting."

"I hope that means the city cops are looking after our girl," I said after they left.

"I hope so too, Sir, but I couldn't very well ask."

"Back to Dilbeck, you started to say what brought him down."

"Yes, Sir. He got caught taking kickbacks on City contracts, thanks to our friend Bradley and his boss. FBI was tracking him, but the newspaper article put them over the top. Other witnesses came out of the woodwork and the whole thing collapsed. He's now serving time along with some of his staff."

"Sounds like a possible."

Gully suddenly pointed at the church. Kids and teachers were spilling out for their morning break. The more active children ran for the playground equipment. Three teams of teachers pushed plastic over-sized strollers through the double doors and up the sidewalk for a walk. Each held a dozen or so little ones. It was chilly out, so they were all properly bundled. My eyes were on the playground and I finally spotted her, seated at the base of a tree. I borrowed the binoculars and checked her out. She was alone, stroking a stuffed kitten clutched against her chest.

I handed the glasses to Gully, "She's sitting under a tree, wearing a light-blue anorak."

"Got her. Pretty girl, but she looks kinda sad."

"Yes. She's had a rough go of it and I'm sure she feels like she can't do anything about it. About the way I feel, also."

"Yeah. Well maybe we can keep at it 'til we get some breaks. At least we'll do our best to keep her safe."

"I know you will. Can you meet at my place at 5:00? We need to hear from the rest."

"Sure, Boss. Hey, here comes my guy. Good timing."

A very large, scary-looking African American guy came down the sidewalk and approached my window. As I rolled it down, he bent over and thrust in a hand the size of a catcher's mitt. "I'm Sam Owen. You must be the man." Then, "Hey, Gully."

"Gideon Grant. You came at a good time. Our girl is outside. She's sitting under a tree. Light blue hooded jacket."

He took small binoculars out of his pocket, squatted by the truck and studied her. "Real sweetie. I'll look after her." He rose and patted my shoulder with his big, meaty hand.

Gully said, "Sam, we'll be going. Now that you've seen her, we need to know where she lives. Is Morris on tonight?"

"Yessir. I'll call him when I'm following her."

"Good. You can take this parking space when we pull out. My cover is that yellow apartment house. I told the cops I was watching a guy named Gonzalez for his wife."

"Got it."

On the way back toward the Bay, Gully dug a folder out of the back seat and extracted a sheet of paper. "Here's the info on Brad's parents."

I fished out my cell phone and dialed Joseph Dickerson's office number. After going through several layers of screening, I got what must have been his personal assistant. When I explained my mission she put me on hold for several minutes, then surprised me by saying he would see me tomorrow, Friday, late afternoon. She further said that Mrs. Dickerson would be contacted and an appointment set for 3:00 p.m. If any difficulty occurred, I'd get a call within the hour. Very efficient.

We pulled up in front of my condo building by the time I'd arranged my flights for the next day.

"Gully, I'm sure you know that Grace can't know what we're doing, in case she comes this evening."

"Sure, Boss." He waved and pulled away.

I found Gran and Reggie in the kitchen putting away a couple of deliveries of kitchenware and groceries, and starting lunch preparation. They were both happy to host a meeting of our task force that evening.

I put off the call I dreaded and called Julia's office number, leaving a message. Then I called her cell and she answered on the first ring. After my greeting, she said she was in her car. "I'm good for five at your place. I just heard from my new friend Greg Peak. He says they may have something on the black boat, and will call me later this afternoon."

"Good. See you then." I dialed the number I dreaded, Grace's direct office number. I couldn't help a little thrill when I heard her soft voice, "Hello, Grace speaking."

"Grace, it's Gideon. I keep making excuses for my behavior, but there are no excuses. Will you forgive me...again?"

"I will if we can leave it behind us and you can promise to understand that I'll do anything I can for Abigail within the bounds of my profession."

"I'll take the oath. I'll treat you with respect and with my admiration, which I've had from the first time I saw you."

"Then we're good. I've never been one to bear a grudge."

"With that in mind, will you come to a meeting of our task force at 5:00, so we can all catch up on any new developments? Gran and her fiancé will be there. You really must meet him."

"Well...I'd planned to have a drink with friends, a regular Thursday thing, but for the sake of our new beginning and for our little girl, I'll be there."

"Wonderful!" I gave her the condo number. I was seated, so I couldn't do the Fred Astaire leap and heel click.

# CHAPTER 19

Grace, Gully, and Julia arrived promptly on time, greeting each other as they entered. Gran and Reggie were behind the kitchen counter and she proudly announced to the rest, "Hey, everyone, this is my fiancé, Sergeant-Major Reginald Thurston, late of the Coldstream Guard."

They came forward and shook hands over the counter, and both women went around it to give Gran a hug. Gran and Reggie put out trays of canapés, and drinks were poured. We moved into the living area. Grace looked about her and said, "This is really great." Then to Gran, "You've done a wonderful job, especially in so short a time."

"Thank you, dear."

Jemima trotted into the room and leaped up on the arm of Grace's chair, then crawled into her lap. Grace smiled at me when I shook my head and shrugged.

"Well, thanks to all of you for coming. I'll begin by summarizing all I know, then we can hear from everyone else. Interrupt me if you have questions.

"First, I was summoned to the police station early this morning to be threatened by Lt. Haney to 'butt out,' but I was able to turn that around and convince him we're on the same side. Gully had given me the info that Haney'd lost a daughter to a pervert and it had understandably affected him.

"Next, if you saw the paper this morning, the story is now public, so it puts Abigail in more danger. If you have any idea who leaked, let me know."

Grace spoke up, "I have no specific knowledge but it could have come from somewhere in our organization, and I'm sorry I was defensive about it."

"It's okay," I said.

Julia said, "Greg said it could have come from the police. Some of them look to score points like that."

"Well, what's done is done," I said. "What matters now is protecting our girl.

"Continuing, I've interviewed a trainer at the club where the Dickersons belonged. She hinted at some interplay, with emphasis on the word 'play' among the Dickersons, Brad's boss, Bart Richie, and others. I don't know yet how far it goes, but have talked to Richie and intend to again. Richie bought the Dickerson's townhouse when they sailed, after his wife had kicked him out of his house.

"And last, I have reservations for tomorrow to fly to Atlanta to talk to Brad's parents. It's really strange to me that they have no interest in Abigail.

"Okay, who's next? Julie?"

"The only news I have is what I mentioned to you on the phone. Detective Peak says they had a report from a couple of fisherman last night off Half Moon Bay. They said a big black cigarette boat went roaring past, almost running them down, then exploded about a quarter-mile away. Coast Guard investigated, found an oil slick, and is still looking for whoever was on board."

"Interesting. Anything else?"

"No. He says they really don't have anything yet and neither does the FBI. They all seem to be concentrating on interviewing friends and looking into possible enemies."

"Grace, do you have anything?"

"Just a report that Abigail seems to be fine, according to her foster parents. They say she is quiet and causes no trouble, but they worry that she's not very happy. I guess that's understandable. I called the police and they assured me they are watching her. They said that a pickup had parked by her school with two men in it, but they checked out okay."

"Good. Thanks." Out of the corner of my eye I could see Gully posing as an innocent person, gazing out the window. "Any progress on a private security firm?"

"No. I haven't figured a way to do that."

"Would it make any sense to let her have Jemima?"

"I'm sure she would like it, but the foster family has other children and it might cause conflict. But I'll check."

"Thanks. Gully?"

Gully sat erect and glanced about the room. "Well, Sir, we talked earlier…uh, by *phone*…about Emil Dilbeck. For the rest of you, he was a corrupt city manager who got caught largely through the efforts of Mr. Dickerson. He's now in San Quentin and should be there for a long time."

"Is there any way we could talk to him?"

"I doubt it, Sir. We'd have to get the cops to go with us."

"That might be tough. Julie?"

"He's right. I'll think on it. You'd have to get the cooperation of your friend, Haney."

"Can I read the transcript of his trial?"

"Yes, but it would fill a big file box."

"Can you set aside some time to scan through it for witnesses, or anyone who might have heard Dilbeck's reactions?"

"I'll see what I can do."

"Uh, Sir," said Gully. "There was one strange thing that happened before the trial. An assistant of Dilbeck's fell off a cliff and died while he was hikin' near Pirate's Cove. Couldn't prove a connection, but there were suspicions."

"Hmm. Does sound suspicious. Anyone else? Oh, I beg your pardon. Maureen and Sergeant-Major Thurston have become engaged to be married, as you heard from Maureen's introduction, and I am honored to welcome him into our small family."

Everyone stood up, clapped their hands, and cheered. The future bride and groom looked suitably pleased and embarrassed at the attention.

"Do either of you have anything to say, or to add to our search for answers? Oh, by the way, I also meant to say what a great job Maureen and Reggie have done making this place into a home so quickly."

Gran and Reggie stood, and Gran said, "Thanks to all of you for your good wishes, and as to this condo, it was a pleasant experience. I will say,

Gid, that I think your visit tomorrow will be interesting. When your dear parents were lost to us the only solace I had was my great love for you. If...if I hadn't had you, I don't think I could have gone on." She wiped tears from her cheeks, and Reggie hugged her, whipping out a gleaming white handkerchief for her.

Reggie spoke in his deep bass, "May I add my thanks, also. I am new to the situation but it seems you are doing what you can. If there is anything I can do, I stand ready."

"Thank you, Reggie. Now, does anyone have anything else?"

All shook their heads.

"Tomorrow's Friday, and I'll be getting back late. Can everyone meet here, same time Saturday evening?"

Grace raised her hand, "I'm sorry, but I'll be out of town; but if I hear anything, I'll call you."

"Well, let's reconsider. I don't want to put you on the spot, but could you make it Sunday? I think your reaction to whatever I find in Atlanta might be important."

She thought a moment. "I suppose I could. What time were you thinking?"

"Whatever you say. I have an idea. Would it be agreeable to everyone to make dinner here at 6:30 or seven, then meet?"

"How about 7:00?" Grace said.

All nodded. "Sunday at seven it is, then. Thanks. Now, speaking of dinner, I have dinner planned tonight for the betrothed and invite all of you to join us. I know it's short notice, but you're welcome to hang out here and we can all go together. Julia, we're going to that Italian restaurant you took me to."

"Gee, I wish I could go, but I have a hearing tomorrow early, and I have to do a little work tonight. I'll call the restaurant and put in a good word for you."

Gully rose, nodded at Gran and Reggie and said, "I wish you the best, but I have a surveillance going and I have to check on it."

Grace was next, looking uncomfortable. "I add my best wishes to what Mr. Tolliver said, but I think it best if I don't intrude on a family gathering."

Gran said, "We'd love to have you with us, dear. We three are not exactly a 'gathering' and your interest in Abigail makes you family to me."

"Thank you, but I really must be going. Have a nice dinner." With that, she displaced Jem, grabbed her purse, and headed for the door.

"Oh, Grace," I said. "Could you bring or send the forms for me to fill out for adoption or foster care?"

"Sure, but nothing has changed." With a little smile she was out the door.

Julia sidled over to me and spoke softly, "What did she mean, nothing changed?"

"I shouldn't be dumb enough to tell you this, but you'll pester me until I do. When I first met her to discuss Abigail and perhaps fostering or adopting, I asked her to marry me. Just a marriage of convenience to make me a better prospect for adoption. Of course she set me straight."

"I hate to say this, Gideon, but that was really stupid. A sure case of premature infatuation."

We were greeted warmly by the maitre-d and shown to a comfortable booth. A waiter appeared in minutes, bearing a tray with three frosty martinis. "Bombay martinis, very dry, compliments of Miss Julia," he announced. In moments, the hostess arrived with a dozen white roses I had ordered.

"My goodness!" said Gran. "This is wonderful!"

I raised my glass, "My very best to both of you. I owe everything to you, Gran; and Reggie, I am so happy you two have found each other. I wish for you both a long and happy life together."

We clashed our glasses and drank our toast, then Gran said, "You really care for her, don't you, Gid."

"Who?"

"You know who. Abigail, of course, but I'm talking about Grace."

"It really doesn't matter how I feel. She's not available."

She put her hand on mine, "I know. I saw the ring. But I know also that you have feelings for her. I saw your look of disappointment when she couldn't join us."

"I'll forget about it."

"I don't want to see you hurt."

"Sometimes life is like that." I wish she hadn't brought up the subject. And to add to my gloom, poorly concealed, the sound track was playing Tony Bennett again, this time *Young and Warm and Wonderful.* I wish he'd shut up about it.

Reggie cleared his throat and spoke, "Son, I hesitate to intrude with my opinion, but in the Coldstream we always said, 'The battle is not lost as long as one of us is still standing.'"

I don't know exactly why, but his words lifted my spirits. I smiled and shook his hand, "Thank you, Reggie."

We had a wonderful dinner together, on the surface. Gran and Reggie were happy as teenagers and I kept my thoughts to myself. Inside, I tried to keep the clouds away, but I thought about the coming weekend when Grace was without doubt going to see her fiancé. It was perfectly normal in the way things are supposed to work. Still, I tortured myself with it. And then there was Abigail, sad to be alone, but not as sad as I was, not being able to see her and comfort her. My plan to get away from the trials of life ashore seemed of another age. Now I wanted nothing other than life ashore.

# CHAPTER 20

I landed in Atlanta's Hartsfield International Airport a little after noon local time, about right to get my rental car and make my appointment with Mrs. Dickerson at three. We taxied up to the end of the most remote rung of the terminal ladder. It was a pretty good hike to the center spine to catch the little underground train to the main terminal. Art Buchwald once wrote, upon traveling through Chicago's O'Hare Airport, that terminals were becoming so large that they would soon be connected to each other. Then we could just walk from one city to another without the bother of planes.

In my nondescript Ford, I exited the airport into the flow of traffic on Interstate 85, soon to conjoin with its mate, Interstate 75. I surfed the river of traffic north through the center of downtown, around the boulders of lane-changers and slow vehicles. The gleaming towers of the New South overlooked the turbulent flow.

Soon I left the city center and the Georgia Tech campus behind, zoomed past the departure of I-75, and began looking for my exit north into the Buckhead area.

I had journeyed to Atlanta several times in my past life. Most of my long hours there were spent in conference rooms downtown, negotiating contracts with Internet and communications companies; transportation and financial firms.

Threading my way west on Paces Ferry Northwest, I was amazed at the wealth and power displayed by the elite estates along the way, what I could see of them behind the fences and landscaping. Modesto, California, hadn't prepared me for this.

I'd done some homework on the Dickerson family. They were listed in numerous publications feeding public fascination of the rich. Joseph Gaines Dickerson was listed in the top five hundred richest U.S. citizens.

His wife had inherited the family holdings of huge chunks of real estate, most of it in the family since before the Civil War, and a significant amount within the I-285 Beltway around Atlanta. By the time of Atlanta's major growth spurt in the 1960s, Joe Dickerson was established in his family's construction business. Then with his wife's inheritance in hand, he built a real estate empire and expanded into banking and insurance. He now had his local headquarters high atop the Peachtree Center downtown.

He met his wife, Abigail Montgomery, a daughter of the Deep South, while in college at Ole Miss. From what I could glean from the family biography, she was one of those pampered debutante types in her youth, descended from a wealthy plantation heritage. Marrying Dickerson seemed a step beneath her, but no one could fault her judgment in picking winners.

I cruised the area in order to arrive at my exact appointed hour. Why she'd agreed to see me was a mystery. Maybe I'd ask her if the opportunity presented itself, but for now, I'd take it. When I buzzed at the wrought iron gate and identified myself, the massive gate silently retracted, allowing me to enter a long sweeping brick drive, past velvet grass, and beautiful landscaping. The scissor-edged lawn had the smooth texture of a bent-grass putting green. Two black men in neat khaki uniforms were raking leaves the old-fashioned, silent way around a grouping of magnolias.

The white-columned mansion bespoke a yearning for antebellum times. It looked like what *Tara* would have wanted to be when she grew up. I parked the Ford on the bricks in front of the curved steps ascending to the verandah. Anywhere else, I would have thought of it as a front porch. Two black jockey figures held out rings, on the off chance that I'd ridden up on my hunter after harassing a fox.

I was surrounded by a forest of white columns, like redwoods with their clothes off. Keeping to the theme, a polished brass fox head door-knocker was centered in the oak door, forming the center of a brass escutcheon with all of the vines, flourishes, and figures of a family crest. I lifted his nose, rapped it a few times and waited. In a few moments, the soft rustle of footsteps preceded the sound of a lock and the opening of the massive door.

A slender, middle-aged maid in black livery beckoned me inside and said softly, "Please follow me, sir." She had a lined mahogany face, carefully devoid of expression, and a lilt of the islands in her speech. Apparently I was the only expected guest that afternoon.

She led me down a long parquetry hall and rapped on a closed door before opening it to admit me to a room cloaked in darkness. My hostess was seated in a high-backed wing chair before a Georgia marble fireplace. The flickering fire provided the only light in the room except for a dim lamp over her left shoulder, casting her face in shadow.

The maid performed a semi-curtsey and announced me, "Mister Grant, Madame." The woman in the chair nodded and spoke in the voice of a little girl.

"Bring us coffee and brandy, Matilda." The maid curtsied again and rustled out of the room.

This was a new situation for me. I winged it by stepping in front of her and bowing slightly. She lifted her hand and I grasped it without kissing it. We'd just met, and I thought that might be a little too forward.

"Thank you for seeing me, Mrs. Dickerson."

That little girl voice replied, "Thank *you*, for coming all this way, Mr. Grant, although Ah must say that name puts me off a bit."

"My name? Oh, I don't think Ulysses and I are related."

"That's a good thing."

My eyes were adjusting to the gloom, so that her features began to emerge. Her eyes sparkled black, her thin face seemed unwrinkled, the skin stretched unnaturally tight over her cheekbones. Her hair was done in a crown of tight curls, with a trailing cape of straight hair ending in curls at the nape of her neck. It was an unnatural black. She was wearing a dark velvet dress with a queenly lace collar, to project the effect of royalty.

The maid rustled in with a silver coffee service on a tray, accompanied by a crystal decanter. My hostess asked, "What is your pleasure, Mr... though we've just met, may Ah call your given name? So's Ah won't have to..."

"Of course. It's Gideon."

"Oh, that's fine! Ah love Biblical names."

"Just coffee, black, please." She stared at me, waiting in mid-pour. I got the hint. "And a splash of brandy will be fine."

She relaxed and smiled, more like a grimace, showing small teeth between thin lips. She made no attempt to conceal her own coffee-brandy combination, more than half the latter.

"I doubt Gideon was a popular name in the land of the Midianites."

"You are probably correct, Gideon. My, he was quite a man!"

"God was on his side, I believe."

Mrs. Dickerson nodded, and changed the subject as the maid bowed and retreated.

"We bring in all of ow'ah help from the islands—Dominican Republic, Jamaica, and so forth. Ow'ah nigras have gotten too uppity to go into service properly."

I almost choked on my coffee, but I determined to ignore such things until I got what I wanted.

"Ah understand you are the one who found my son's yacht?"

"Yes, and that's the reason I wanted to—"

"And Gideon, do you have a family?"

"Just my grandmother. She raised me after my parents died in a car crash when I was little." Where did that question come from? She ignored my answer.

"Would you be so kind as to tell me of this adventure?" She took a slug of coffee and dashed brandy into the cup to recover the level.

I told her of encountering the yacht, seeing the cat, pumping out the water, then the discovery. "And then I found your granddaughter—"

"I have no granddaughter!"

I was startled by the vehemence of her statement and the black glitter of her eyes.

"I'm sorry. I assumed that her name, being with your son—"

She stared into the dim recesses of the room. "Well, you couldn't know. Ow'ah son was always well-behaved. Did what we told him. But this time he defied us. We told him not to do it. Told him we'd disown him. Joseph just couldn't go through with it." She turned back to me, "But we could surely ignore anything or anybody else involved, like that dark person!"

I struggled to keep my feelings in check. "I didn't mean to upset you, but she's a beautiful little girl. Would you like to see a picture—"

She interrupted again with a wave of her hand. "Absolutely not. Ah don't care what she looks like. She's of mixed blood. My family can be traced back through the generations to a land grant from the king of England in the sixteen hundreds. All of pure blood. Ah'm not about to sully it now."

"Okay. Just so there are no future misunderstandings, would you and your husband be willing to sign a document severing all claims to the little girl involved? That is, of course, in the sad event that her parents are not found alive."

"Of course. Now tell me what you think may have happened to my son. Be blunt. Ah'm tough. Had to be."

"All I know is what I saw. He and ... No one was on board except the little girl. The electrical panel had been destroyed by gunfire and a valve had been opened to the sea. Later I found that the anchors and chain were missing."

She placed her arthritic knuckles against her mouth and began a strange keening, rocking back and forth in her chair. Almost as suddenly, she stopped and sat upright, reaching a trembling hand for her cup. No tears flowed down the parchment cheeks from the black, expressionless eyes.

I had to fight an urge to flee. "Mrs. Dickerson, can you think of anyone who would wish ill of your son?"

"Ah really know nothing about his life out there in that strange land. Ah think he wrote for a newspaper. Could be he stirred somebody up."

Also one of our theories. I'd wait for my audience with Joseph. "Well, thank you for your time. I'll head downtown to see your husband at his office. He said he'd want to hear my story."

"Do you have that paper you talked about?"

"Yes, I brought it just in case."

She reached for a black Waterman pen on the lamp table, and signed the document I presented without reading it. Then she rang a small bell and the imported maid appeared at my side.

I clasped the proffered hand again, and was ushered out the door. Although I had another appointment, I felt the need of a shower to decontaminate. Maybe I'd feel the same way after I met the other half of the couple. Thank God they had no interest in Abigail.

I stashed the car in an underground parking garage and made my way into the gleaming granite lobby of the twin towers. I signed in with a guard and rode an express elevator to the top floor. Plate glass doors were labeled with gold leaf proclaiming "Dickerson Enterprises."

I pressed a button and was asked by a soft voice to identify myself. A buzzer rang, unlocking the doors. The apparent owner of the voice smiled at me from behind a curved granite desk. She was lacquered with perfect makeup and blond hair, the other end of the female spectrum from Mrs. Dickerson. With a manicured finger, she indicated a guest book, smiled a news anchor smile, and bade me sit in one of the overstuffed leather couches.

In moments, a clone of the receptionist came in, gave me the same smile, and said, "Follow me, please, Mr. Grant. I hope you are enjoying your visit to our city?"

"Yes, of course," I lied.

"Will you be staying tonight?"

"No, I'm afraid not. Too much going on at home."

"Oh, too bad. I'm sure you would love an evening in Atlanta." She pouted her lips. Probably gave all visitors the same tease.

I followed her into a large office with floor to ceiling walls of glass on the north and east. The perspective from this height flattened the terrain, making Stone Mountain stand out in the distance to the east. The city was laid out below us like a full-scale map, the rivers of rush-hour traffic animating the scene. A man behind a carved antique desk was facing away from us, a telephone held to his ear. We stood on the luxurious carpet, waiting. With the dimensions of the room and his soft speech, security was maintained.

The west wall of the office was covered with pictures and plaques, a shrine to the occupant. There were pictures of Dickerson and a toothy Jimmie Carter, ranging from Governor Jimmie to President Jimmie. There were pictures of Dickerson with golfers, with a large dead fish, speaking at a dinner, getting a plaque, in a hard hat standing in front of some construction, and on and on.

I was startled out of my inspection by a shouted *'You can go to hell!'* and the slamming of a receiver. The man in the chair wheeled about and rose to face us. "Mr. Grant to see you sir," said the babe.

He walked around the massive desk and met me halfway across the room, smiling a benign smile, the explosive words left behind. "Thanks for coming Mr. Grant. Welcome to Atlanta. That'll be all, Charlotte."

"Thank you sir, and thanks for seeing me." He was medium height, but heavily built, muscle mass beginning to turn to fat around the waist. He wore a dark suit, liberally sprinkled with dandruff from beneath a black toupee. The piece looked to be of high quality, but he had no fringe of his own hair to blend with it; so it gave the impression of a squirrel clinging to the white branch of a sycamore.

I shook the blunt hand and followed him to a grouping of leather furniture at the south end of the office. He strode to a bar and began to fill crystal glasses with ice. "Please be seated Mr. Grant. What will you have?"

"Scotch is fine, but a small one. I'll be driving when I leave here."

"Don't worry about it. You're in my town." To emphasize the point, he swept his hand around the glass walls.

North-south streets were cast in dark relief from the setting sun. Head- and taillights became visible as the day neared its end. He clashed his glass against mine, seated himself without a word, and took a long drink.

"Well, I'd like to hear what you found when you discovered the boat."

"First, I'm sorry about what may have happened. I guess no one knows yet exactly what did happen...or I suppose someone does."

His pale gray eyes seemed to narrow. "Well, let's hear it."

I went through the narrative, leaving out any comments about evidence, or opinions about what I had seen. When I told of finding Abigail, his face was impassive.

"What do you think happened, based on what you saw?"

"I'm afraid it looked like someone had kidnapped or otherwise harmed your son and his wife."

He snorted, then finished the rest of his drink. *"Wife!"* he said, through clenched teeth.

The last flashes of gold lit the buildings to the east, then all was dusk. I waited while he refilled his drink, and shook my head at the proffered decanter.

"What was she like?"

"Didn't know her place. Wrong background. What more can I say?"

"Did you have a bad relationship?"

"None at all. Never met the woman. Never wanted to."

"That must have been hard for your son."

"Ya make your bed, ya sleep in it. Literally so, in this case."

"Did your son have any enemies that you know about?"

"How would I know? He was a muck-raker. Some of the shit he stirred may have come back to bite him. Who the hell knows?"

"How about his wife, Solene?"

"Same thing. Who knows? She flaunted herself in public. Like I said, didn't know her place."

"Flaunted herself?"

"Yeah, yeah. Magazine covers, prancing around on stage without enough clothes, that kind of crap."

"You mean her modeling career? How could that make someone harm her?"

"We don't know what else went with it."

"No, I guess not." There seemed to be something beneath the surface, but I didn't expect him to reveal it.

"There is something else I discussed with your wife. The FBI told me you were not interested in any contact with your son's child."

"Right. Is it money you want?"

"Money? No. I want to see to her welfare myself. I've brought a paper for you to sign, if you're willing, giving up rights to her, if the worst case is confirmed."

"Why the hell would you want anything to do with her?"

"She's a wonderful, precious little girl. Maybe it's the old tradition that if you save someone, you're responsible for them."

He clenched his teeth and shook his head. "Give it to me. I'll have my lawyers look at it, and get it back to you."

"Thank you. And thanks for seeing me. It you think of anything else, my contact information is with the document."

We stood and shook hands. The city below was now laced with rivers of light from the ceaseless flow of traffic. The secretary babe arrived to see me out.

Harking back to my past life, I joined the commuters outbound from the city to the airport, turned in my car, and went through the hassle of the airport for my flight home. What had I experienced? Perhaps the strangest encounter of my life. How could such a sweet, bright little girl be carrying the genes of those two in her bloodstream?

# CHAPTER 21

I was awakened by a light disturbance on the foot of my bed. Stealthy footsteps padded on the blankets covering my foot, then up my leg and body, pausing on my shoulder. I opened my eyes to find Jem staring at me from inches away.

"Hi, there, tiger. Are you wanting breakfast?"

I got an answering "Meerrowrr," so reluctantly got out of bed and padded into the kitchen. The coffee was already perking. Reggie must have set it for five o'clock, as it was a few minutes after. The cat food was organized in a lower cabinet and Jem watched my every move as I got out her dish and served her on a small rug Gran had arranged for the purpose.

The flight the night before was delayed, so the condo was dark and still when I crept into my bedroom. My dreams were indecipherable, involving a wild mix of a surging ocean, sinister people obscured in darkness, angry police, and tangles from my past career. It left me with a feeling of weariness.

As I drank my coffee, I thought about Grace, and tortured myself imagining how she might be spending her weekend. And I thought of Abigail, never far from my thoughts. It seemed an age since that emotional parting in the hallways of the police station. Was that only last Sunday? It was. Less than a week. I'd not wait until the seven o'clock meeting on Sunday to see what Gully had to say. I wanted to speak again to Black Bart Richie and Lieutenant Haney, but I didn't' think 5:30 a.m. phone calls would make fans of anyone.

The shower had been running, and now Reggie entered from the bedroom, silently closing the door after himself. He was perfectly shaved and groomed, in contrast to my tousled hair, wrinkled pajamas, and need of a shave.

"Good morning, Gideon," he said, *sotto voce*. "I trust you had a good journey?"

"I don't know how I should describe it. It was a late night and strange visit. Thanks for the coffee, Reggie. I'll catch a shower, then I'll tell you about it."

"Jolly good. I'll get us breakfast."

When I returned, refreshed, the kitchen was filled with the aroma of bacon, kippers, eggs, and toast. Reggie had retrieved the paper from the entryway, but put it down when I came in. He rose and filled our coffee cups. As we ate, I told him of my encounter with the grandparents.

He made no comments through most of the narration, but occasionally shook his head, mostly staring at me until I finished. He looked down at his coffee cup, then up at me. "You don't suppose..."

"What?" I asked.

"No. It couldn't be." He pinched his lower lip.

"You're wondering if they could have something to do with it?"

"It was a fleeting thought, but I can't think of a motive...except hate, of course. Still, their own son. I simply couldn't imagine that." He shook his head and reached for his coffee.

"I suppose I must consider everything, but you're right. They seemed to have written him off completely and were getting on with their miserable lives."

"We cannot see into the minds of others, especially those that are warped. Knowing how I felt about my own son, and how losing him destroyed me..." his voice broke and he quickly took a drink of coffee.

Gran came padding in, greeted us, kissed us each on the cheek. "Judging by the far-away expressions, your trip must have been something."

"How right you are," I said.

"Dear, I'll have a cup of coffee out here and Gid can tell me about it. I'll do my puzzles later."

I went through it again for her. She listened intently without speaking, with eyes wide and a worried frown.

"Well, what do you think?"

"I'm speechless. That woman seems trapped in the worst of a pre-Civil War attitude. She should be committed!"

"I agree. Do you see a murder motive, though?"

"Who can say, but I think *I* now have one."

Reggie fixed her some toast and refilled our cups.

"I feel like I'm not getting closer to any theories that make sense," I said. "There are a few things I need to pursue, and I've got to figure how to approach them. First, a little secret for the two of you. I've had Gully trying to find out where Abigail is, and he found where she goes to school."

"Oh great!" Gran said. "What will you do about it? I'd love to meet her."

"I did it so I could hire extra security to watch over her, and we have a team on duty. I can't really do anything else at the moment. It would create a mess if I let her see me."

"I understand, but have you seen her?"

"From a distance, when she was on the school playground."

"Must be hard."

I nodded. "But back to the problem. I'd like to talk to Bart Richie again, and also see if there's any way I can talk Lt. Haney into interviewing the former mayor and letting me go along. I want to find out if Gully was successful in finding where Abigail lives, and I had another thought. I wonder if the police have talked to Richie's ex-wife?"

Reggie spoke. "All of those points sound worthwhile. From what I've heard of detective work, one pursues everything until something happens. Never give up, I say!"

I called Gully first from the privacy of my bedroom.

"Good morning, Sir," he replied. "How was Atlanta?"

"Pretty strange. I'll fill you in when I see you. Did you track Abigail to her home?"

"Yes, Sir, Sam Owen did the same day you met him at her school. We've been watching twenty-four hours a day. Nothing goin' on so far."

"Great. I'm going to see what I can set up with Bart Richie and also see if I can make any headway with Lt. Haney on Mayor Dilbeck. Then I'd like to get back to you and see if I can see where she lives."

"Very good, Sir."

My call to the Central Police Station came up empty on Lt. Haney. He was off duty, but the desk sergeant promised to contact him and ask him to call me.

The same thing happened with my call to the newspaper. Bart Richie was not in the office, but they promised to have him call. Saturday didn't seem to be working for me.

I called Julia. "Hey, beautiful. How's Saturday going?"

"Pretty miserable. This person I used to call a friend has me sequestered with a bunch of boring paperwork."

"Poor thing! You say 'boring'?"

"They pretty much had Dilbeck dead to rights. That guy who fell off a cliff didn't seem to be necessary—to the trial, that is. I'm making an outline of the case for you. It should help if you get a chance to see him."

"Great, and thanks, Julie. I'll see you Sunday evening."

My cell rang soon after I disconnected. It was Black Bart.

"Thanks for calling back. I wondered if we could talk again. I just got back from visiting Brad's parents in Atlanta."

"Sure. Can you come to my place around four o'clock today? I have a couple of things to take care of, but will be available then."

I agreed and we rang off after he gave me his address.

Again my phone rang as soon as I disconnected. It was Lt. Haney, "If you want a callback, stay off the goddamn phone! This is the third try."

"Good morning, Lt. Haney. Thanks for returning my call. I just got back in town and several contacts to make."

"Well, whattaya want?"

"I know you want me to sit at home and wait, but I can't do that. I just got back from Atlanta where I talked to the grandparents. It might be of interest to you. Also, I'm seeing Bart Richie again this afternoon. I'd like to sit with you when you have time and go over the results."

"Well...it's not procedure, but I guess I'll listen. How about tomorrow morning? It's Sunday, but every day is alike to me."

"Sunday's fine. Nine o'clock at the station?"

"Nine o'clock." The phone went dead.

# CHAPTER 22

I found Black Bart's townhouse with little difficulty. Considering the price of real estate in San Francisco, it must have cost a chunk of money. It was Spanish Mission style, a row of six, new construction. It was blessed with a double garage slightly below ground level, with three stories stacked above. Without benefit of a tour, I guessed that an entertainment deck was on the roof because I could see some green things up there, and a safety railing. Probably had a great view of the Bay.

Since each unit had its own entrance, there was no doorman or security hassle as in many apartment buildings. I gave that little thought until I walked up a few steps to the ornate carved oak door and found it slightly ajar. I pressed the ivory doorbell and heard the answering chimes inside. I waited. I rang again. I waited. I could hear jazz music playing inside and could see lights on in the entry hall.

I rapped loudly on the oaken door. "Mr. Richie!" I shouted. No answer. I tried again. At that point, I should have called the police, but hindsight is a wonderful thing. Instead, I went inside and climbed a few steps to a landing, again shouting, "Anyone home?" Directly ahead of me was an opening into a beautiful kitchen of granite, stainless steel, and Italian tile. To my left was an archway leading into a large room, echoing the Spanish influence of the exterior. The furniture was massive oak, the upholstery in woven Navaho or Mexican woolen colors. A huge wrought iron chandelier hung in the center of the room, and a natural stone fireplace took up most of the wall opposite the furniture group that had its back to me.

I called out again, but expected no answer. An open bottle of red wine sat on a silver tray on the coffee table with two glasses. One was empty, the other lying on its side, with a partially dry stain of wine spilling across the table. One more step into the room, and I saw a man sprawled on his back on the sofa.

Bart Richie was staring up at me with one glassy eye. The other was gone, with a flow of blood, partially congealed, coming from where it had been. His head rested on the sofa cushion in a mass of blood soaking into the fabric.

The shocking scene froze me where I stood. I fished out my phone and dialed 911.

"911. What is your emergency?"

"This is Gideon Grant. I came to see a friend and found him dead."

"Are you sure he's dead, or do we need to scramble emergency medical? What is the nature of any injury?"

"I'm sure. Looks like he's been shot. I haven't touched him, but I'm sure."

"We'll scramble anyway. What's your location?"

I gave it to her, spelling out the street name.

"Is anyone else on the scene?"

God, I hadn't thought about that. "I don't think so. Can you get the police here right away? And can you notify Lt. Haney at Central?"

"I'll pass your request on to the police dispatcher. Please stay on the line. I have personnel on the way."

While I waited with the phone pressed to my ear, I stepped forward and forced myself to survey the scene. Bart's head was at my end of the couch, and I could see a bloody mess sprayed on the back where his head must have been when the shot was fired. He was dressed in jeans and a yellow pull-over sweater, now stained with red-black blood. With some knowledge gained from movies and television shows, I could see black stippling around the wound in his eye. Whoever shot him had surprised him at close range.

"Sir, are you still on the line?"

"Yes, I'm here."

"Hold on. The police should be there in moments."

"I hear them coming up the steps."

I turned to see two uniforms burst into the room, guns drawn.

"Put your hands in the air," commanded a beefy sergeant. Trailing behind him was his partner, a slender dark-haired woman.

I complied. "Look, this is what I found when I got here."

He stepped behind me, holstering his gun while his partner continued to hold hers. He stepped quickly to Bart's body and pressed his fingers to the carotid artery. He looked at his partner and shook his head. Then to me: "Keep your hands up, sir. I'm going to search you until we sort this out."

I closed my phone and complied. "I suppose you must. I'd appreciate it if you would call Lt. Haney at Central."

"Already done. The dispatcher called him. He's on the way. Okay, you can lower your hands. I'm going to bag them and cuff you until we can check for residue. Did you touch anything?"

"Cuff me? What the hell for?"

"Procedure."

"*Procedure?* No, Of course I didn't touch anything after I saw him. The doorbell, maybe the railing outside, the outside door handle."

As he taped bags over both my hands and handcuffed them behind me, two young EMS men arrived, carrying a stretcher.

"You won't need that yet," the sergeant said.

"Okay," one of them said. "I know you've probably done it, but I'll check the victim. Procedure. We'll hang outside."

Haney and Alvarez arrived in minutes. He gave me a look, "Well, Grant, here we are again. What the hell are you involved in now?"

"In case you didn't know, this is Bart Richie, Dickerson's boss at the paper. He'd agreed to meet me and talk about the situation."

"Looks like an interesting discussion, at least with somebody."

Haney turned to his partner, "Alvarez, you keep an eye on Grant, see he doesn't do anything. Officer—he peered at her nametag—Rice, get a lab team on the way, then secure the area outside. Sergeant, you and me'll clear the building."

They left, with guns drawn. Alvarez looked at me with a crooked smile, "Well, Mr. Grant, we meet again. Conchita will take care of you. Have you been a bad boy?"

"Not guilty. But we'll both be in trouble if Haney catches us talking."

"Hokay, hokay, another time."

Haney and the sergeant returned, guns holstered. We'd heard them in the upper floors shouting "clear" at each other. Haney said to the others, "Sergeant Ross, I'll leave you in charge of the scene while the lab people do their thing. Detective Alvarez will stay here. I'll take Mr. Grant in for a statement. We'll swab his hands there. Okay? After I'm through with him, I'll bring a couple more people and we'll search the entire scene."

On the way to his unmarked Ford, I said, "how about taking these damn cuffs off, so I can at least sit in the car?"

"Can't do it. Procedure. Tell you what, I'll cuff them in front of you."

"Big deal. I'll take what I can get, I guess."

When we were on the way, he turned to me, "Now, want to tell me what the hell's going on?"

"You have a lawyer trussed up like a chicken and you expect him to talk to you? You should know better? 'Procedure,' you know."

"Don't be a wise-ass."

"Look, Lieutenant, I've tried every way to cooperate with you. I want to know what happened to these people, so I'll know what happens to the little girl, who I care about. That's my only objective in this. Would I be stupid enough to silence someone who might clear it up? Now, that's all you get until I'm assured I'm free from all suspicion, which means not wearing cuffs, among other things."

We went through an abbreviated booking, since I'd been there before. "Welcome back, Mr. Grant," the desk sergeant said.

I was un-cuffed and un-bagged, and my hands were swabbed by a young woman in uniform, with the proper documentation filled out. Haney led me to an interview room, after calling over his shoulder for coffee to be delivered. After it arrived, I thanked him, "And thanks also for not chaining me to the eyebolt in the floor."

"Yeah, right," he said. "Are you ready to talk now?"

"After four things: The GSR test comes back clean, which it will, Julia arrives, you agree I'm clear, and we go someplace where we talk off the record."

He stared at me, thinking. Finally he got up and opened the door, shouting, "Peak, come in here."

Detective Peak arrived in seconds.

Haney pointed at me. "Grant here is in custody until we check for GSR. There's been a shooting. Fill ya in later. Keep an eye on him. If GSR comes back clean, he can go. If not, put him in a cell." Then to me, "I have a murder to take care of. If you're clean, you can leave, I'll see you here at nine tomorrow as we planned."

# CHAPTER 23

When I returned to the condo Saturday night, I was exhausted by the ordeal of finding Bart Richie dead, then waiting to get cleared to come home. Gran and Reggie were out to dinner. I drank a large Famous Grouse while Jemima kept me company. When they returned home, I went over the events of the evening while they listened in astonishment. We talked for hours, speculating on what it might mean without coming up with anything. Gran brought up something I hadn't thought of: What if the timing had been different and I arrived before the killer left?

On Sunday morning, three of us assembled in a back booth of the diner near Central Station; Julia, Lieutenant Haney, and me. It hadn't been easy to convince him to leave the environs of the police station, but I wanted to speculate freely with no recording devices around. Only paranoia would make me think the booth was bugged. Haney began; looking at me.

"I have my questions, but what made you want to get together?"

"I know things have changed since I called you yesterday morning—"

"Ya think?"

"I guess it's an understatement, but I wanted to tell you about a trip to Atlanta to see Abigail's grandparents, and see if I could make a trade with you."

"A trade?"

"According to what we've found so far, ex-Mayor Dilbeck looks like a candidate. If you haven't talked to him, I'd like to listen in when you do."

"Probably won't happen, but let's hear what you have to say. First, though, let's get into yesterday."

"Just a minute, if I may. Julia, what have you found so far, reading Dilbeck's case?"

"I'm about through it. Neither Richie or Dickerson were called to testify since their stuff was hearsay. But there's no doubt they are the ones that convicted him by their investigation."

"Well, there was no doubt the son of a bitch was guilty," Haney said. "Now, who knew you were going to meet with Richie, and why were you?"

I glanced at Julia, and she nodded. "I told my investigator, Tolliver, and my grandmother and her fiancé, who are staying with me. Oh, Julie might have known in general, but not the specific time."

Haney glanced at her.

"As he said," she replied.

Haney waited until the waitress had refilled our coffee cups, then continued, "Now the reason you were talking to him?"

"I wanted to understand the relationship of the players, and maybe that's an operative word. Richie was Dickerson's boss, but was also a member of the same sports club. From what I've been able to determine, there was a rather tangled social scene going on there, then Richie gets a divorce, Dickerson leaves town, and Richie buys his condo. Mrs. Richie heads back to Chicago with a large chunk of Richie's net worth in her pocket. Has anyone talked to her?"

"Not until last night." A glance at Julia, "Your Detective Peak talked to her, said she didn't seem to give a rat's ass."

"Interesting," Julia said, "But he's not my Detective Peak. I believe he pretty much belongs to you."

Haney glared at her without replying.

"Don't get uptight," I said, "but if it were me, I'd see if he called anyone before he wound up dead. I suppose you already did. But another thing I got to thinking about. What if he was bugged? What if someone thought he might talk to the wrong people?"

He gave me a withering look. "We checked his phone records, but we didn't sweep for bugs. That's a little far-out. There was an incoming call we're tracking down. Came in right after noon."

"I just wondered. Strange someone killed him a little before I came. The blood and the wine had just started to dry. It's just too much of a coincidence to think it's not connected to the Dickersons. I'm glad he or she left before I got there."

"I told you to keep your nose out of it," Haney said. "Now tell me about Atlanta. Why'd you go?"

"I knew the FBI talked to the grandparents and they expressed no interest in Abigail. I took a document with me getting them to decline all claims to her. Got it back by registered mail yesterday. I found them to be really weird people, both of them..."

I went through every detail of my visit with both of the senior Dickersons, describing them as best I could. Haney listened, shaking his head several times. After an hour and some coffee refills, I concluded: "I came home thinking all of the bitterness and weirdness might have led them to violence. They have more money than God, as Tolliver says, so they could hire it done. However, Richie's killing seems to point in another direction."

"It would seem so," Haney agreed. "But what if they held Richie responsible for killing their son, and did him to get even? They could'a found out any of the stuff you've been talking about. Being rich and weird, they could'a been investigating their son for a long time."

"It's a mess," Julia said. "I've just been listening and thinking. I wouldn't rule out the parents, but it seems to look like one of two things: either the investigative reporting, as Brad and Bart were both involved; or the tangled relationship issues, as in who was screwing whom. And who is still out there with an axe to grind, and are they done?"

Haney scratched his head, squirmed in his seat, "This whole mess wasn't simple. If it is tied together, it had to have some horsepower behind it. Just think: steal the boat, hire some creeps to track the sailboat, get rid of the boat and the creeps, somehow off Richie. Takes money and planning."

He squirmed again, took a deep sigh, and looked at the table top. "Look, this isn't easy for me. I've been on your ass from the start, but I appreciate what you're going through to help the girl. Okay?"

He held out his hand to shake.

"Okay, and thanks," I said, gripping his large hand. "Another thing: I've hired extra security to look out for Abigail. I told the guys to let your people know who they are. I've been worried sick about her, in case whoever went after the sailboat finds out where she is."

"As long as they don't screw things up. Now I've got to get the hell out of here; see if we're getting anywhere on this."

After he left, I asked Julia, "Julie, what do you think?"

"I just don't know. What bothers me is, there's a murderer out there and we don't know who and with what motive. Watch your back. I'll see you at seven."


With some of Sunday left, I called Gully. He answered quietly on the second ring.

"Gully, I hate to bother you on Sunday, but I'd sure like to see where Abigail and her foster family live. When can we do that?"

Again he spoke quietly, like one of the announcers describing a birdie putt at a pro golf tournament, "Now's a good time. They live on a street bordering Alta Plaza Park. You know where that is?"

"Sort of. I can find it."

"I'm on duty myself today. They're walking up to the top of the Park with the girl and two other kids, a boy and a girl. So I'm doing the same thing. Quite a few people out, so it's easy to blend in. Unfortunately, somebody else could too."

"I'll call you when I get there and you can tell me where to find you."


I refreshed my memory on a city map and zipped across town to the park. I pulled over and checked with Gully. In his golf course voice he replied, "Come around to the north side, Jackson Street. We're coming down the horseshoe-shaped walk toward Pierce Street."

I eased out, drove up the west end, turned the corner and found a spot halfway to the steps. I spotted the family immediately; parents, a pre-teen boy, and trailing behind, a girl perhaps six years old leading Abigail by the hand. A few yards back, wearing a hooded sweatshirt and dark glasses, I saw the diminutive, muscular figure of Gully.

They crossed the street, turned toward me, and walked right by me on the other side. I scrunched down in my seat and saw them enter a beige and white three-story apartment building. After they'd crossed the street, Abigail was no longer holding hands. She walked slowly with head down, clutching a small stuffed cat. I called Gully again. "I'm across the street from their building, a little toward the steps you came down."

"Yes, Sir. I've got you. I'll come over."

When he got in, I said, "Well, it looks like a really nice family, and goodness knows, nice digs here."

"Yes, Sir. He's an upper manager in a CPA firm downtown, probably does all right."

"Thanks, Gully. I really do appreciate what you've done. Are the police here also?"

"Yes, Sir. They mainly watch the house, but they would have followed the family if I hadn't been here to do so."

"Good. I'll see you at seven?"

"Yes, Sir."

I headed back to the Condo. Selfishly, I worried about the way they looked like such a nice family. No one would ever know, looking at them, that Abigail wasn't their daughter. Should I encourage her adoption, if that's what they had in mind? I wanted her to be happy, above all else, but I wanted her to be with me.

# CHAPTER 24

Julia and Gully arrived at the same time, a few minutes before seven. Gran and Reggie were in charge of preparing dinner, laughing and talking excitedly with each other most of the late afternoon. I served as bartender, since they shooed me out of the kitchen. The two chefs were having champagne. Julia opted for a martini; Gully, scotch, neat. I couldn't concentrate on anything as I listened for the intercom and worried about Grace.

At last, her arrival was announced. I glanced at my watch, and it was only six minutes after. Foolish me. I had the door already open when she came down the hallway.

"Grace, I'm so glad to see you." I couldn't contain my relief.

She seemed to force a smile in return and said, "I'm glad I could make it."

Her cheeks glowed from the outside night breezes and her 24-karat hair shone in the lights of the hall. But her demeanor was not what I expected. She'd just returned from a weekend with her fiancé, which should have been positive, but now she seemed preoccupied. Perhaps sad she had to leave there?

"May I take your jacket, or would you like to keep it?"

"I'll keep it for now, thank you."

"Grace is here, everyone." Then to her, "May I fix you a drink? The 'kids' in the kitchen are drinking champagne but anything else is okay."

"No, no. No champagne for me. Perhaps red wine?"

The others came forward to speak with her while I fixed her glass. Jem came from nowhere and rubbed against her ankles.

When we were all seated for dinner, the atmosphere was more that of a dinner party, avoiding discussion of the reason we were together. I insisted Reggie should sit at the head of the table, with Gran at the foot. Grace and I sat on one side, Julia and Gully on the other. Reggie had put together a delicious dinner of roasted chickens, caesar salad, and a side dish of oven roasted potatoes. Gran contributed soft dinner rolls I remembered from my childhood. I served a crisp *pinot grigio* from Napa Valley.

Reggie and Gran insisted on clearing afterward and urged us to start our meeting.

"Grace, for your benefit, I have some shocking news that the others already know."

She'd been staring into the distance, but now looked at me, her eyes wide.

"You remember Bart Richie, Brad's boss?"

She nodded.

"I had an appointment to talk to him again at four o'clock yesterday, and when I got to his townhouse I found him dead, apparently shot."

"My goodness!" she said. "Were you in danger?"

"I don't think so. I did have to be hauled to the police station until they could check me out."

"You were suspected?"

"Well, I was the only one at the scene. 'Procedure' they said. I even got to wear cuffs. However, I was clean of gunshot residue and motive so they let me go."

Speculation ensued, and I asked Julia to summarize all of the things we discussed with Haney. She mentioned my trip to Atlanta, but left details until later.

"Anyone have anything to add?"

Gully said, "I think the wife shouldn't be ruled out. We might investigate what kind of divorce it was."

"There might be a chance," Julia added. "Detective Peak said that she's coming to town to see about things. Not to mourn, according to what she said when he called her."

"Good," I said. "Will you see what he can arrange, sort of off the record? I don't want to cross Haney any more than I have to."

"I'll see what I can do. Oh, by the way, the phone call Richie received before he was shot? Came from a 'burner' purchased from Wal-Mart for cash a week or two ago. No help there."

"Anything else?"

Grace spoke up for the first time since dinner, "I'm looking forward to hearing about the grandparents."

"Good. I'll get right to it. Refill your glasses if you wish."

No one stirred, so I launched into the strange tale of my visit. After I had finished, Grace spoke again, "I agree with you that it's hard to explain the genetic connection between people like that and a sweet little girl like Abigail. In my calling I have seen everything you might imagine, however. It's still hard to understand. I think we should keep them on the list of suspects."

"I agree," Julia said.

Grace spoke again, "Something that concerns me: We don't know if Abigail's parents really are dead, both of them or either of them. People have been known to disappear on purpose, but I can't believe they'd desert Abigail to die."

"They'd have to be insane," I agreed. "Let's take a break. And Grace, may I speak with you alone for a few minutes? There's a sitting area in the master. Will the rest of you excuse us?"

Grace looked puzzled, but followed me into the master bedroom. I'd told Gran what I wanted to do. When we were seated, I began, "The others already know what I'm about to tell you, but I didn't want to spring it on you in front of them."

"Is it bad?"

"I don't think so. I've been so concerned about Abigail's safety, since this situation is so weird. Gully has found out where Abigail lives and we've put extra security agents to watch over her. I hope you aren't angry with me."

"Of course not. I'd like to know how he found her, but you probably won't tell me. You can't interfere with her, you know."

"We won't. And I don't know exactly, but it wasn't a leak in your office. We're very careful not to let anyone know except the police, who are supposed to be watching. They don't mind. In fact, they appreciate the extra eyes. I've seen her myself from a distance, both at her school and at her foster home."

She looked at me with her beautiful eyes, "Gideon, I've come to know how much you care for her and how dedicated you are for her safety. It's taken me a little while to trust, but I know you'll do what's right."

"I'm so relieved! I've upset you more than once, and it's the very last thing I want to do."

We rose together and she smiled at me. We were close together and I smelled the clean scent of her. Impulsively, I put my arms around her and gave her a quick hug. She seemed not to resist this first physical contact.

When we rejoined the others, still seated in the living area, I told them what we had discussed. "I wanted to tell Grace in private because I wasn't sure if we had done the right thing. She's good with it."

Gran and Reggie were with them, and they all smiled. I added, "Of course, a reminder that this is totally confidential.

"Now to wind things up, first my thanks to the chefs."

We applauded and cheered.

"Next, a quick list: We'll keep watching Abigail; I'll try to be in on the interview with the ex-mayor; we'd like to interview Richie's ex-wife; we'll find out what we can about the Richie case; and I haven't heard squat out of the FBI. Julie, can you see if you can hear anything?"

"Will do."

"Anything else?"

Julia snapped her fingers, "I forgot. A body washed up on the beach in Half Moon Bay. Pretty bad shape, but has to be from the black boat that blew up. More later, after autopsy."

"Thanks. Is that all?"

"Oh," Grace said, "I have the adoption forms for you."

"Great. Thanks. I know it's getting late, but would you have a few minutes to let me glance at them to see if I might have questions?"

"Of course," she said. Gully and Julia said their farewells, thanking Gran and Reggie again.

We sat alone at the table, and I scanned the forms, "Name, address, date and place of birth, et cetera, et cetera. It asks for income. I'll have to put 'variable,' but will it work to include a copy of my last income tax?"

"Yes. If they want more later they can ask."

"I see they want my short marital history, no criminal record, no children. I will put Gran's name in 'other persons in the home.' That's where you were supposed to be, in my first stupid and clumsy encounter with you."

She smiled.

"There's a 'Child Desired' section. Naturally, I'll put Abigail in there. I don't know her date of birth. And can I attach a detailed letter to explain 'relationship to applicant'?"

"I'll get her birthdate for you, and yes, I think a detailed explanation is totally appropriate."

"Thanks. I'll have to scare up some references, and that should about do it."

"Good. You can send it to me or bring it by the office and I'll see that it doesn't get lost."

"Grace, I really do appreciate it. Now may I take another chance?"

"What is it?"

"I don't want to pry, but I sense that you're a bit down tonight. To me, you're always a picture of depth and serenity, with a positive outlook. That is, when I'm not doing something stupid. When you got here, you looked deep in thought. 'Introspective,' might be the big word."

She gave a little smile as she looked into my eyes, "I don't mind the analysis. You're very perceptive."

"Anything I can do?"

"No, it's just some family issues. Nothing serious."

"I hope not. May I follow you home? ...And return here, of course."

She actually laughed. "No, I'll be okay. I would settle for another hug. A brotherly hug."

"I'm more than happy to oblige."

With that, I saw her to the door and safely down the elevator and to her car. She could call it "brotherly" if she wished. Despite that diamond still on her finger, that brief moment of holding her in my arms kept me awake for a while, alone in my bed.

# CHAPTER 25

On Monday morning Gran and Reggie left for Modesto to spend a couple of days seeing to their properties, taking Jemima along. Precisely at nine the telephone rang.

"Good morning, Gideon, it's Grace."

"Oh, thanks. I hope you got home okay. I thought about you into the evening, and this morning."

"Well, thanks. But you really shouldn't."

"Maybe not. Can't help it."

"I have something for you. Abigail's birthday is this coming Saturday. She'll be four."

"I'll put it on the form, but is it possible for me to give her a card and a little gift? Could you get it to her?"

Grace sighed. "I don't know. How little?"

"Not much. Perhaps a Barbie Desiree, if I can find one."

"How do you know about such a thing?"

"Abigail told me. She said her mother looks like Christie and she looks like Desiree."

"Aw, that's cute."

"Also, if you go along with it I could get something for the other kids. Maybe a soccer ball for the boy, and could you suggest something for the girl?"

"I can't see any harm. That way she'll know you're still around, even though it might raise questions again why she can't see you."

"Let's work on it then. Maybe the card can say something about my love for her and how the police are helping me search for her mother. Okay to mention Jemima? I'll let you approve all of it."

"Okay. I'll find something for the girl. And Gideon? Be really careful. Someone is still out there."

"I will, Grace, and I can't wait to see you again."

The moment the phone was disconnected, it rang again, Julia this time.

"Hi, Julie. What's up?"

"You have an appointment with Mrs. Richie at noon today."

"Great! How did you do that?"

"Well, Greg put me in touch with her. He's her police contact. Her name, by the way, is Christine Jensen. As to how I did it, she was a fellow student of ours at Stanford, a coupla years ahead. I didn't know her, but she knew me because she's a basketball fan. I'm famous, you know."

"Yeah, right. Seriously though, thanks. Noon today, and where?"

"At the Fairmont, the original on Mason, in the Laurel Court Restaurant and Bar. I agreed to come, too. She may bring her lawyer, just to give advice if she needs it."

"Again, thanks, Julie. I'll get there a half-hour early, in case you want to give me any advice."

I just had time to go into the kitchen and pour a cup of coffee, when the phone rang again. This time it was the curt voice of Special Agent Scott. After an exchange of greeting, he said, "I understand you found the body of Mr. Richie."

"Correct."

"You seem to have a knack for involvement in distressing situations."

"Not something I'm proud of, but it is what it is. What do you want?"

"As part of our ongoing investigation, I'd like to discuss it with you. Can you come into the office today?"

"I have a mid-day appointment, but three o'clock might work. You'll get a callback if Ms. Mangini can't make it."

"Your lawyer won't be necessary."

"Yes she will. See you at 3:00."

Traffic was light as I drove south on Brannon Street, then across on 5$^{th}$. As I passed under Interstate 80, a black Firebird dipped into the right

lane a couple of cars back. Hadn't one like it been around before? Is paranoia entering the picture? When I picked up Powell to head up toward
the hotel, it was still there. Maybe just a coincidence.

My watch said 11:15 as I handed the keys to a valet in front of the
magnificent hotel. The Fairmont sits atop Nob Hill like a king on a
throne. From its birth in the early 1900s to the present day, it has repre-
sented the very best San Francisco has to offer, both in spirit and in beauty.
The devastating earthquake and fire in 1906 failed to bring it down.

Julia was waiting for me at a corner table for four in the Laurel Court.
A waiter appeared immediately and I ordered a bottle of white wine.

"Anything I should know before she gets here?"

"Not much. She's the only child of a commodity trader in Chicago.
Rolling in money. She may know a little about this situation, but I think
she'll want some reassurance of your motives and of confidentiality, of
course."

"No problem. Oh, by the way, can you go with me to see the FBI at
3:00? I know you have other clients."

"Sure. I didn't know how long this would take, so I cleared my
schedule."

Christine Jensen made her entrance at precisely twelve o'clock, making points with me. She was striking in appearance, tall and runway-
model thin, with cropped platinum hair. She wore a shimmering blue
silk dress, with alligator heels and purse. Trailing behind her was an
older man, several inches shorter, with snow-white hair and goatee to
match.

Julia and I both rose. She held out her hand to me and I took it.
"Hello, I'm Christine Jensen."

"Thank you for coming. I'm Gideon Grant. I believe you know Julia
Mangini?"

"We've not actually met in person," she said as she took Julia's hand.
"I'm pleased to meet you."

She turned to the distinguished gentleman who had waited patiently,
"And this is my attorney, Mark Sheffield."

"I know Ms. Mangini, of course. How are you Julia?" Then to me, "A
pleasure to meet you Mr. Grant. I knew of your firm also."

"The pleasure is mine. Please be seated. I ordered white wine, which I see approaching. Or feel free to order for yourselves."

As we were settling in, my impression of Ms. Jensen brought the word "narrow" to mind. Her face was attractive, but narrow to match her stick-like frame. The ice-blue color of her eyes matched her dress. Her smiles of greeting never quite reached her eyes. On her left wrist dangled a glittering multi-carat tennis bracelet and on her right ring finger, a large diamond ring. Made me glad for my upgrade to a blazer and tie.

"May I begin?" I said, as drinks were poured and Sheffield started on his martini. "Thank you for meeting with us. To save everyone's time, perhaps we can talk while we have lunch."

"Fine," Christine said. "I have little information to offer, I'm afraid, but came out of courtesy and curiosity."

"Thanks. I have no official capacity and will treat everything said with total confidentiality. My only objective is to sort through what might have happened to leave a small child stranded on a sinking boat out in the Pacific Ocean. During that adventure, we became quite attached to each other, and I can't walk away without seeing that no harm comes to her. I don't remember the origin, but there's tradition that if you save someone's life, then you're responsible for them."

"Please continue. I'll help if I can. Little Abigail is an innocent."

We paused to give the waiter our lunch orders, then began again. I told a brief version of finding the yacht and arrival back in San Francisco.

"The police and FBI are investigating, but they don't seem to be getting anywhere. Not that they'd tell me if they were, but meanwhile Abigail is stuck in foster care and I'm impatient to find her parents, or reach some kind of resolution."

Our lunches arrived, allowing a momentary break as we were served.

"Tell me, Mr. Grant, what do you want to happen?" Christine said.

"First choice would have to be finding her parents safe, and re-uniting the family. If that doesn't happen, I'd like to adopt her myself and take care of her. I have no children."

"Noble sentiments, but you don't expect the first choice to happen, do you?"

"Probably not, to be honest. But it has to reach a final answer."

"So what do you expect from me?"

"I know that Dickerson and your ex-husband worked closely together exposing potentially dangerous people; I know that you both belonged to the same club. Anything you can tell me would be of great help. How did they get along, for example?"

Christine picked at her salad, sighed, and glanced at Sheffield. He gave a slight nod. We waited in silence.

Finally she began. "In the beginning, quite well, I think. They were both driven. Bart was the boss and Bradley his protégé. I know less about Brad, but gossip said he was disowned after he brought home a black woman. Imagine that being a problem in the nineties! Bart went through the foster system, but was blessed with great looks and intelligence. He made the most of them, but never left behind his feelings of rejection, if I may psychoanalyze. I'm afraid I acted like a bitch when the police called, but I do have feelings of regret for such a waste. And you found him? Had you talked to him before?"

"Yes, we'd met previously for background on my story in exchange for what he could tell me about the Dickersons. He'd agreed to meet me again at his place the day he was killed."

"Any idea who or why?"

"No idea. It could have been tied up with the Dickersons' disappearance or something else entirely."

The two lawyers both sat silently and watched the dialogue until Christine said, "It could have been any number of jealous husbands."

Mark said, "Christine, I'd advise against too much discussion along those lines."

"Sorry, Mark, but you know it's true, and the tabloids have plenty of stuff—"

"It's still not a good idea."

Christine turned to me and persisted. "You know how attractive he was, how it might affect women. It certainly did me until our marriage became too crowded."

"What can you say about Solene? Excuse me. I've given you little chance to finish your lunch."

"It's all right." She looked down at her salad, and forked a small piece of romaine, then put it down again. "How to begin? She came here out of chaos in her home country, and was quite humble; thankful to Bradley for giving her the chance to come here. Bradley seemed to take great pride in having her at his side. It inflated his self-esteem.

"I liked her from the beginning, and did what I could to introduce her into the community. I helped her make the connections to begin modeling. She met society by joining me at various charity events. Her problem, if you want to call it that, was that she blossomed like a desert flower after a rain."

"Her problem?" I asked.

"Yes. Her radiance eclipsed anything Bradley might do. She didn't seem to notice, but you could see him become withdrawn. And perhaps women can't judge such things except by observation, but there was a sexual magnetism about her that caused men to act like teenagers. It was amusing in the beginning, watching them trip over their tongues. Eventually, though, it caused many strained relationships, including mine."

"You blame her for your divorce?"

"No, I don't. I never lost my regard for her and never was able to prove that anything wrong took place. But she was one more distraction that convinced me I didn't need to continue pretending and looking the other way."

"Ms. Jensen, I'm sorry for dredging up bad memories—"

"It's okay. If anything I say helps clear up what happened, then it's the least I can do. The police don't seem to be interested, except to nail down my alibi. Give me a break!"

"Do you know of *anyone* whose enmity might rise to what happened to Bart? Or what happened on the yacht?

"No, I have no idea. They made enemies with their news reporting, but that's a big field."

"One more thing. How were they toward each other when Dickerson decided to leave?"

"'Estranged' might be a way to describe it. They were working together, but somehow things were different."

"Then I find it strange that Bart bought the townhouse from him."

"Oh, he didn't buy it directly. Bradley and Solene had already left, and he might not even have known who bought it."

That made me wonder how he financed the yacht, but it wasn't something she would know. There seemed little else we could discuss. We shook hands around, the women hugged, and we said our farewells. Julia and I made our way to the lobby with almost an hour to go for our appointment with the FBI.

# CHAPTER 26

We found a quiet corner in the Fairmont lobby to wait, "Well, Julie, what do you think? Did I miss anything?"

"No, Gid, I don't think so. I couldn't think of anything else to ask or I would have done so. She surely presented a picture of unhappy relationships."

"Yeah. A lot of it going around. But does any of it rise to murder?"

"In some cases it does."

We arrived at FBI headquarters at the appointed hour and were met in the lobby by a sharp young man in the dark suit and white shirt uniform of an agent.

"I'm Special Agent Lattimore," he said. "Please follow me."

Are they all Special Agents and not just Agents? I wondered as we were ushered to a second-floor corner office.

Special Agent Scott rose from his leather chair behind a large mahogany desk. "Thanks, Stuart. You may close the door as you leave."

He shook hands with both of us and motioned toward the guest chairs across from him. His office walls were full-height windows on two sides. The others were covered with plaques, pictures, and certificates. An American Flag stood in a corner. Scott still presented the fierce eyes, bald head, and hooked beak of an eagle, recalled from our first encounter. This time he managed a small curl of his lips that passed for a smile.

"We may not have gotten off on the right foot when you were here the first time. I'd like to see if we have any information to share that may move us forward on this case. You're both members of the bar, and I trust you can keep anything we say in confidence."

"Correct. I have no inclination or motivation to do otherwise," I replied. "Lieutenant Haney now seems to see that it's best if we work together."

"Haney has briefed me on the Richie murder, but I'd like to hear about it from you—anything you can think of as to why you were there, what you found, thoughts on who was responsible."

"I'll tell all I know, although an answer to the last question is not evident." I went through it all again; our first meeting in detail, how the scene appeared in Richie's condominium and my interrogation by the police.

"You made a rather curious comment to Lieutenant Haney. You suggested a sweep for bugs. Why?"

"It seemed a weird coincidence that the murder occurred in a narrow time frame between setting up the meeting and when I arrived."

"Your speculation was prescient. It was bugged."

"*Really!*"

"Yes. We're in the process of tracking down the sources of the equipment."

"Good luck with that. While we're on the subject, a few times I've noticed a black GM car behind me. May be coincidence, but maybe not, since someone seems to have been keeping track of Bart Richie. It's a Firebird or Camaro, black with obscure windows."

Scott made a note on a yellow pad. "We'll check it out."

Julia had been listening, but now spoke, "Gideon, I think we should talk about today's meeting."

"Sure. Why don't you handle it?"

Julia handled the presentation with the precision and detail of a trial lawyer making a closing statement. SA Scott listened without comment, scratching a note on his pad from time to time.

"The two of you seem to be focusing on personal relationships as the key to the Dickersons' disappearance and the murder of Richie."

"It makes some sense to get to know the players in the game and we hear that most murders are by people we know. The other possible suspects, those that were ruined by the newspaper investigations, are a little out of the reach of private citizens. Is that the main thrust of the FBI, or can you answer that?"

Scott doodled on his pad. "I will say this much. We are going back through the archives and had interviewed Richie ourselves about threats. An agent has talked to the former mayor, Dilbeck. Slimy guy, but no connections yet."

"He's one I wanted to talk to, but Haney hasn't made any promises. There's also the city manager of Sacramento a few years back, the serial sexual harasser and finally rapist. Don't know much about him yet, but my private detective suggested him."

"We've talked to him also. Nothing so far."

"Is there any hope we're getting closer?"

Scott shook his head. "Nothing significant. We've confirmed the sunken cigarette was likely the one and we know Lyon was killed in the explosion. Someone is definitely covering tracks, and they seem to know what they're doing."

"Haney probably told you about my visit to the grandparents in Atlanta."

"Right. And your conclusion was that they are weird, but seemingly detached from caring. Fair enough?"

"Fair enough. Well, are we done?"

"I believe so. Anything else, Ms. Mangini?"

"No. But I hope you'll keep us in the loop."

"Before we break up, there is another matter," I said. "What about the boats? Can they be released? I'd like to get them both to a boat-yard to be hauled out and refitted. I'll pay the tab on them. Whatever becomes of Abigail and family, they deserve to have it ready. And God only knows what I'll do with mine. Probably sell it."

"I'll see what I can do," Scott said, rising and extending his hand to each of us. He escorted us down to the front lobby and watched us leave.

Outside, Julia turned to me. "I know you're frustrated. Maybe it just takes time and more digging."

"You're right. As to digging, it seems like we are more likely waiting for something else bad to happen. The Bart Richie thing shook me. Up until then, it was a matter of talking and thinking."

She patted my shoulder. "Well, let's hope you're wrong. I gotta go to a client's office. See ya back home."

Traffic was heavy heading south on Van Ness, but moving swiftly. Cars changed lanes and took every advantage to gain a few seconds. If anyone followed me, it would be relatively easy to conceal themselves behind others, especially with the mix of a few delivery vans and trucks. It was unlike me to think of something like that, being followed, in danger, but that was before finding a man dead who was supposed to talk to me. The FBI and the police must eventually come up with *something*.

I reached the clover-leaf entrance to the Central Freeway and jockeyed for position to climb the perfect circle to enter the merge into traffic. Across the way, a vision sent a chill down my spine. A black GM sports car was two or three cars back, unable to hide around the curve.

I sped up onto the Freeway and did my own lane-changing, gaining every advantage possible to put as much distance as I could between myself and my pursuer, if indeed that's what he was. He didn't show himself as we merged onto the northbound lanes of Interstate 80.

Not wanting to telegraph my intentions, I stayed in the second lane until the last minute, before cutting off another driver in a van, to dart into the 4th Street exit ramp. The rear-view mirror was suddenly filled with a dark shape coming behind me from behind the van at a high rate of speed.

As I entered the curve, he slammed into my right rear bumper with a crash that sent me into a hard left, into the wall with a loud clang. The airbags blew and my faithful Land Cruiser rolled over with shattering glass and screeching metal against concrete. It bounced over the wall to the street below.

# CHAPTER 27

Soft voices. Muffled voices. A man and a woman, speaking words that made no sense to me. Who are they and where am I? I struggled to open my eyes. Was this another dream, another hazy scene I could not understand?

The woman said, "Look. I think he's waking up. His eyelid fluttered. Oh, I hope so! Dear Gideon, come back to us. Please wake up."

Her words penetrated my consciousness and I forced my eyes partially open in the bright light. I squinted at the woman leaning over me. She had red hair but she was not young—maybe a mother or grandmother? Something familiar about her. I tried to speak, but a big plastic tube was stuck down my throat and taped in place. I wanted to say, "What happened; where am I?" but nothing came out but incoherent sounds.

She took my hand "Gideon, sweetheart, if you can understand me, try to squeeze my hand."

With an effort, my hand obeyed. She called me Gideon.

"Good," She said. "You're going to be all right. You were in a car accident, but the doctor says you'll be fine. You're in San Francisco General. Reggie is here with me."

Who is Reggie? Nothing made sense.

"You've been asleep for over two days. You had a bad bump on the head and the doctor kept you sleeping until the swelling went down." I squeezed her hand again.

Car accident? How did it happen? Too much trouble to think about it now. Time to go to sleep again.

More voices, different people. "Okay, Mr. Grant, time to change your bedding. You just relax and let us do all the work."

This time I was able to open my eyes and see a robust nurse smiling at me and a male orderly at the foot of the bed. My chest was wrapped tightly in a binding that restricted my breathing, and my left arm was encased in a cast suspended from a frame over my bed. The nurse and the room came into better focus. She had dark hair in tidy curls and a name tag said "Martha."

"We're going to unhook your cast and roll you on your left side and make this half, then roll you back. Don't worry, we'll be careful. We've done it a few times while you were taking a long nap, Rip Van Winkle."

Pain shot through my rib cage, but not unbearable. Must be on painkillers. I realized for the first time that my head was bound in a large turban of bandages.

When they had me all fixed, Nurse Martha bent over me. "I'll see if the doctor will let me take out the tube, now that you're awake and your $O_2$ level is good. Then you can talk if you want."

Someone touched me on the shoulder, waking me again. This time a man with rimless glasses looked down at me. He smiled and said, "Hi, Mr. Grant. I'm Doctor Pagano." He gently grasped my right hand. "We're going to get the tube out of your throat, and then get you up."

Get me up? What the hell is he talking about? My head aches and my ankles hurt and my ribs hurt.

Then he spoke to the nurse, "Martha, you can take the tube out, then let's get him rigged with a sling and try for a walk to the bathroom. He's going to have some pain in his ankles, so we'll take it slow. I'll come back in a few minutes and talk to him."

"Right, Doctor."

She went to work on me, gently removing the tube and giving me a mouth rinse, wiping my lips with balm. "Both of your ankles are sprained but not broken, so they may hurt a little when we get you up. You have some fractured ribs and your left arm is broken. Otherwise, except for your head, you're in pretty good shape."

I smiled in spite of myself. "Thanks," I croaked.

We managed the slow trip, despite dizziness and pain, to the bathroom with the help of the orderly. They encased both my feet in

Velcro-strapped boots and trailed an IV stand behind me. Unfortunately, there was a mirror in there. Both my eyes were bloodshot and ringed in black. With my turban bandage, I looked like an Arab raccoon.

After I was resettled, Dr. Pagano came striding back into the room and stood over my bed.

"Well, Mr. Grant, how do you feel?"

"Okay, I suppose, considering. Thank you for patching me up." My voice was coming back.

"Good. Your most serious injury was a blow to the head. You had some brain trauma, so we kept you sleeping to let the swelling go down. We kept a measurement of intracranial pressure, and didn't have to drill any burr holes. You'll find stitches in your upper forehead under those bandages, but it's doing well. Do you remember the accident?"

"No, I don't think so. Everything's pretty fuzzy right now, but thanks for not putting any more holes in my head."

"It'll come back to you. We'll back off on the medication as much as we can, but let us know if you need help with the pain. We'll keep the visitors under control for a day or two and let you rest. There's a police lieutenant pestering me."

"Maybe tomorrow? I don't even know what time of day it is—or what day it is, for that matter."

"It's Thursday, mid-morning. We've let your grandmother keep close by."

"Does she have red hair?"

"That's her. It'll come back to you." He patted my hand. "Okay, good. I'll see you on evening rounds." With that he was gone.

A nurse's aide brought a lunch tray in to awaken me the next time. They must have been feeding me through a tube or something, because I found myself eager to eat. After coffee and food, I began to feel alive again. My thoughts, however, were disturbed by a vision or dream that I couldn't bring into focus.

When Nurse Martha came in later to check my vital signs, I decided to see if she could help.

"Martha, can I ask a question?"

She nodded watching the dial on a pressure cuff.

"Was I near death at any time?"

"Why, no, not that I know of. Why such a question?"

"Well, as my mind begins to clear, I'm remembering a vision or a dream that I've heard described by those near-death people."

"Really? How so?"

"I remember a bright light over me, and there was an angel."

"An angel?"

"Yes, I think so. My mind is hazy, but it seemed that her face was floating above me, but it was in shadow. She was dressed in white. There was a bright glow, or halo, around her head. She touched my face, and she kissed me."

"An angel kissed you? A nice dream, at least."

"What about the light?"

"The overhead in Recovery is brighter. Maybe it was when you were there." She smiled. "I'll ask them about the angel."

"Thanks. I hope they don't think I'm nuts."

She breezed out of the room and it was back to sleep for me.


Nurse Martha came by to check on me again at mid-afternoon. As she briskly went about her business, hanging a new IV, checking blood pressure and other vitals, she said, "I checked with the people downstairs and solved your mysterious angelic visitation, I think. They said that police had checked out your cell and called a couple of numbers. When they brought you to recovery there were a couple of women and a muscular little guy waiting. They wouldn't normally let a visitor in, but your fiancé insisted. They gave her a couple of minutes as you were waking up, before they sedated you again."

"My *fiancé?* I don't think I have one. At least I should remember something like that."

"Well, I don't know what to say. That's what they told me. Said she was a beautiful blonde and showed them her engagement ring. Made her wear a white robe so it could be what you saw."

"Somebody pulled a fast one, unless it really was an angel." Some of the fog in my brain began to lift. A thought occurred that made me smile.

She peered over her glasses. "You know who it was, don't you?"

"I have no idea. Must be my brain trauma."

She looked me in the eye. "Well, you'd better remember by tomorrow. I'm going off duty now, and it won't be an angel haunting you when I come back in the morning."

She left after helping me out of bed so I could moon the room as I hobbled to the bathroom in my gown.

They brought me my dinner tray in the early evening, holding off any visitors until they took it away. The first to arrive were the red-haired woman and a large man with white hair.

She kissed me lightly on the cheek. "Gideon, I'm so relieved to see you awake and looking so good. How are you?"

"My mind is foggy. Help me understand who you are. You're my grandmother?"

She took my hand and there were tears in her eyes. "Oh, Gideon, I'm your grandmother Maureen. I raised you from childhood."

"I knew you were. Hearing your words is bringing it back. Oh, Gran. Please forgive me."

In response, she took my hand and kissed me on the cheek.

"Physically, I'm okay for the shape I'm in. A headache and some pains, but not too bad. Maybe I'm lucky."

"You truly are. That little Gully told me you were pulled out of the wreckage before it caught fire."

"Wow! And I don't remember a thing."

"Just as well, young man," said her companion. "I'm Reggie, by the way. Memory shuts down sometime to protect us from fright. May I also say how happy I am to see you? Maureen's been beside herself the last couple of days."

"I confess," she said. "I couldn't bear it if something worse happened. This is bad enough. Miss Julia is the one who called me. I was terrified. Made Reggie break all the speed limits getting over here."

"Sorry for your scare, and thank you for always being there for me."

"Welcome, but we have to go. They made us promise to stay only a few minutes. They let me sit with you all day when you were asleep. Now it's too 'stimulating'. By the way, Miss Julia, your friend and lawyer, and Grace, a woman you care about, are waiting to come in next."

"Thanks for the heads up. I'm really okay, but we'd better do what they say."

Immediately after they left, my two women visitors came in. Thanks to Gran, I recognized both immediately.

"Is this real, or am I having a dream?" I said.

"Sounds like you're on the road to recovery. Saw your Gran outside. She says your memory is a bit clouded. Just to give you a little help, I'm Julia and she's Grace." Julia kissed me on the cheek.

Grace looked hesitant, then did the same. "Gideon, all of us were really worried about you."

I reached for her hand and she allowed me to take it. "Thanks for caring, and I'd like to talk with you when we can."

She blushed and moved away to allow Julia to come closer.

Julia said, "I can stay only a minute, which will make the nurses happy. We had to beg to get to see you, and I have a court appearance."

"I'm glad you came. It means a lot to me."

"I talked with Greg, and can tell you more about the wreck, but let's not do it now."

"Okay. My mind's still a little fuzzy."

"Do you remember talking with the FBI?"

"Yes, actually I do. I remember driving in my car...."

"Don't try to think about it now. Give your brain a rest. Get a good night's sleep. Lieutenant Haney's coming by in the morning. Wait until then. Well, gotta go. Be well." Julia patted my hand and was gone.

Grace looked uncertain.

"Grace, will you stay a moment? You can get that side chair and bring it over."

"Yes, I suppose so."

When she was seated close to me, with our faces at the same level, I could smell the wonderful clean scent of her. She looked concerned, but a little uncomfortable. I expected my blood pressure monitor to start beeping.

"May I tell you a little story?" I asked.

"Of course."

"I was unconscious for quite a while, but when my mind began to focus I told my nurse that it felt like I'd had a near-death experience. It actually worried me."

Her eyes widened.

"I described to her a vision of a bright light and an angel hovering over me. She had a golden halo and she touched my face and kissed me. Do you know what I found out?"

She blushed crimson, and it was beautiful. "I can't imagine." She covered her face with her hands, and peeped between her fingers.

"The recovery room people told her my *fiancé* demanded to see me. They described her. Turns out it really was an angel."

"Well," she said softly, taking her hands away and smiling at me. "You *did* ask me to marry you."

"So it was only half a lie, right? Does that mean I can still anticipate an answer?"

She ignored my question. "We were all worried, and it worked, didn't it? You didn't look great, but at least you were alive. You're not very pretty now, if I may be truthful. Now, I must go." She caressed my face, kissed my cheek, and flew away.


Dr. Pagano came in for evening rounds, checked my reflexes, listened to my heart and lungs, and checked my chart. He gave orders to remove the padding around my head and redress my wound, pronouncing himself satisfied with my progress.

# CHAPTER 28

Haney burst through the door the next morning right after they took away my breakfast tray. By then, I knew who he was. He managed to appear rumpled even early in the morning. He also looked hesitant for the first time since I had met him, as though being in the presence of an invalid put him off stride.

"How ya doin'?" He growled.

"Getting better, thanks," I said. "Pull up a chair."

He complied, then got right down to business. "Do ya know what happened to you?"

"It's coming back. First, all I could remember was leaving the FBI and driving away in my car. Since I woke up this morning, I remember worrying about the black car following me. That's about it."

"Let me fill ya in on a few things. Witnesses say it looked like on purpose, a hit and run. You rolled over and off the exit ramp. Some guys on the street below pulled you out before your car caught on fire and burned up. You were lucky."

"I'd like to find them and thank them. Was it the car I'd seen a few times?"

"No doubt. It was a Firebird and it lived up to its name. Later that day, we got a report of a car fire down in the Central Waterfront area, behind a vacant warehouse. Burned to a crisp, so no fingerprints, no DNA. We ran the VIN and it matched a stolen car from six months ago. Plate was stolen a couple of weeks ago."

"So, any leads?"

He nibbled on the overhang of his bushy mustache. "We ain't got squat. We did run pictures on TV and in the newspapers to see if anyone knows where it's been. Have to wait and see...well, we *are* canvassing that area of storage units and buildings to see if it's been hidden around there."

"Good hunting. I sure feel helpless in here. You know, this thing just keeps getting bigger. Look at what had to be done just to get rid of Dickerson and...the other guy...the newspaper guy?"

"Richie."

"Right. Did they steal and hide the car knowing how this would go? Imagine hiring someone to steal that boat and follow him out to sea. Then killing the guys on the boat to get rid of witnesses. Scary."

"We'd better take this serious. He was trying to kill you. I'm gonna put a man here as long as you're in the hospital."

"You think that's necessary?"

"Yeah, I do." He gave a crooked grin. "Might be, you'd be bait to catch him."

"That's a comforting thought. Maybe two guys?"

"I'll think about it. And we'll talk about it after you get out. But we'll get the sonofabitch eventually. They always slip up somewhere."

"I hope so."

"By the way, you look like hell."

After he left, the staff came in to work me over. They gave me what passes for a bath when you're helpless and wrapped in various dressings. Afterward, I lay on my back on the bed and an aide washed my hair, working carefully around the bandage. It felt great. San Francisco General Spa and Hospital. Even the IV was removed.

"Now," said Martha. "Let's hear it."

"Hear what?"

She just stared at me over her glasses.

"Okay, okay. The angel was Grace O'Quinn, who works for Child Protective Services. She is a fiancé, just not mine, unfortunately. It's a long story. She came by after you left yesterday and confessed."

"Well, something's going on, but I have work to do. You can tell me about it later."

Gran and Reggie came by in mid-afternoon. They brought another huge bouquet, a couple of detective novels, and some magazines, *SAIL* and *Wooden Boat*. I could be cynical about the latter and say, "That's what got me into this mess," but I'd be joking.

Gran said, "I can't believe how some people drive in this city! And that fool left the scene!"

Julia hadn't told her the real story.

Reggie told me they had postponed their travel plans, which I'd forgotten, until I was fully recovered.

I thanked them sincerely and promised to get going as soon as possible. We visited quietly and softly. They left after an hour to let me rest.


Sleep took away the rest of the afternoon, and consciousness came with the delivery of dinner. When I had finished, something wonderful happened. Grace walked into the room. She came to my bedside and gave me a kiss on the cheek, reprising the angel visit.

"Gideon, I'm so glad to see you recovering. I was worried. Now I have a surprise for you. I've brought visitors, and you may want this." She slipped a gaily wrapped package from a shopping bag she'd concealed.

"What's this?"

"It's a birthday present."

"What?" My fogged brain wouldn't compute.

"For Abigail." She went to the door and opened it. Abigail peeped around her, then came bouncing into the room.

"*Kitteeee!*" she squealed, and come rushing toward me, but stopped and stared. "Whaaaat *happened?*" She said.

No way could I forget her. "I was in a car wreck, Sweetheart."

"Your eyes are *blaack* and you have a plastic arm."

"I got hit on the head to make my eyes black, and my arm is broken. That's why it has plaster on it."

"Oh," she said, then came over beside me and smiled a mile wide.

I was overcome with emotion and couldn't speak for a moment as I put my arm around her slender waist.

"Sweetheart, it's so good to see you! I've really missed you." Tears were coursing down my cheeks, but she wouldn't let go of my good hand so I could wipe them away.

"I missed you, too. I wanted you to come and get me, but they said you couldn't. Why couldn't you? Why are you crying?"

"It's happy crying, because I love you. You can get me a tissue."

While she did so, I could see Grace needed the same service.

After we were all under control again, I tried to explain. "Abigail, I didn't want to stay away from you, but I've been helping the police try to find your mother and father. We're still trying. Are you doing okay?"

"I'm okay, but I'm sad. I want to see you and I want to see Jemima, and I want to see my mama."

"I'm sorry you're sad. Miss Grace is a wonderful person for bringing you to see me." I looked at Grace and could see she was still emotional about our reunion. "I hope we can see each other again soon."

"Can I stay here with you?"

"No, Sweetie, only sick people can stay in the hospital."

"Can I be sick?"

"We don't want you to be sick. Maybe you can come to see me again soon. Right, Miss Grace?"

Grace smiled, "We'll see."

Abigail mumbled, "We'll see. We'll see. Big people always say, 'We'll see.'"

Grace and I laughed together, but I winced in pain from my ribs.

"Abigail, I understand someone has a birthday—is tomorrow Saturday?—here's a little something from me."

"Oh, goody! But I can't open it until tomorrow. Can you come to my party?"

"I don't think so, Sweetheart, but I'll be thinking of you. Will you save me a piece of cake?"

"We'll see."

Grace and I both laughed, and Abigail smiled, proud of herself.

"I've brought two others for you to meet," said Grace. "I'll go get them."

She reappeared a few moments later, followed by a middle-aged couple. "Gideon, I'd like you to meet Clifford and Wilma Epperson. Mr. and Mrs. Epperson, Gideon Grant."

They stepped forward, smiled, and each shook my hand. Abigail turned loose of my hand only for this operation and grasped it again, one little hand around my thumb, the other my first two fingers.

"How are you doing?" said Clifford. "Sorry for your trouble."

"Better, thanks, but it may be hard to believe, based on how I look."

Clifford smiled, "I'll use my imagination."

Wilma stepped forward, holding a potted plant. "I brought you a little flower to cheer you up, but it looks like you have one attached to your hand."

Grace said, "Abigail, we have to go for now because they broke the rules a little to let us all in together." She smiled, "And I promise to bring you back. No more of that 'we'll see' stuff."

"Oh, pleeeeeze," she said. Grace shook her head and grasped her arm to take her away. Abigail relented and kissed me on the cheek. "Bye, bye, Kitty. I'll come back tomorrow."

Grace smiled and mouthed the words, "We'll see."

Clifford said, "Miss Grace, I'll lag behind a couple of minutes if I may." Then to me, "May I bring over a chair?"

"Of course."

He seated himself and began, speaking softly. "Abigail is a sweet little girl, but it was amazing to see her light up when she came into this room. When she talks, it's always about you…well, occasionally about her cat or her mother…but always back to you."

I felt my emotions rising.

He continued, "We originally thought about trying for adoption if her parents weren't found, but after Miss Grace told us all about your time together on the ocean, and seeing how Abigail is, Wilma and I talked. We'd not stand in your way if you have the same thoughts."

"I can't thank you enough. You're both very kind to do what you do in the first place, caring for her."

"Well, it's what we do. Our first two children came to us the same way. Others have gone back to family members after being with us awhile."

"There's a special place in God's Kingdom for you both."

"Well, thank you. By the way, I know you in a way. I'm a CPA and our firm has worked with some of your former clients, so I've seen your firm name in some of their papers."

"Meeting you has been a great pleasure and an honor."

We shook hands and he departed.

# CHAPTER 29

The doctor released me the next morning, but before anything else could happen, DeeDee Marshall walked into the room. She was dressed in a tight top and a skirt the size of a handkerchief.

"What are you doing here?" I asked.

"Heard you were injured, and thought you might need a little therapy." She gave me a crooked grin.

"I believe I'll trust that to the hospital staff. How did you know I was here?"

"Saw it in the paper, I think. I bet they can't do for you what I can do. Gee, one arm's tied up already. I could tie up the other one—"

"I don't think so."

"Well, at least tell me what happened. Did you see who was in the other car?"

"How do you know about another car?"

"Uh, it was in the newspaper article."

There was a tap at the door and an aide with a wheelchair came into the room, followed by Gully and Gran.

"Crap! We'll talk later." DeeDee said, hurrying past them.

Nurse Martha came in and took charge of the operation. I was allowed to dress in normal clothing Gran brought, discarding the regulation drafty hospital gown. Gully served as my valet, finally fitting a sling for my cumbersome cast. The word had gotten out to all my task force. He wheeled me into a waiting room where I found Reggie, Julia, and most surprisingly, Grace. There were also two husky young men in suits, trying to look inconspicuous.

"Good morning everyone," I said, looking mostly at Grace. "Thanks for coming. I don't see Two Men and a Truck, but this is quite a moving crew."

They all smiled, but Grace was the one to speak. "We're all happy to see you going home. A scare for us, but a happy ending." She walked over and knelt beside my chair and whispered, *"Who was that I saw coming out of your room?"*

*"That was the person I talked to that works at the North Beach Club."*

*"Person? What was she doing here?"*

*"Wishing me well, I guess. Damned if I know. We're attracting attention."* She stood.

"Thanks for being here, Grace. There's someone here you should meet. Nurse Martha, this is the angel visitor, Grace O'Quinn. Grace, this is Martha, who took good care of me."

"Aha! Now I understand," Martha said as they shook hands. "Nice to meet you."

Grace blushed.

"Understand what?" Gran demanded.

"I'll explain later," I said. The rest of the party looked puzzled.

"I'll not be going down with you," Martha said.

"Is a hug allowed?"

"You bet."

I gave her a clumsy one-armed hug. "Thanks for taking care of me." They called it a lightweight cast, but it was still cumbersome. Dr. Pagano explained that the break was above the elbow, so they put in a titanium plate and screws.

Reggie went ahead to bring the car around. One of the undercover cops went down with him. The rest of us came down in a scattered herd, bearing flowers and potted plants. After they got me safely on the sidewalk, I was allowed to stand. The aide took away the chair. It was a bit awkward, as no one seemed to know what to do next. Reggie drove up, came around, and opened the door. My guardian joined his partner in a plain-looking cop car behind Reggie.

Time for me to speak. "Thanks again, all of you. It means a lot to me. Maureen and Reggie will get me home, so all of you probably have things to do, since it's Saturday. Let me get my battered head into the ballgame, then maybe we can have a meeting to catch up on everything.

Let's shoot for Monday at 5:30 at my place, unless something comes up. If it does, just let me know."

They all nodded agreement, and Julia and Grace each gave me a quick hug. "One more thing," I said: "We don't know what's going on, so please, please be careful."

"I'm seeing Greg tonight," Julia said. "I'll see what I can find out without being obvious."

"Me, too, Sir," said Gully. "Uh, I don't mean seeing Greg. I mean, I'll rattle my sources."

"I'll see if there is a way to bring Abigail to see you, perhaps this afternoon at your place?" Grace said.

"That's great...all of you. And Grace, just give me a ring if you get it arranged."

We were soon settled in my condo, me in my leather recliner with a soft afghan Gran had knitted tucked around me. My first act was to telephone the insurance carrier and start in motion getting a replacement car. He said he'd get right on it, after getting the details.

Gran and Reggie had gone out and Jemima had settled in my lap, purring contentedly as I stroked her patchwork fur. I began to think about Grace. There was something different about her; not only how she treated me, but something else. My mind wasn't functioning at its highest level since the hit-and-run. Slowly reviewing everything as in a series of movie scenes, I could see her looking at me. There was that time she covered her face with her hands, and peeped between her fingers at me... *The ring!* She wasn't wearing it! Maybe she'd taken it off for some reason. But then, last meeting we had at the condo, she had come back from Los Angeles a little distracted. She was wearing the ring then and she was wearing it as a passport when she came to see me in Recovery. Puzzling, but there was no appropriate way to ask her about it. Might mean nothing. "We'll see," as big people say.

It wasn't a good day to make calls, but I tried it anyway. Special Agent Scott wasn't in, but his answering machine promised to call back. He had several things that my beleaguered brain remembered, among them the bugged telephone in Bart Richie's condo, formerly belonging to the Dickersons. The same thing happened with Lieutenant Haney. He wasn't in, but a desk sergeant took a number for a callback. The main thing on my mind, besides Grace, was the unknown someone out there who tried to kill me, or at least send a stern warning. Would they try again? Could those around me be in jeopardy?

The telephone rang, but it wasn't the expected call from Scott or Haney. Grace was on the line. "Gideon, I'm sorry, but I have to go out of town today. I can't bring Abigail by as we had hoped."

"I'm sorry, too. Is everything okay?"

"Well...yes, I think it is. It's one of the reasons Big People have to say, 'we'll see.' I'll do my best to make it up to Abigail and you."

"I won't pry, but you sound uncertain."

"I'm certain. Look, I'll be back Sunday evening. Maybe I can explain it to you then."

"That would be great. Take care of yourself, and let me know when you're back."

"I promise. And thanks."


Gran and Reggie returned and made chicken noodle soup for lunch, the universal curative for invalids. The phone didn't ring. I took some aspirin for my headache, sore ribs, and sore ankles. Without planning on it, I slept in my chair for several hours.

The ringing phone awakened me at a little after four in the afternoon. It was Gully, "Hello, boss. How are you feeling?"

"I'll get there eventually. What's up?"

"Well, Sir, I won't keep you, but I found out something interesting. My backdoor to the FBI tells me that the bugs on the phone in Richie's condo were paid for by Solene Dickerson."

"*What?* They've got to be kidding."

"They were serious as a heart attack."

"When was it done?"

"Several months ago."

"What do you think it means?"

"I couldn't say, Sir, but I'd guess it was to catch a cheating husband."

"Would it stay alive that long? I suppose it gets power from the phone line."

"Correct. If it transmits over RF, with the right receiver it would work until somebody found it. You can wire the transmitter into house current, and there you are. Several ways to do it. Not complicated."

"Thanks, Gully. We'll talk more about it Monday evening."

Gran and Reggie were in the kitchen area, bustling about for the evening meal, but came in after hearing my side of the conversation.

Reggie said, "We couldn't help overhearing part of what you said. Is everything copacetic?"

"Just strange," I replied. "Recall I speculated Richie's condo might be bugged? FBI confirmed that it was, and found out the installation was paid for by Solene. What do you make of that?"

"I wouldn't venture a guess. How about you, Maureen?"

"Same here. You said it used to be the Dickerson's, so I'd guess it was to check up on her husband. But why would they go away together and leave it that way? And could someone else know about it and start using it, or is one or both still alive?"

"That would mean someone would have to have no qualms about leaving Abigail to die. That, I can't imagine. We're certain they were both on the yacht.

"Now let me change the subject. I'm worried about Grace. While you were out earlier, she called and said she couldn't bring Abigail to see me. Said she had to go out of town."

Gran came over and touched my bandaged head, "Did she say why?"

"No. Said she was okay, but didn't sound like it. I couldn't pry. Promised to call me tomorrow evening."

She stoked my cheek. "I've known from the first time I saw her that you were smitten. Don't worry."

"Smitten? Guilty, I guess. I'll just have to wait."

Gran went back and sat on the couch, but got that determined look on her face I remembered from my youth. "Now let's hear about the 'angel visitor' comment at the hospital."

"It sounds foolish now, but in the fog of drugs when I woke up in the recovery room, it was like a dream, or a vision." I told the whole story and they listened with rapt attention. I said nothing about the missing engagement ring the next day.

Gran looked at Reggie, "Makes sense to me, Dear, don't you agree?"

"Righto. A lovely mistake, I'd say," and he beamed at me.

It was time for cocktails—I didn't get any—then dinner followed by the struggle to bed me down for the night. I was awake late into the night, stewing over the missing-persons case, but more about what Grace would tell me the next day.

# CHAPTER 30

R eggie tapped on my door the next morning. "Gideon, are you awake? Well, I presume you will be after I knocked."
"Sure, Reggie. I was lying here thinking about getting up."
He entered with a mug of coffee. "Here you are. There's a Leftenant Haney on the telephone, says he's downstairs and wishes to speak with you."

"Thought I heard it. I'll be right there."

I threw on my robe, picked up the receiver from the kitchen counter, and spoke.

Haney's gruff voice, "Mr. Grant, are you able to come down, or should I come up there?"

"If you don't mind, come on up. We have coffee."

Reggie met him at the door and introduced himself. They appraised each other, and seemed satisfied with what they saw.

"Please have a seat. Sergeant-Major Thurston is retired from the Coldstream Guard, and is engaged to marry my grandmother. Lieutenant Haney is lead on the case I'm involved in." They both nodded in acknowledgement and sat at the table.

Haney spoke first. "I worked with your security to program a one-touch phone to 911, and a second button to my cell number. I think we're good to rely on more frequent patrols on the street rather than putting men in the building."

"Sounds good to me," I said.

Haney took a drag of coffee. "However, if you feel the need to leave the building, give me a call first and I'll have someone shadow you. Here's my cell number." He handed me a card.

"I don't know that I'll be going anywhere, but thanks."

"There's another thing or two," Haney said, and glanced at Reggie. "Maybe we can talk when you feel like coming down to the station."

"We're good here. Sergeant Thurston knows everything I know, and I rely on him completely."

Haney shifted in his chair, and stared at his coffee cup. "We've found where the Firebird was garaged."

"Do you have a name?"

"We do. Scott Donaldson."

"Well, do you know where he is?"

"We know exactly where he is. His ashes are in an urn on the mantel of his mother's house in Sausalito. He died in a car wreck six years ago."

"Can it get any worse? I don't suppose anyone has seen this imposter?"

Haney took another drink, and wiped his mustache. "We haven't found anyone yet, but we're working on it. Best the guy can recall, they did the rental on the phone, but it was done some months ago, about the time the car was stolen, natcherly. He couldn't remember if it was a man or woman on the phone."

"It figures. But the rental was in the name of a man, at least. Reason I asked, though; you've heard from the FBI about the bugs in Richie's condo?"

He stared at me. "Yes, but who told you?"

"I have resources. But Solene paying for them doesn't mean much even with fake Donaldson running around. He could have been a hire. One other thing, it slipped my fogged mind, but you recall we had a deal for me to go with you to see Mayor Dilbeck?"

"Yeah, I remember. FBI talked to him, didn't get much."

"They also talked to Bradley's parents. How about it?"

"I'll think about it." Haney stood, pushing back his chair. "Don't get up. I'd better get to it. Thanks for the coffee." He shook hands and Reggie showed him out the door, refreshed our coffee and sat back down.

"Reggie, what do you think about all this?"

"Confusing, I must say. A crime of passion or greed. I'm no Sherlock Holmes, although some may say I sound like him." He winked at me.

"Well, we know they're still around, whoever they are."

Reggie prepared our breakfast and Gran joined us. Reggie filled her in on Haney's visit. She was pleased with the added security. In a busy morning, the intercom said we had another visitor, this time Gully. I gave the word to send him up and Reggie ushered him in. The physical contrast between the two could not have been greater, but both carried themselves in a similar, military manner.

"Good morning Sir," he began. "I hope you're feeling well."

"Thank you, Gully. Have some coffee and tell us what's happening."

"Thank you, Sir. I have some concerns about your safety. The police tell me they've added presence, but I brought you something."

He reached in a leather satchel and brought out a pistol. "You need personal protection. Do you know how to shoot?"

"Yes, I've done a bit, but aren't we being a little too cautious? And I don't have a permit."

"No, Sir, I don't believe so. And as to a permit, no one need know. Here's an ankle holster, but instead of using it like that, let's try putting it around your cast, inside the sling. Should be perfect."

We did, and it was. It was a small, blue-black .380 Beretta, with an alloy frame.

"Thanks, Gully. We'll see how it works out. And let's think about diagramming all we know in the meeting tomorrow."

He departed, with the promise of seeing to the guarding of Abigail.


I fidgeted in my chair, picked at my lunch, tried to read, tried to nap. All I could think about was Grace's call. Gran and Reggie tried not to notice my discomfort, but they would glance at me from time to time. Gran knitted, Reggie read. At last the telephone rang.

I snatched it up on the first ring. It was for Gran, a grocery delivery.

At mid-afternoon, her call finally came through. Her voice was soft, but showed a trace of strain. Or was it defeat? "Gideon, are you okay?"

"I'm fine, but anxious for your call."

Gran and Reggie left the room.

"I'm about to catch the shuttle, so I'll be there soon. Can we meet somewhere to talk, as I had promised you? Are you able to go out?"

"Of course. Will you have dinner with me?"

"Yes, if we avoid soft light and romantic music. Just a place in a crowd, to talk."

"Good. *Scoma's* okay?"

"Yes. Shall we make it for eight? I'll call when I get home and we'll decide how to get there."

Her call filled me with anticipation, so I hurried to make all the arrangements. First was a call to *Scoma's*, a fixture for many years on the Wharf. They promised a table with some isolation, plus a table for two a few feet away for my separate "guests." No reason for my watchers to go hungry. Haney took my call and promised to inform his team.


Grace called at seven, and we worked out that she would park as a guest in our secure parking garage and we would cab together to the restaurant. We met in the lobby and she wore that strained expression she had the last time she returned from Los Angeles. Still, she was beautiful; her shining, golden hair, creamy skin, mouth like a rose. She wore a long plaid skirt, high heels, and a cape-style coat with a velvet-lined hood.

As we started to enter our cab, I saw the unmarked car at the curb. I went back to speak to them and the guy in the right seat rolled down the window. "As you know, we're going to *Scoma's*. I've booked a table for you, so come in after us. Dinner's on me."

"Thanks, Boss. Take care."

We said little on the ride down the Embarcadero to the Wharf. The atmosphere was subdued and also there was a third set of ears, although the driver was tuned to Latin music, beating time on the steering wheel.

The hostess greeted us and immediately noticed my sling and discolored face. "Mr. Grant, I hope you're okay?"

"Recovering nicely, thank you, Susan."

Our table was discreet, indeed. Other diners were not far away, but we had a corner. Our watchers came in and were seated a dozen feet away. They ignored us.

I sat next to Grace so we could speak softly in the noisy environment. A veteran waiter old enough to be my father, in starched white jacket, approached us immediately, bringing menus and water. I placed an order for a bottle of *pinot grigio*. Champagne would have been pushing it.

Grace looked down at the table, rearranged her silverware, took a sip of water, and finally turned to me. "You may wonder why I am telling you about this…"

She took another tiny sip of water. I kept my mouth shut.

"I don't want you to hear things and get any wrong ideas. I know you care what happens to me, but I believe in laying it on the line."

What was coming? Best to wait for it. "It's true. I do care about you."

The waiter brought and poured our wine. We placed our orders, both for sole amandine. I waited for Grace to continue.

"I'm no longer engaged, which you might have guessed. I thought it only fair to tell you, I'm not a rebounder." She looked at me with fire in her eyes. "I'm mad as hell, and I'm disgusted with the whole situation, and I won't be good to be around until I get it out of my system."

"I can't imagine what happened, but remember I'm in your corner. I'll be around you any time I get a chance, no matter how you are." I covered her hand with mine.

"Thank you," she said. "I had a lot of time invested…or I should say 'wasted'." My parents think I'm nuts. That's because I couldn't tell them the truth. They think I'm the problem."

"Sorry, parents, not important what you think, and time invested doesn't count."

"My parents know his parents, he's a 'good catch,' and so on. But you're right. I'm just disgusted, and I need to hear encouraging words."

"I have lots of 'em. The future is yours. You're beautiful and talented. A man would have to be a fool to lose you. And anyone who could gain your love would be the luckiest man on earth. Shall I go on?"

"'Fool' wasn't the word I used. More to do with canine parentage." She mumbled.

The waiter brought our food, filleting the sole with the skill of a surgeon. I began to eat, which I could handle with my one good hand.

Grace looked down at her plate, picked up her fork and gently prodded her fish, then laid it down again and took a tiny sip of wine.

"Are you okay, Grace?"

She continued to look down and shook her head. "I shouldn't do this to you," she whispered. "It's okay. Drink your wine and eat your food. You'll feel better."

"Yes, mother." She forced a small smile.

"I won't ask any questions and I won't celebrate."

She nodded, and made an attempt to do as I asked. We spoke little for the rest of the meal. When the time came, the waiter seemed puzzled, but brought me the bill for the two strangers at the other table. We got a cab outside and reversed the quiet ride back down the Embarcadero. She held my hand all the way this time. We didn't speak until we were standing beside her silver Mercedes coupe.

"Nice car," I said.

"My father gave it to me. Probably thinks I don't deserve it now."

"No more negative thoughts. He can't help loving you." I took both her hands, but resisted the urge to take her in my arms. She sensed my thoughts as she looked up at me.

"It's not fair to you, Gideon, to tell you my troubles. I…I can't think now about anything but anger."

"Anger? That bad?"

Her voice was almost a whisper. "I told you his specialty was plastic surgery. Well, he proposed that I be modified, physically." Then she raised her voice, and the fire in her eyes returned, "I'm not some God-damn corpse donated to science!"

Modified? I could think of only one thing…well, actually two things. "Did you tell him that?"

"Yes, I did."

"In those words?"

"Exactly."

"I've never heard you use profanity."

"You haven't given me a reason. But I have to admit, I've never used those exact terms before. It felt right for the circumstance. There's nothing wrong with the operation but it's a personal choice."

"I agree." This time I couldn't resist. I put my clumsy "plastic arm," as Abigail called it, and my good one around her and held her close to me. "Jesus, Grace, what a fool. I'm truly sorry. I know the time isn't right, but someday I'll hold you like this and tell you what I'm really thinking."

"Maybe that time will come," she said. She gave me a quick kiss and was in her car and gone.

I saw a Grace I had not seen before, indignation intruding on her usual sunny dignity. It made me admit to myself I loved her even more.

# CHAPTER 31

G ran and Reggie left right after breakfast for Modesto to check on Gran's house and visit friends. They'd be gone overnight, but I assured them I could take care of myself. Doctor Pagano wanted to see me in his office at one o'clock, and a taxi would take me there, followed by my security detail.

The office visit was uneventful after the good doctor and his assistant got over the surprise at finding a pistol strapped to my cast. They accepted my explanation without further questions. Pagano instructed that the elastic wrap could be continued for my sore ribs if it made me feel better, and chastised me for using a coat hanger inside the infernal itchy cast. My eyes and face were now zombie shades of gray and green. The cut on my head, now a week old, had knitted nicely so he plucked out the stitches and put a light bandage over it.

The great room was all set for the evening meeting. An office supply store sent a guy over with a white board on a stand, with a handful of colored markers. Now all we had to do was think of intelligent things to write. With all afternoon to ponder where we were, I sat and made notes on a yellow pad, trying to make sense out of what I did and didn't know. The former was sparse; the latter could fill several pages. I had to reach around Jcm, who had curled in my lap, to write what few notes made it to the pad. My mind wandered over the last several days...

The telephone woke me. The yellow pad had slipped to the floor and it took me a moment to orient myself.

"Hi, Gideon."

"Grace. What's up?"

"I'd promised to take Abigail shopping after school and help her buy some clothes. I had to miss her birthday party because of my *wonderful*

Saturday in LA. The shopping is one of those 'we'll see' promises? I'm in a city bus on my way to pick her up at school. Mrs. Epperson was kind enough to give me some time with her."

"Sounds like fun. You be careful. Don't trust anyone. Oh, by the way, you can bring her here if you like and it's okay with the Eppersons. Let her see Jemima."

"We'll see…do I say that a lot? Anyway, we'll stay totally in the public eye. I should have plenty of time, but don't worry if I'm a little late to your meeting. I'll get there as quickly as I can."

"Okay, but remember what I said. I couldn't…Never mind."

"What?"

"I was about to say something unauthorized."

"You're speaking in riddles."

"Remember what I said to you last night. That someday—"

"Oh. I understand. It's okay. I'll see you later."

I immediately called Gully and was thankful he answered on the first ring.

"Gully, just to alert you, Grace is going to pick up Abigail at school and travel by bus to go shopping for clothes. Thought you'd like to give a heads-up to your guy."

"Will do, Sir. Sam's on duty. I'll give him a call."

After I hung up, I called Haney, but had to leave a call-back.

I paced the floor and waited for Haney's call. It was time for Abigail to get out of school and the police needed to know her plans. They should have visual contact to follow her anyway, but nothing should be left to chance. I called 911 and received little encouragement when I explained the situation. The response, thinly veiled, seemed to be, "Your emergency is a shopping trip?" Well, at least Sam Owen was on duty.

Jemima trotted along beside me as I continued to pace all around the condo. After a few laps she gave up and retired to a corner to groom herself. Couldn't blame her. Nothing exciting happened and I didn't go near the can opener and her food dish.

At last there was a knock at the door and I opened it to Gully and Julia, but no Grace.

"You didn't see Grace?"

Julia answered, 'No, we didn't see her, but we're a little early if anything."

"Well, come in and let me fix you a drink. As Gully already knows, she was taking Abigail shopping after school, so she might be a little late."

I poured a glass of Shiraz for Julia from the bottle that was already open and breathing. For Gully, it was scotch, neat, and scotch for me, but over ice. Since my doctor visit, there were no meds in the picture except for this attractive alternative.

We munched on snacks and nuts, enjoyed our drinks, and chatted about mundane subjects. The Carolina Panthers are in town next weekend to play the 49ers. Weather was a dull subject—always beautiful but due to change. I looked at my watch twenty-five times.

"Well, shall we get started? She said she might be late. I'll catch her up when she gets here. Before I try to chart anything, why don't we bring up anything new since we last met? Julie?"

"I finished grinding through the files of the Emit Dilbeck case, and have to say I didn't get much out of it. Sure, he was corrupt and a miserable creep, but I just couldn't get much of a feel of violence out of him. Bradley did have a hand in exposing him, of course."

"There was that death of a witness," Gully said.

"Yes, but he didn't rise to 'key witness' level. There was plenty of other evidence."

"Thanks, Julie. I'll keep him in the mix, but not high priority. Anything else?"

"Greg says the police continue to check out all known associates of Buddy Lyon, but aren't hopeful. They still don't have anything on Bart Richie's murder. Also, he told me about your hit-and-run ghost whose ashes are in an urn."

"Oh, Gully, I apologize. My mind wasn't working when you came by to give me the gun. Haney had been by earlier to tell me more about the Firebird." I proceeded to fill him in on all we knew.

"That's okay, Sir. Sounds like a dead end, anyway."

"Yes, but someone went to a lot of trouble ahead of time. Where the heck is Grace? She's forty-five minutes late. Excuse me a minute."

Her cell went immediately to her message, so it was either turned off or she was on the phone. I left a message to call me.

I refreshed our drinks and decided to lay out what I'd been thinking about all afternoon. "I don't want to jump the gun, but let me lay out a possible scenario and let you shoot holes in it."

They both looked surprised, and Julia said, "You think you know what happened?"

"Well, I don't *know*, and we still don't have much information on the various news scandals, but when I look at what we know at this point—"

Gully's phone rang. He whipped it out and looked at the screen, then held up his hand and answered. "Yeah, Sam?"

A pause, "This is Gulliver Tolliver. Who's this?"

Gully looked stricken as he listened. "How is he?"

Another pause. "I'll be right there."

When Gully closed his cellphone and turned to us, his face was white and his hands were shaking. He gulped for air. "I don't know how to tell you this. Sam Owen has been shot and is in the emergency room in critical condition. I don't know any more—"

Oh God oh God oh God. "You go to him. I'll try to get hold of Haney. How'd they find you?"

"The hospital had his cell and called the last number that had called him."

"Okay. Go, go. Call me when you know anything. Julie will you try Greg Peak? I'll call Haney."

We went to our respective corners and started making calls. I could hear Julie leaving a message while I was doing the same on Haney's cell. Either it was off or he was using it. Next I called Central and asked for Haney or Alvarez. The female desk sergeant promised to leave a message for them. "Please, this is urgent, a real matter of life and death," I said. "There's been a shooting somewhere in the city, a bodyguard protecting two people very important to me. Do you know anything about it?"

"I'm sorry, Sir, I can't comment on any police matters except to tell you that both Lieutenant Haney and Detective Alvarez are out on another matter."

"Please, however you have to do it, tell them to call Gideon Grant."

"I'll try, Sir."

"Any luck, Julie?"

"No. All I could do was leave a message."

"Will you call the FBI guy? Scott?"

"Will do."

I looked for the Eppersons in the directory, but they were unlisted. Julia was talking on her phone so I waited.

"Okay, thanks," she said, then to me. "I got Scott. He says there was an armored car holdup downtown, and the police have all scrambled to set up a net. That's why no one is answering. He promised to check on the shooting, and call back."

"Damn! What can I do? I'll ask the guys in the lobby to push their buttons."

A few minutes later security called back. They'd had no luck raising anyone either. So much for my handlers.

"What shall I do, Julie?" I was getting frantic.

"All we can do is hang in here until we get a call from somebody. We wouldn't know where to go and we don't really know what happened."

"I'm scared to death that something has happened to Abigail and Grace. What if they called off Abigail's surveillance for this God-damn robbery?"

"We can't get ahead of ourselves until we hear something."

"I'm getting another drink. Want one?"

"No. And don't overdo it."

I paced, drank, and looked at my watch every few seconds. Jemima fell in behind me again, suspecting something was going on. Julia sat with her phone in her hand and watched me.

Finally, finally, my phone rang. It was Gully. "I'm here at the hospital. Sam's in the operating room. They came and told me they thought he'd make it, but they're not done yet. He caught one through the lung and lost a lot of blood. Nobody seems to know anything."

"Thanks. And I'm glad he should make it. Didn't any police come in?"

"No, and I don't know why. They were supposed to be there, too. We don't normally wear body armor for assignments like this, but that's my mistake. Won't happen again."

"Don't beat yourself up. And from what we've heard from FBI, there was an armored car holdup downtown somewhere, and apparently it sucked in all the police."

As I was relaying our conversation to Julia, her phone rang.

"Hi, Greg. I called to find out about a shooting...It was a bodyguard looking after the little girl I told you about...You have?...Good...Can you check?...about an hour ago...Okay."

She clicked off. "He'll check it out and call right back. They think they have the holdup gang bottled up now."

She just finished telling me when her phone rang again. She answered, then listened and nodded. She looked at me and there was pain in her expression. My heart sank.

"Gid, I'm sorry. Witnesses say it was a kidnapping of a woman and a girl. They have a couple of squads at the scene."

"Did he say where, or how?"

"Said it was over on Market, didn't know where."

She came and put her arms around me. "We'll find them and get them back, Gid. Hang in there."

"We have to, Julie. We just have to. I couldn't bear it..."

She took my arm. "Let's go. I'll drive. I'm betting on Westfield Centre."


Julie was right. It wasn't hard to find where it happened as we drove down Market. There was a squad car with flashing blue and red lights parked crosswise in the combination bike lane and bus stop. Another squad was guarding the other end of the scene. Traffic cones and crime scene tape were up, out as far as the trolley tracks and all the way across the broad brick sidewalk to the building. I asked her to drop me off while she searched for a place to park. She then squeezed into the traffic going around the site, all slowed by gawkers wondering what had happened.

They had blocked the exit from Bloomingdale's, but crowds had gathered outside the tape on both sides. I squeezed through the crowd and worked my way to one of the uniformed cops guarding the tape. He was a beefy young Hispanic and gave me a somber stare and an order, "Stand back, Sir."

"Officer, may I please approach? I'm connected to the victims."

"What's the connection?"

"The bodyguard was in my employ and the woman is my…my fiancé." Lying works both ways.

"I'll get the sergeant. Step inside the tape, but wait right there." He pointed his baton at a spot by the curb.

He returned with the sergeant, who had been supervising some techs over by a tall three-sided sign, the kind where they place gallery showings and playbills. They may have been taking samples of Sam's blood. The sergeant was wearing a grim expression. She was about an inch taller than I, an African American. She strode within inches of me and spoke softly, "Okay, talk to me."

I also kept my voice away from the crowd along the tape. "My name is Gideon Grant. I've been working on a case with Lieutenant Haney at Central. You know him?"

She nodded.

"To make this quick, I rescued the little girl on a yacht out in the Pacific. She's under the supervision of CPS, and one of their supervisors was with her. I hired a private firm to guard the little girl. We just heard he'd been shot and I'm desperate to know what happened to the woman and girl."

"All I can tell you, Sir, is bystanders say they were taken away in a dark van. We're still trying to find out more. Give me their names and descriptions."

I complied and she wrote in her pocket notebook. "Let me step away and get this on the network."

Julia arrived, breathless. "Any news?"

"Not much. The sergeant over there is calling in names and descriptions I gave her. Otherwise they're talking to witnesses and sweeping the scene."

"What happened?"

"The worst. She says witnesses say a woman and a girl were forced into a van."

"Oh, God."

Sergeant Taylor returned. "Who's this?"

"My friend, Julia Mangini, who's also my lawyer."

Taylor nodded, "Counselor. Do you know anything about this?"

"Nothing more than he does. I've just talked to Special Agent Scott, who is familiar with the case, and Detective Peak at Central, to see if we can find out anything."

"I can assure both of you we'll do all we can. Now please step outside the tape. I've got to get back to it."

"Thank you, Sergeant Taylor."

A feeling of desperation gripped me. "What can we do, Julie?"

# CHAPTER 32

Standing there on the street, surrounded by the buzz of the crowd that had gathered, I felt helpless and alone. But there was Julia. She put her arms around me and spoke softly in my ear. "Don't give up, Gid. We'll find them. They're alive and will continue to be, or they'd have been shot also."

"Thanks, Julie. I'm glad you're with me. It's just so hard to avoid second-guesses. But you're right. It won't solve anything. Why don't we go to Gully and plot what to do next?"

We found Gully in the waiting room for Intensive Care, where I'd been only days before. He jumped up when he saw us coming down the hall.

"How is he, Gully?"

"They think he'll make it, Sir. He's out of the OR and hooked up to breathing and everything else, just like you were."

Julia gave him a hug also, causing him to turn red, perhaps because his face was crushed to her breasts. "I'm glad he's going to be okay," she said.

"Gully, they have Grace and Abigail. It happened in front of Westfield Center. We just got back from there."

"Oh, God, Boss. I'm truly sorry. I'm supposed to protect them." He hung his head.

"It was a matter of circumstance. There was an armored car robbery, and they pulled off your police backup. Sam was alone."

We were standing in a corner and speaking softly, but there were others looking at us with curiosity. "Let's go somewhere to talk."

"I'll make a quick check with the desk," Gully said, "then we can go to the coffee shop."

We found a table away from others, carrying our coffee in paper cups. "I have no experience with this kind of thing, thank goodness. Can either of you tell me what might happen next?"

Julia looked across at Gully, "I have a little experience with kidnapping, but not this kind. Do you, Gully?"

He rubbed his stubbled chin in a characteristic response. "Yes. There are several motives. To name a few: estranged parents kidnap their children from each other; crooks kidnap people from moneyed families for money; terrorist kidnap for money, prisoner exchange, or to strike terror. And there is kidnapping of witnesses to silence them or for bargaining power."

"Okay. Now don't try to protect my feelings, both of you. What do we have here?"

Julia spoke first. "The FBI and police will try to keep all the options open, which they should do, but I believe this just has to be connected to Abigail and her parents. You have money and Grace's parents are loaded. However, I don't believe in the coincidence of your hit and run and Richie's murder, followed by this. I mean, *get real*."

"Miss Julie is right," Gully said. "And if she is right, what can we expect next? With your permission, I can speculate a bit." He drained the last of his coffee.

"Please go for it."

"If it's connected to Abigail and her parents, you'll get a phone call or some other contact. If it's a random thing about money, Miss Grace's parents will hear first. That's my prediction. And I think it will be you."

"So we just *wait*? How will they know how to get in touch with me?"

"Well, they have the captives and they have Miss Grace's phone with you on it, I suspect. There's not a lot you can do except hope the FBI and police can track them down."

"I'll get us another round of coffee, then I have more questions."

After a bathroom break and with coffee replenished, we began again. "I haven't watched a lot of television, so I don't know much about how these things go down."

Julia spoke first. "Any involvement I've had has been related to high-profile custody disputes, so I doubt it applies. I do know the FBI will be on it."

"Right," Gully said. "Again, I won't mince words. Kidnapping is a dangerous and touchy situation. If there's to be some kind of exchange, it's really hard to do. The perps don't want to get caught, and the police have to be really careful it doesn't blow up in their faces. That's why the perps will always make threats about 'no police involvement, or else' if they call you."

"So what do I do?"

"It has to be your call. Why don't we wait and see what develops with the FBI and police? They'll want to patch into your cell, also Miss Grace's parents' phone. Maybe even the Eppersons."

"We just wait?"

"That's right. You can't do anything tonight. Try to get some rest; you'll need it. As we speak, police are tracking down all the witnesses they can, getting in contact with the O'Quinns, putting an APB out on the van, and so forth. I'm going to hang in here for a while and see if Sam wakes up. I suspect the police will be by."

On our way back to our condos, my cellphone rang. It was Special Agent Scott. "Where are you now?"

"Julia Mangini and I are in her car, heading home from the hospital. Just checked in on our bodyguard."

"Right. Can you divert down to my office?"

"Julie, can we go to see the FBI?" She nodded. "Yes. We'll be there in about fifteen minutes."

We were met at the entrance by a female agent and escorted to Scott's office. He came to meet us and shook hands. "Let me say how sorry I am this happened. We'll do all we can to get them back."

"I appreciate that, but I'm interested to hear how that's done."

He led us to a conference table and sat across from us. "Now, tell me where you were when this came about and how you found out about it."

"We were in my condo, along with Gulliver Tolliver, my investigator. Ms. O'Quinn was expected to join us. She'd called earlier and said she was taking Abigail Dickerson shopping."

"I see."

"Ms. O'Quinn was late for our meeting, then Tolliver got a call from the hospital on Sam Owen's phone, telling us he'd been shot. Anyway, he went there and we started making calls, including to you; went to the scene and talked to the police there."

"I assume you found out some details of what happened?"

"Basically. I also gave the sergeant a description and names and she put out the word."

He fixed us with his eagle stare. "So you claim no knowledge that this might take place?"

I burst from my chair, "*What the hell do you mean, 'claim no knowledge'?* Of course not!"

"Calm down. It's the kind of question we will be asking everyone connected with the persons abducted."

"It's an incredibly stupid question. Julie, shall we go?"

Scott looked a bit uncomfortable. "Perhaps I could have phrased it more delicately."

"You don't have to be delicate. But for Christ's sake, use a little common sense."

"Okay, objection noted. Now, do you have contact information for Ms. O'Quinn's parents?"

"Of course not. I do know that her father is Geoffrey O'Quinn, the Hollywood producer, and they live in Beverly Hills. Maybe the vast resources of the FBI can find him."

He just looked at me without reacting, and went to his desk phone. He pushed a button and told someone to get the LA duty officer on the line. Before he got back to our table his phone rang and he answered. "This is Special Agent Scott in San Francisco. We have a situation here..."

As he droned into the phone, I asked Julia, "Are we wasting our time here?"

"Yeah, probably. He doesn't know any more than we do, probably less, and he's just going to grind along for a while."

We both stood as Scott approached. "Why are you standing? We're not finished here."

"I think we are, unless you can come up with something productive."

"Sit down, sit down. I have a team going to notify the parents. They may want to come up here. And I want to give you some idea what to expect."

We looked at each other and resumed out seats.

"Either you or the parents will probably be contacted—"

"We know that."

"We'll want to patch in to your telephone."

"I'll think about it."

"What's to think about? It would be a big mistake to think you can handle this on your own."

"Go on. What else do you have?"

"They may want money, or it may be something else. We'll try to track them down in the meantime. We'll make plans to set up surveillance and get ready to put a net around them if they want to arrange a drop."

"That's what scares the hell out of me. We were supposed to have a team watching Abigail, and that really worked great. Right?"

Scott just stared.

"I know you have to do your job your way. Someone needs to call Clifford and Wilma Epperson, Abigail's foster parents. I don't have a number for them. Child Protective Services should know how to reach them. Meanwhile, we're going home."

"I won't stop you, but I'm sure we'll want to talk again tomorrow."

"You know where to reach me."

With that, we shook hands and left.

It was a restless night full of tossing and turning and second-guessing. I dreaded the day to come when I'd have to call Gran, and I might have to face Grace's parents. If the robbery hadn't taken place, the cops might have been there. If I'd been stronger in discouraging Grace from making the shopping trip…If Sam had worn a vest…If, if, if. But looming largest of all, the fear that harm could come to Grace and Abigail in spite of everything I could do.

I finally gave up at five o'clock and brewed coffee. It was useless to call anyone at such an hour. If I did get a call from the kidnappers, I would do anything they asked. Further, it would seem to me that my safest approach would be to keep the police and FBI out of it. Maybe Gully could be my backup in some way. Maybe they'd hit up Grace's parents, but I doubted it. I didn't believe it was about money. They might want me, a trade I was prepared to make. They tried for me once and came close to success.

Jemima had her breakfast and kept me company. No food for me, just coffee. The hours ground slowly until seven-thirty when my phone finally rang. It was Gully.

"He's awake, and seems to be getting better. Still groggy."

"Good. Selfishly, does he remember anything?"

"Not much. It was a dark mini-van, probably Dodge, with obscure windows. There were two guys wearing ski masks. Sam was afraid to fire directly at them. It was too fast and they were too close to the girls. He did shoot at the tires and at the windshield. Got off two shots before they hit him."

"I guess the police and FBI have all of that?"

"Yes, Sir. An agent came by this morning. Big guy named Liggett."

"I'm just idling here. About time to call Gran. Julie and I talked to Scott at the FBI last night. He expects Grace's parent may come up today. When you feel free to get away, maybe we can talk over a few things. Meanwhile, I'll run downstairs for a paper."

"Sure thing, Boss. I'll head on over now."

*The Clarion* was a disappointment in that the big, bold headlines shouted "**ARMORED CAR HEIST**," with smaller sub-heads, "DARING HOLDUP IN MARKET DISTRICT" and "POLICE SCRAMBLE ALL UNITS." I quickly scanned below the fold. A smaller headline said:

## WOMAN AND GIRL KIDNAPPED

At about the same time police were occupied with the armored car robbery, a woman and young girl were seized from the sidewalk in front of Westfield Centre on Market Street. Witnesses say a dark van pulled to a stop at the curb in front of Bloomingdale's and two men wearing ski masks dragged the two into the van. Shots were fired at the van by a man later identified as a private security guard. The abductors fired back at him, and word is that he is listed in serious condition at San Francisco General.

As of press time, a police spokesperson refused to reveal the identity of those captured pending notification of next of kin. They also refused to speculate on a motive for the bold public abduction during a normally busy time of day, and declined to link the abduction to the armored car robbery taking place downtown.

Police have put out an All Points Bulletin on a description of the van and of the woman and girl kidnapped. They also ask any citizen who might have any knowledge of the incident or the victims to contact the police hotline...

Nothing new here. Reporters were probably caught up in the larger news story and got after the kidnapping later in the night. With shaking hands, I dialed Gran's number in Modesto and heard her cheerful voice.

"Hi Gid, Sweetheart, how is everything?"

"Sorry, Gran. Really bad news. Last evening, Grace and Abigail were kidnapped—"

"*Oh no! Oh, no!* Reggie, pick up the extension!"

After they were both on, I briefed them on the whole situation as I knew it, and apologized for bringing them such bad news. They tried to comfort me and promised to be on the way back to San Francisco within the hour.

As I hung up, my doorbell rang. I'd told security to send Gully up when he arrived. I invited him in and we sat at the kitchen table with coffee.

"The paper didn't have anything worthwhile yet. Talked to Gran and they're on their way over. Haven't heard anything out of the police or FBI. You got anything new?"

"No, Sir. I've thought a lot about what may happen next. It would help if we had any idea what they're after."

"I've been thinking, too. It has to be connected to the whole mess we've been in. Just couldn't be coincidence. Therefore, my conclusion is they want *me*. Not money, not anything, but *me*. Maybe Abigail, if they think she's old enough to shed any light on what happened on the boat. Grace is a way to bargain for me to give myself up—which I'll do, by the way."

"Don't give in too easy, Boss. I'd rather we rescue them and also get the sonofabitch."

"The question is, how?"

"Well, let's game the thing a little bit. Can I talk through it?"

"Go ahead. I'll just listen."

"Here we go: They'll call you and make their demands. When the time comes for exchange, maybe money being the excuse, they'll call again and have you go somewhere right then, maybe two or three changes to try to shake you loose from police. Unless I miss my guess, and I agree it's probably you they want, they'll get you in a vehicle and take you somewhere. It may or may not be where they have the girls, and they'll lie to you if they feel like it, about letting them go."

"I don't like the sound of that last part. Seems to me the assumption is they may have no plans to let anyone go. And the thought of the police and FBI tramping all over this scares me. I know they're the pros, but they have less to lose than I do."

"That's what we're up against."

"Scott already said they want to patch into my phones."

"I don't see how you can very well refuse, Boss. But think about this: maybe the crooks will be smart enough to shake them off you."

"Then we have to have a way for you to follow me, Gully. I trust you to do it right."

"Thank you, Sir. I would do my very best. I have another guy to help me, and we owe them for Sam."

"So I've been thinking. How about a tracking device on me? And I know just where to put it."

"Your cast?"

"Right. We can get Dr. Pagano to do it right. How long do the batteries last?"

"Plenty of time. This will go down in a matter of days."

"Then let's do it."

The telephone rang. It was Special Agent Scott of the FBI

# CHAPTER 33

Scott asked me to come in to his office at ten o'clock to meet with the family of Grace O'Quinn. It was not something to be welcomed under the circumstances. I called Julia and she agreed to pick me up. We were ushered into a large conference room on the same floor as Scott's office. Everyone in attendance was standing around the table, waiting for us to enter.

Scott took charge. "Please, everyone, take seats and I'll introduce you. You will have a chance to speak with each other if you wish, after our briefing. Get coffee or drinks, if you like."

We complied, although no one took refreshments. We were all looking at each other as we took seats. The Eppersons were there and nodded gravely at me in recognition. It was easy for me to identify Grace's parents, but there was a young man and a young woman I did not know.

Scott began, indicating each person with a wave of his hand. "This is Ms. O'Quinn's father, Mr. Geoffrey O'Quinn; her mother, Mrs. O'Quinn; her fiancé, Doctor Kurt Luttrell; and Mr. O'Quinn's assistant, Stephanie Kelly..."

All nodded, looking grim, as they were introduced. But fiancé? Did he forget he'd been discarded? Kurt Luttrell was handsome in the Gentlemen's Quarterly sense: tall, with close-cut moussed black hair, navy blazer with pink dress shirt, open at the collar to display a gold chain; smug demeanor. Geoffrey O'Quinn looked the part of the successful man he was, gray-streaked blond hair combed back, thinning on top, rimless glasses, commanding presence. Mrs. O'Quinn appeared to be in her middle-fifties, red-blond hair, still beautiful, but with worry lines around her eyes.

"...On the other side of the table, we have Mr. and Mrs. Epperson, who are foster parenting Abigail Dickerson while we seek an answer to the disappearance of her parents. More about that in a moment. Next is Ms. Julia Mangini, Mr. Grant's attorney, and Mr. Gideon Grant, who rescued Abigail from a sinking yacht out in the Pacific. On my right is Special Agent Liggett.

"Now, I'm sure you have many questions. We spoke briefly earlier to Mr. and Mrs. O'Quinn, but let me say to all of you that we and the police are doing everything in our power to locate the suspects and secure the release of your loved ones. We cannot automatically assume anything, but believe it is most likely related to the disappearance of Abigail's parents..."

Scott droned on for the next half-hour, laying out the sequence of events since I found Abigail in the yacht. He appropriately left out the murder of Bart Richie, my "accident," and any speculation about motives in the disappearance of Abigail's parents. Finally, he asked for questions.

Geoffrey O'Quinn looked directly at me, "What is Mr. Grant's role in this? In other words, specifically why is he here?"

Scott looked uncomfortable.

"May I answer?" I said. Scott nodded. "After I found Abigail alone on a sinking boat, we spent several days together making our way back to California. I became quite attached to her, and she to me, since she had no one to look after her. I've since done everything I can to help locate her parents or find out what happened to them. In fact, I hired private security to supplement police protection because of my concerns that whoever was involved might consider she would know something."

"Do you think she does?" O'Quinn asked.

"I do not," I said. "She's a bright and beautiful little girl, but she's only four, and she was hiding on the yacht at the time. The police, with the help of your daughter's organization, have questioned her thoroughly. But I worry that whoever it is may not believe that."

O'Quinn stared at me again, "Are you responsible for my daughter's kidnapping?"

Mrs. O'Quinn grasped his forearm, "Geoffrey, please—"

"Sorry, Mina, I'd like to hear his answer."

"Mr. and Mrs. O'Quinn, I am desperately sorry this happened and I will do whatever it takes to get them both back. I'll trade places with her if I can arrange it, or pay any amount. We'll have to wait to hear from them."

Luttrell spoke for the first time, glaring at me, "We'd better get her back safely, or you'll be sorry you ever met me!"

Scott spoke up, "Threats are uncalled-for and counterproductive. I'll outline how these situations generally progress…"

He droned on again about phone taps, setting up nets to capture perpetrators during any exchange, and so forth, until the meeting lost its momentum. As we broke up to leave, the Eppersons came around the table and hugged me in turn, knowing how I felt about Abigail and suspecting what my feelings were for Grace.

Next I found myself facing the O'Quinns. Mina spoke first. "Will you take some time to talk with me about Grace? She spoke about you to me, you know."

"Of course. Whenever you wish."

Geoffrey glanced at his thin gold watch. "How about having lunch with us?"

He saw me hesitate and look in the direction of Kurt Luttrell.

"We'll make it just the three of us if you like."

"That would be good."

"Fine. Let's make it a half-hour from now at the Fairmont, Laurel Court."

Laurel Court was getting to be a habit.

Before we left FBI Headquarters, Scott extracted from me, the Eppersons, and the O'Quinns permission to monitor our phones. Julie dropped me off and I went up to the Laurel Court. As I got off the elevator, I saw Kurt in intense conversation with the O'Quinns outside the restaurant. Geoffrey was shaking his head and Kurt was looking flustered. The assistant, Stephanie, was standing by, plucking at Kurt's sleeve. He shook her off and turned away in my direction. He glared at me and whisked by, Stephanie at his heels.

The O'Quinns and I simply nodded at each other and were led to a table in the corner, at the request of Geoffrey. After we were seated, Geoffrey said, "Wine okay?" I nodded and he placed his order.

"Now," he began. "You can understand that we're devastated by what has happened to our Grace. I apologize for my bluntness, but we'd like to hear more from you, away from the FBI."

"I understand. This is not how I wanted us to meet for the first time. I don't know how much Grace has told you about me."

Mina spoke, "Not very much, but a mother can suspect certain things. She did talk to me about your love for Abigail, and what you were doing to keep her safe and solve her parents' disappearance. Beyond that, as time went by, I sensed something else might be developing."

The waiter served our wine, after approval of our host.

"I hope this won't cause you even more concern, but I must be honest with you. I have come to love her very much. It wasn't something I could avoid. It happened very quickly. I intend to tell her as soon as we're together again."

Mina reached for my hand. "Say what you must, but you do know that she is engaged?"

"She didn't tell you?"

She gave a dismissive wave of her hand, "Oh, I know they had a tiff of some kind, but those things usually have a way of working out."

Our lunches were served, allowing time to change the subject. I reviewed in detail our plans to meet the evening before Grace's call to tell me about the shopping trip.

"It concerned me, but I immediately called my security personnel to alert them and also tried to alert the police, but without success. Later I found out about the armored car robbery. There should have been a police detail also watching Abigail."

"So…bad luck?" Geoffrey said.

"Who can say what might have happened, but now that it's come to this, we'll get them back. I believe Abigail and I are the actual targets."

"My view is that we do exactly what the FBI tells us," Geoffrey continued. "If they ask for money, or whatever, I'm prepared to comply."

"So am I."

"I think I remember a little about you," said Mina, "but what is your family situation?"

"I have no family, other than my grandmother, who raised me when my parents were killed in an accident. She lives in Modesto, but is engaged to marry again. When I brought Abigail back from my planned voyage, I bought a condominium to stay here until her parents' situation is settled. My grandmother is staying with me until then. I visited Abigail's paternal grandparents in Atlanta after finding they wanted nothing to do with her. I got them to sign away all claims to her, and I've applied to be her guardian and eventually adopt her if her parents are never found."

"That's remarkable," said Geoffrey. "You *are* serious."

"I am. Although I was married briefly years ago, I never had a child. Abigail is beautiful and bright. Wait 'til you see her."

"I hope it is soon," said Mina.

"We all do. And speaking of that, I'd better get back to my place and wait for a call…unless you have other questions. Let me give you contact information."

We exchanged telephone numbers, including cellphones for both of them. I thanked them for lunch, urging them to call me if they had any questions.

As I cabbed back across town, I called Gully.

"I'm headed back home. Shall we get going on that transponder?"

"Already got it, Boss."

"Why am I not surprised? I'll see when Dr. Pagano can see us."

"Good. Also, I want to bring my guy by to meet you."

"Anytime."

Dr. Pagano's scheduler agreed he could see me in his office at five o'clock, after some back and forth and questions about the nature of the visit, with pauses while she consulted with him.

Gran and Reggie were there as expected when I came in. Gran was all over me with concern in her eyes and a break in her voice. "Whatever shall we do? Will the FBI find them?" and "They are both so precious. We simply must get them back safely."

"We intend to, Gran. We just met with the FBI, and Gully and I will be making some contingency arrangements. He's coming over with a friend and we'll have to have some privacy."

"We'll clear out when you give us the word."

"I may be old," Reggie said, "but I've been around. Use me in any way I can help.

I called Gully and told him of the five o'clock appointment. He promised to be over within a half-hour. He rang from the front desk in twenty minutes and they sent him up.

"Gran, you don't have to leave the apartment. You have a sitting area and TV in the bedroom. We'll just be a little while."

"Okay, Gid. We'll do that."

The doorbell rang and Gran and Reggie disappeared.

Gully entered with a man of about fifty, and introduced him as Vincent Jacob. Jacob stepped forward with a firm handshake. "Pleased to meet you, Mr. Grant."

"Call me Gideon, or Gid. I'm glad you're here. I assume Gully has filled you in on the situation?"

"Yes, Sir, he has. Sorry for your troubles."

Jacob was about my height, but more muscular, with dark, crew-cut hair and closely trimmed beard sprinkled with gray. He never smiled and his dark eyes had a sorrowful depth.

"Let's sit and talk tactics a bit before Gully and I have to leave for my doctor appointment."

"Vince is ex-Special Forces," Gully said. "He now has his own security firm. He travels the world with various high-profile people to areas that are prone to kidnapping. He's been in on a few rescues."

"Sounds perfect."

We went over the same ground Gully and I had covered. The way we figured it would go, I would be constrained and taken to an unknown location. Gully and Vince could attempt to follow me, but would rely on the transponder if it became risky to get too close. We knew the FBI would also try to see where I was taken and we hoped they wouldn't interfere. We had to hope to God the kidnappers called me.

When Gully and I showed up at Dr. Pagano's office, there was some confusion about who my companion was. I told the receptionist I would explain to Dr. Pagano, so she showed us to an examining room.

Dr. Pagano tapped on the door and entered. He looked at us in surprise. "Are you having some kind of problem, Mr. Grant?"

"Yes, but not with the broken arm. Can we talk privately?"

Dr. Pagano continued to look puzzled. "Well, yes, I suppose so. Marie, we won't be needing you for now," he said to his nurse. "Let's go into my office."

When we were seated, I began. "This is Gulliver Tolliver, a private detective in my employ. You may have heard of the kidnapping of a woman and girl last evening."

"Yes, I did," Dr. Pagano said.

"Well, the woman is very dear to me and the little girl is also. I rescued her from a sinking yacht in the Pacific and hope to adopt her if her parents are not found. And the truth about my "accident" is that it was no accident."

"I remember reading about the little girl and the yacht," Dr. Pagano said. "I had no idea it was you."

"Now for why we're here: I really expect they want me, because I've been digging into the disappearance of the little girl's parents. If it's me they want, they'll ask for money or something, but take me. I'm willing to trade myself for the woman, Grace O'Quinn, but we want the girl also, of course. And I wouldn't mind if we get me back, too."

Dr. Pagano nodded. "You're putting yourself in jeopardy? Where do I come in?"

"We want you to implant a GPS locater in my cast. We'd try it ourselves but it's better if you do it. I suppose doctor-patient privilege will cover such an operation?"

He smiled, "Of course. What about the police?"

"They tend to overdo everything. We're trying our best for low-key."

"Well, I'll do my part, and the rest is up to you. I'll go send the office help home."

We moved to an examining room where he had the tools of the trade. "Let's see the device."

Gully produced it and handed it to him. It was small, maybe a little over a quarter-inch thick and two inches square.

"That should be no problem. I've seen TV cop shows where they stick these things on cars." He turned it over in his hand. "I assume it's reasonably waterproof?"

"Yes, Sir." Gully said. "It has a membrane switch."

Dr. Pagano examined my cast. "I first thought about removing the cast and starting over, but I think we can cut out a square with the Stryker saw and just put another layer of saturated fabric winding around the whole thing. After it sets, you can rub some dirt on it to age it a little."

He proceeded to perform the operation, after Gully got out a laptop computer and tested the device. Dr. Pagano set it in a nest of cotton on the inside of my forearm near the elbow. After it was all done, and the plaster had set, the change was invisible and the signal was strong. All we needed now was a phone call.

# CHAPTER 34

The call came at 8:52 p.m.

When Gully drove me back to the condo, two FBI agents and Detective Greg Peak were seated at my kitchen table drinking coffee. They had laptop computers open, presumably to monitor my phones and those of the O'Quinns who were staying at the Fairmont. Julia was there also, to help monitor the phones and be with Detective Peak at the same time. We all sat and waited for two and a half hours, tense and bored at the same time. I laid my phone on the table, staring at it, wondering if it would ring. Gran hovered over us, urging refreshments.

The call was on my cell. Everyone was instantly alert, like birddogs on point.

I answered. An electronically modified voice spoke:

*LISTEN CAREFULLY: GATHER ONE MILLION IN USED BILLS, HUNDREDS. NO BUGS OR MARKERS OR SOMEONE DIES. NO POLICE. WAIT FOR INSTRUCTIONS. YOU HAVE TWENTY HOURS.*

"Hold on. No deal unless I speak to the woman you have in custody. You could be anybody."

*YOUR CHOICE. YOU WILL HEAR FROM ME TOMORROW.*

There was a click and a dial tone. "He hung up on me. Now what?"

Special Agent Liggett spoke, "It's up to you, but we'll probably have to just wait for the next contact."

"I think you're right. Couldn't be a crank call because he had my cell number."

"Right," Julia said. "It was probably the real deal."

"Well, I think everyone can clear out and wait for tomorrow. Detective Peak, I assume the protection detail is on duty?"

"Yes Sir."

"That's it, then. Tomorrow morning, I'll go to my bank and start gathering the money. It's a small price to pay if we get them back."

"I wouldn't be too hasty, Mr. Grant," Liggett said. "We want to get these dudes."

"You can do what you do," I replied. "As for me, my total focus is on Abigail and Ms. O'Quinn."

When they all left, I dialed the number Grace's father had given me. He answered firmly by stating his last name.

"Mr. O'Quinn? Gideon Grant here. The call just came in. The voice was modified electronically and they asked for a million dollars—just about like we expected."

"What can I do to help? When do they want it? I can get money together tomorrow."

"Thanks. I'll do the money first thing in the morning. I had set aside significant liquid assets for my abortive sail to the South Pacific. They gave me twenty hours."

"Please. I'd like to help."

"I understand. If you'd like, why don't you come here in the morning? The FBI and police will be back. We can wait together to see what comes next."

"Thank you. Mina and I would like that."

I gave him the address and went to my recliner to think, to ponder the coming day. It could be my last day or my most triumphant. Whatever came, it was rife with unknowns; not only what the beast that did this would do, but also the unpredictability of various law enforcement agencies.

Jemima seemed to sense my turmoil, so she came and jumped into my lap. She stared at me, as though trying to penetrate my brain. Then she reached out a paw with the claws slightly exposed and slapped at my right arm. Holding the stare, she switched paws and made a few more swipes at my arm.

"What is it, girl? Can't be hunger, you've been fed. You know something's wrong?" She gave up, hopped down off my lap, and walked away.

Gran brought me a cup of hot chocolate. "Remember when you were a little boy and I'd fix chocolate for you?"

"I surely do, Gran. I love you and all that you have done for me. It should be something I say more often."

She patted my cheek. "You say it enough, but you needn't say anything. I know because I've always felt your love. But let's not get maudlin. It's going to be okay."

"I hope so, but you should know that if anything happens to me, all I have is for you. The only request I now have is for you to see that Abigail is cared for if she makes it back."

"You have my promise, but I don't want to even consider such talk."

I rose and gave her a hug and a kiss on her cheek. "I'll not bring it up again. Goodnight, Gran."

It was another night of tossing and turning, trying to visualize what might happen on the coming day. The glowing numbers on the clock turned slowly. I tried to close my eyes and resist looking at it.

*I was in darkness and rain on the surging deck of a sailboat. Lightning flashed and thunder exploded. Grace and Abigail were both lost overboard and I couldn't find them. I was desperate and I shouted into the darkness...*

There was a knock on my bedroom door, and Gran opened it, clad in her robe. "Gid, are you all right?"

"Oh, yes, Gran. I guess so. I was just having a nightmare. Please go back to bed, and thanks."

The infernal clock said five o'clock. I waited for her bedroom door to close, then got up and went into the kitchen and flipped the switch on the coffeemaker that Reggie always loaded the night before.

Risking the sound of running water, I shaved and showered, then dressed in comfortable khakis and running shoes for my day of trial. I buttoned a cotton shirt over my good arm and around my cast, now rubbed with just enough dirt to make it look its age. By the time I got to the kitchen, Reggie was there getting out breakfast fixings.

"You don't have to do that every morning, Reggie."

"It's my pleasure, Gideon. It's the least I can do to support our household."

"Well, I want you to know I appreciate it."

He nodded and went about his work. Soon we were breakfasting on fruit-filled crepes, with bacon on the side. How does he do it? He repeated his offer to do all he could to help and I assured him it would be a comfort to me if he held down the fort here and took care of my grandmother. He got on the phone to a market and ordered quantities of pastries, fruit, and soft drinks.

I resumed my post in my recliner and watched the slow roll of time. At precisely seven-thirty, I dialed the home number of the bank manager who watched over my checking and money-market accounts. We'd become friends over the years and had seen each other on occasion outside the bank.

His wife answered and I asked for Paul. He had not left for work.

"Paul, I wouldn't bother you at home, but I have a big problem."

"Gideon, it's good to hear from you and don't worry about the call. What is it?"

"You may have heard about the kidnapping of the woman and girl downtown Monday night?"

"Don't' tell me you're involved."

"Sorry, but yes. They were both very close to me and I'm the target. In fact, I've received a ransom call."

*"You have?"*

"Yes. As soon as you get to the office, I need you to start rounding up a million dollars in used bills. Hundreds."

"I can do that. When do you need it?"

"Before noon if you can."

"Are you sure? Do the police know? And are we putting in dye packs or anything?"

"Yes, they know, but absolutely not on the dye or anything. I'm doing as they say."

"Okay. I'll leave right now and call as soon as I can."

The intercom from downstairs spoke and our visitors began to arrive, first the FBI, then the police. This time Lieutenant Haney replaced Peak with himself and brought Alvarez. She didn't look at me directly, realizing this wasn't the time for her nonsense. Haney strode forward and held out his hand, "Sorry for the trouble," he said.

"Thanks. We're just waiting for the next step. I've started gathering the money."

"We'll be on top of it."

"I just hope everyone is damned careful. You guys may concentrate on catching the creeps, but above all, please, please stress safety of the victims."

"Of course."


The police and FBI took over the kitchen table, opening laptops and attacking coffee and pastries. The O'Quinns arrived just before nine. I met them at the door and ushered them in to the living area, where Gran awaited.

"Mr. and Mrs. O'Quinn, please meet Maureen O'Brien, who raised me from a child. Gran, meet Grace's parents."

Handshakes and greetings were exchanged, with hugs between Gran and Mina.

"Please call me Mina, Mrs. O'Brien. It's actually 'Wilhelmina,' but I try to keep that a secret." She smiled, the same beautiful smile of her daughter.

"And call me Maureen."

We all sat, the men in one corner, the women in another. Reggie came in to offer drinks and was introduced also. Mina graciously congratulated him on their engagement. Reggie went for a tray of coffee service.

O'Quinn asked me about plans for the day and I invited him to come along when my bank called. Otherwise, I filled him in on the events of the past few weeks. I became conscious of another conversation from across the room, as Geoffrey and I continued our own.

I heard Gran say, "I've seen you in the movies. Weren't you in *Errant Knight?*"

"I'm afraid so. I'm surprised you'd remember."

Gran again, "Oh, yes. You were a beautiful young damsel. And you are beautiful still."

"You're very kind."

Then Gran predictably said, "And that daughter of yours! My, my. The first time I saw her, I had those predatory impulses that any grandmother would have if they had a grandson like Gideon."

This was getting embarrassing, so I tried to tune it out. With some difficulty, I focused on my own narrative. O'Quinn listened with interest.

"Grace didn't tell us all the details of this case. It's quite distressing. Someone out there is troubled and dangerous."

"I'm afraid so." I refrained from telling him about the murder of Bart Richie. No need to add to his distress.


Time passed, coffee and pastries were consumed. Haney made his exit, leaving Conchita Alvarez in place to observe. Julia came by from her condo and soon left after seeing Alvarez instead of Peak. Gully arrived and was introduced to the O'Quinns. Gran and Mina became fast friends, sharing concern about the coming events. Finally, at almost eleven, my cell phone rang. Everyone tensed, and all eyes were on me as I answered. It was Paul Holland.

"I have the money ready, Gideon. I assume you want to pick it up here?"

"Yes. We'll be right down."

"You have security?"

"Yes. See you in a few minutes."


Gully drove us in my new replacement Toyota to the branch on Powell Street. He had a bulge under his sport coat that could only be the .45

Colt Commander he preferred. I adjusted the holster around my cast for my .380. O'Quinn was unarmed.

We all three entered the bank and went straight to Paul's office. He rose and was introduced to my companions.

"Let's go back to the vault. I see you brought a bag."

I signed a withdrawal slip with a surprising number of zeros, and Paul stacked the bundles of money on a table to confirm the count. It was a quick transaction to walk out with a sports duffle full of a surprising weight of cash, more than I'd seen in one pile. This part was simple; the real trials were yet to come.

# CHAPTER 35

When we returned to the parking garage, O'Quinn paused beside the Toyota and turned to me. Gully walked away to a discreet distance.

"Gideon, Mina and I will be returning to our hotel to wait. You have enough on your mind without entertaining guests."

"It's okay. Reggie will be setting out a lunch of deli stuff. You're welcome to stay."

"No, it's best we go. Listen, I want to apologize for my attitude at the FBI meeting."

"Not necessary. I understand. Your daughter is in danger."

"No, I was out of line. Grace has done what she always does: try to help others. She was just doing her job to help the little girl."

"Well, it's true I guess, but it was I who started the whole mess."

"No, it was the person who abandoned the little girl. What you did was rescue her. Now let's not try to redo the past. You have a trial facing you and I wish for you God's protection." He surprised me by embracing me.

"Thank you, Mr. O'Quinn." "Please call me Geoff. All I ask is a phone call when the next step is taken."

Reggie was indeed continuing his host duties, laying out a spread of sandwich materials, fruit, and a vegetable tray, along with coffee and cold drinks. Detective Peak had returned to replace Alvarez and surprise; Julia had returned.

Gully declined lunch and spoke softly to me away from the others. "Vince and I will gear up and wait. If you have a chance, give me a call when something breaks. If you don't I'll track you anyway. It's working fine this morning."

We shook hands. "I'll see you on the other side of this," I whispered.

Nothing in my past compared to the tension and tedium of the next few hours. Gran or Reggie would come by from time to time and speak a few words of encouragement to me. Julia did the same, but it seemed that everything had been said that could be said. There was one interruption of a ringing phone, which brought everyone out of their thoughts. It was SA Scott of the FBI reporting that they and the police were re-interviewing all of the witnesses, but no new leads had been discovered.

Grace, where are you? I hope you are not being mistreated. I couldn't take it if you are. Do you wish you had never met me? Where is Abigail? Is she with you? Both of you must know that I will do anything to get you back. On and on, these thoughts were repeated in my mind, endless spirals of futile inaction, waiting for that phone call. Finally, it came.

*DO YOU HAVE THE MONEY?*

"Yes."

*LISTEN CAREFULLY. WITHIN TEN MINUTES, BRING IT AND WALK OUT THE FRONT ENTRANCE OF YOUR BUILDING. WALK NORTH TO THE NEXT STREET, TURN LEFT AND FIND A PAY PHONE KIOSK HALFWAY DOWN THE BLOCK. WAIT FOR A CALL.*

An abrupt dial tone and at last action could take place. Everyone rose to their feet. My first call was to Gully, quickly repeating my instructions from the kidnapper. Gran had come out of the master bedroom at the sound of the phone.

"Here, Gran. Please call the O'Quinns at this number. I'm off to see the Wizard."

She embraced me, "God go with you Gideon. I love you."

"Love you too, Gran. Try not to worry. Gotta run."

I grabbed the bag and rushed out the door, down the elevator, and out the front entrance, determined to do everything by the book. Gully and Vince could be depended on to do what they could. The police would mean well, but the larger the organization, the more chances for a screw-up.

The streets were full at the peak of rush hour, with street noise at full volume. There was a damp chill in the air, with the threat of an early-season rain. I didn't know which side of the cross street to expect the phone kiosk, but caught the walk light and crossed to the north side and punched the button to stop the north-south flow of cars. Pedestrians were also hurrying about, lost in their own missions to end the work day.

We crossed in a herd, dividing on the other side to continue west or head north. The telephone kiosk was on my side, just where it was supposed to be. It was a creepy feeling, knowing someone was watching me. My cell phone was still in my pocket, so the FBI could be triangulating me even if they didn't have eyes on me.

Within minutes, the telephone rang. The same electronic voice spoke:

*GO TO THE NEXT CORNER AND TURN RIGHT. KEEP WALKING. A TAXI WILL PICK YOU UP.*

A click, and the connection was broken. I followed instructions; turning the corner and walking north sideways near the curb, looking back down the street. About halfway up the block an American Cab pulled over with a squeak of brakes. I opened the rear door and started to get in.

"Where to, buddy?" the driver said.

"You're supposed to know, aren't you?"

"*What?*"

"Weren't you sent to pick me up?"

"What are you, nuts?"

"Sorry," I slammed the door and he drove off, shaking his head.

Just as he left, a Yellow Cab pulled over and this time I got in, as the driver, a heavy-set Hispanic man, hid the right side of his face with his hand. Still looking forward, he thrust his hand back to the partition. "Gimme your cell," he demanded.

I complied, and he said, "Lie down in the seat and put that pillowcase over your head. Stay down until I tell ya."

As he pulled away into traffic, he rolled down his window and threw my phone out into the street. A wild ride was about to begin. I tried to trace where we were going, but it soon became impossible. He roared northward until he hit the Embarcadero, it seemed, but then many twists and turns followed and I was thrown back and forth in the seat. Traffic noises were all around us and he occasionally stopped, then started again with the noise of revving engines all about.

Finally we made a sharp turn and light darkened through the thin fabric over my face. A series of sharp turns followed, throwing me about. His tires squealed and we climbed an incline. No doubt a parking deck. Mysterious why, but it was soon solved. He braked to a stop, opened the door and told me to get out.

"Stay low and keep quiet."

I heard the clunk of a car trunk opening. He roughly patted me down, finding nothing on me, and pulled my right arm up and used a plastic tie to cuff it to my left where it exited the cast. He lifted the front of the pillowcase and slapped a wide strip of tape over my mouth, then led me to the rear of a car and half lifted me into the trunk. There was the sound of a zipper and an exclamation, "Holy shit!" It felt like a plastic bag was thrown in on my ankles; evidently he'd changed out the bag of money. The trunk lid was slammed shut and I was in darkness. An engine started, and another ride began back down the spiral ramp of the parking deck. Other cars joined us as we descended. After all, we were in rush hour and downtown workers were heading home.

Apparently we neared the exit, as there was a series of starts and stops. Eventually a muffled male voice said, "Drivers' license, miss." Miss? Who the hell was driving the car?

"Okay, move on."

Our car accelerated out into more rush-hour traffic, making a right turn according to the momentum. After that, it was impossible to track the direction or distance, but it seemed quite some time; perhaps a half-hour before we slowed and stopped. There was a muffled phone conversation from the front, a wait of perhaps a minute, then we moved again a short distance and stopped again. There was a clattering sound of some kind of machinery. Had to be an overhead door closing.

The trunk opened, with dim light penetrating the bag. Strong hands grabbed me by the belt and arm, dragging me over the rear opening. I was unable to get my feet under me and fell to the floor, which felt like concrete. No words were spoken but I was pulled to my feet and led away. The car engine started, and the overhead door clattered again. Apparently I was a delivery, first by the cab driver, if that's what he was, then the woman, if that's what *she* was.

He guided me to a set of metal steps, only three up to a metal grate landing. A door was opened and I was led through it, turned about, and pushed into an upholstered armchair. I felt zip ties being cinched around my ankles and the chair legs.

"Okay, I assume we're here. Now how about taking this pillowcase off? I've fulfilled my side of the bargain."

He finally spoke, his voice low in volume, "Won't happen like that."

"How will it happen? I assume Abigail and Ms. O'Quinn are here. It's time you let them go."

"Won't happen, at least not now. And don't try anything. I have a gun and will use it."

"So you have a gun. But when will they be released? You must have been smart enough to not let them see your face, or where they are."

"True, but it's not that simple."

"They'll find you, you know. You won't get away, not matter what happens to me." I hoped it was true. If my locater was working, Gully and Vince would be showing up soon.

He laughed softly. "How's it been working out so far? I have it all planned. But I won't be taken alive. I couldn't face Mother if I brought that shame on the family."

Couldn't face Mother? Wow! "What's the plan? I assume you plan to kill me. The others should go free."

"True, you're the one that screwed it all up. If you hadn't chanced upon the boat, you'd be free and so would I."

"How could you do such a thing, Bradley?"

"*What? How did you know?*"

The pillowcase was jerked from my head and I faced my captor.

"It took me awhile, but in the end, it was easy. It's a perfect example of someone trying to fake his own death, but screwing it up. And I've met '*Mother*'."

He was standing on the other side of the small dining table. As my eyes adjusted to the light, it became clear that we were in the living/kitchen area of a small mobile home. Darkness outside the windows confirmed that it was inside a building of some kind.

Bradley Dickerson was about six feet tall, generally slender with a small paunch and sloping shoulders. He was wearing Levi's and a black tee shirt. His arms were well-muscled. His wide, staring eyes were blue. His unkempt blond hair and beard gave him a wild appearance. His right hand was placed near a black pistol on the counter.

"Well now you've done it. You've sealed your fate."

"So what's changed? Look, you can still redeem some self-respect by releasing your captives."

"I might keep Abigail this time. Or give her away when we get where we're going if it doesn't work out."

"How could you ever have left her to die?"

"Cleaner break that way. And her drowning would have been painless. Had to get rid of that bitch of a mother, and the girl didn't care about me anyway."

"Why Solene? You can tell me, since I'm gone anyway."

"If you want to know, she used me. Used me to get out of Africa, used me to weasel her way into San Francisco society, screwed anyone she wanted. My parents disowned me, and they have wealth you can't imagine. My mother always loved me, and she took it away." He looked down and the corners of his mouth turned down. He wiped a tear from his eye.

"So she'd give it back if you'd do this? How nice."

He nodded.

I thought about the fake keening sounds with no tears when I was with the weird old witch. Too bad all this couldn't be recorded, in case I got out alive. There was a faint sound from somewhere outside. He grabbed the gun and went to the door. He opened it and stepped out on the landing. There was only silence. He came back in and took up his former stance by the kitchen counter.

"Why not divorce? Why this elaborate murder scheme?"

"She'd still be around to taunt me and people would be laughing at me. Needed to start over."

"I assume Dad financed all this?"

"Yeah, and there's a pile of money waiting for us in the islands."

"Us?"

"Never mind. I've said enough."

"Just a couple more. Where is Ms. O'Quinn, and did you kill Richie?"

"Oh, she's here, locked in a back room, and no, I didn't kill him, although the sonofabitch deserved it."

"I want to see her, and she'd better be okay."

"Won't happen, but nobody touched her. Might set her free somewhere. Haven't decided."

I kept pressing. "Who did kill Richie?"

"I'm through with this shit." He started to turn toward the hall to his left. At that moment, the door lock and handle exploded into the room.

# CHAPTER 36

The door was yanked open and two men in combat gear burst into the room, guns immediately trained on Dickerson. He grabbed his gun off the counter.

*"Don't do it!"* shouted Gully. *"Drop the gun! Drop the gun!"*

In one swift motion, Bradley Dickerson put the muzzle of the pistol under his chin and pulled the trigger. Blood and matter sprayed on the white cabinet behind him and the ceiling above and his body slumped to the floor. The sound was deafening in the small room. It was horrifying to watch the twitching and jerking of his death throes. Vince lowered his 12-guage riot gun and whipped his phone out, calling 911, before the body lay still.

Gully came to me with a large knife and cut the plastic ties. "Aw, geez, Boss. I'm sorry we didn't get to him in time to stop it."

"Don't worry, Gully. It might be for the best. And thank you for your faithfulness."

"You're welcome. Where are the girls?"

I leaped to my feet. "He said Grace was here."

I ran down the hall with him right behind me. We came to a closed door at the end. I tried the handle and it was locked.

"Grace! Grace! Are you in there?" I shouted.

There was a muffled sound in response.

"Stay away from the door if you can." I stood back and kicked it near the door lever and it flew open. There she was, the most beautiful sight I could imagine. She was seated in a straight chair with a gag over her mouth and her hands and feet zip-tied to the chair. I rushed across the small room with Gully right beside me and he cut her bonds while I removed the gag.

She burst into tears and tried her best to speak through her sobs. "Oh, Gideon! The gunshot! I-I thought I'd never see you again!"

As her bonds were released, she leaped into my arms and kissed me the way I dreamed it would be someday.

She turned to Gully and hugged him, too. "Gully, thank you from the bottom of my heart!"

He looked embarrassed and said, "Don't say a word about it. I'm just sorry they got you."

As Grace embraced me again, I asked, "Are you okay? Did they harm you?"

"No, no. Not really, but it was horrible not knowing what would come next. That man hardly spoke, and always wore a mask when I wasn't blindfolded. I feel grimy and I'm worried about Abigail."

"Do you know where she is?"

"No, but there's some woman involved, and I think she took her. How did you find me?"

"There's time for that later. Let's get you out of here. As we walk out, I want you to look left. He shot himself in there and you don't need to see it."

We heard sirens as we walked out. I picked up the plastic bag of money and managed to stay between Grace and the kitchen scene as we went out the front door. Vince had opened the overhead door to the semi-darkness outside, illuminated only by distant street lights, and came to join us. I set the bag down under the front landing.

Gully lent me his phone and I called Gran. "Gran, it's Gideon and I'm okay."

"Gracious, merciful God! How I prayed for you and He answered me! Oh, Gid, I was so worried!"

"Too bad it had to happen, Gran. Grace is safe also. Will you call her parents for me? We'll talk later. We don't have Abigail but I might know where she is, so gotta go."

Grace was still holding tight to me. "You think you know where she is?"

"Just a hunch. When the police get here, 'we'll see,' to quote a certain angel I know."

I huddled quickly with Gully and Vince. "Guys, I think it's best if we don't tell them about the GPS locater. They'll be pissed we didn't tell them ahead of time. The best narrative is that you were able to keep the cab in sight and Gully thought he recognized the woman that drove out. Wasn't sure, but followed her on a hunch."

"They'll still be pissed," Gully said. "And who's this woman I thought I recognized?"

"You don't know her, but she looked familiar. Just a lucky guess."

The screaming sirens drew louder and suddenly a police cruiser came in, his light bar painting the cavernous darkness with red and blue stroboscopic light. An ambulance entered immediately after. Two or three other cars braked to a stop outside. Vince went to find a power panel and in minutes, lights came on. A cacophony of slamming doors followed and a half-dozen uniforms and a couple of suits came in with guns drawn.

Gully, Grace, and I put our hands in the air and Vince joined us, doing the same.

"*It's all over!*" I shouted. Then I was pleased to see that one of the suits bringing up the rear was Lieutenant Haney and the other was Greg Peak.

Haney waved them off. "Put 'em away, guys." As he drew closer, he looked at me. "Well, here we are again. What's the story this time?"

"Bradley Dickerson is in there, dead. Shot himself."

"It was *him*? Okay, okay, okay. Greg, get a lab wagon on the way. You, Sergeant," he pointed at one of the uniformed cops, "Make sure the area is secure and put up tape."

He turned back and extended his hand to Grace. "I'm Marty Haney. You must be Ms. O'Quinn."

"I am, and grateful to be free. Now we need to find Abigail."

"She's not with you?"

I spoke up. "I may know where to find her. Can I make a couple of suggestions?"

"Does it matter what I say?" he said.

"No, not really. Why don't we send Grace to her parents at the Fairmont. She's been through a lot. You can take her statement tomorrow."

He glared at me, thinking. Then he sighed and asked Grace. "Are you all right, Miss? Is there anything that happened to you that might need evidence collection?" A sideways reference to a rape kit, apparently.

"No, Lieutenant. I'm just tired and grimy. I'll see you whenever you say and tell you what happened. Just please find Abigail."

He sent her home with one of the uniformed cops in a squad car and turned back to us. "You three wait right here with Detective Peak." He consulted with the EMTs, standing nearby. One went inside with one of the cops to verify what we'd told him about Dickerson.

Back to us, he said. "I need a preliminary statement from each of you. Detective Peak will take care of that. The lab wagon just got here. They'll swab your hands for GSR, just routine. Anybody fire a gun?"

"I did, Marty," said Vince. "I blasted the door with the shotgun."

"Okay, Vince."

Two men entered the building, wearing navy windbreakers with big white letters "FBI" emblazoned on them. "Wait here," Haney said, and intercepted them halfway to the entrance. They began to talk animatedly, arms waving, fingers pointing. When they looked in our direction, we could see it was Scott and Liggett. They didn't look happy. Apparently the police had not relayed Vince's 911 call.

They approached. "Special Agents Scott and Liggett are taking you to where you think the girl is," Haney said. "First, Scott and I are going inside for a look." As he said this, the lab people arrived in their van and proceeded to shuffle cars so they could drive inside.

When Scott and Haney returned, Haney took charge of the scene and I grabbed the plastic bag and left with the two FBI agents.

"What's that?" Scott said.

"It's the ransom money. They dumped it into a bag and threw away mine."

He stopped. "We need to hold that for evidence."

"If you do, I'll need a receipt from you for a million dollars. Wouldn't it be simpler just to let me take it back and put it in the bank?"

"I'll consult with Haney. Meanwhile, let's put it in the trunk."

Liggett drove, heading for the address I gave him. Scott and I were in the backseat and he turned to me, "What makes you think the girl is there?"

"From the beginning, she's seemed awfully curious about everything I've been doing, pumping me for information, even visited me in the hospital. She hinted involvement with all the major players." 'Pumping' was a poor choice of words, I realized after I said it.

"Is that all you have to go on?"

"That and the fact that my ride from the parking garage was in the trunk of a car driven by a woman, and Ms. O'Quinn said a woman took Abigail away. Grace was blindfolded so didn't get to see her. Oh, and the apartment we're approaching seemed a bit rich for her job so I think she got help with it."

"You've been there?"

"Interviewed her early on."

"By the way, we got the cab driver hiding out in the parking garage. We were trying to track you down and thought he might have gone in there. We lost track of you thanks to ineptitude of the police."

"What did the cab driver have to say?"

"It was all a blind transaction, according to him, and he was paid twenty-five hundred for an hour's work. He'll still face kidnapping charges."

We left the Central Waterfront area and took Caesar Chavez across to the Bayshore Parkway, joining the stream of traffic north, then across on the Central to Octavia and left on Fulton to Alamo Square. Night had fallen, with lights from the downtown area glowing through the light fog. With the overcast, darkness in the shadows was intense.

Liggett parked across the driveway of the apartment building. They told me to stay behind them throughout. Scott pressed the button for the first floor apartment and a woman's voice answered. Scott spoke quietly into the intercom. "Ma'm, this is the FBI. Don't be alarmed, but we have business with another tenant and need you to let us in the front entrance."

"I'll be right out," the voice answered.

We waited as Scott held his badge up in front of the peephole. In a few moments, the lock clicked, and a middle-aged woman in a robe opened the door cautiously, peering at us in wonder.

Scott thanked her and we climbed the stairs to the front door of the apartment. We could hear the faint sound of a television. Both agents drew their guns, waved me away, and Scott rapped on the door and called out, *"FBI, open up!"* The television sound ceased.

Scott hammered the door again with his fist and repeated his demand. Nothing happened.

Then he shouted, *"Okay, we're coming in."* He nodded at Liggett, younger and heavier. Liggett stepped back and slammed his right foot into the door at lock level. It flew open and they charged in with me trailing behind. The place was dark, so they turned on flashlights and held them along their pistols, just like the TV shows, sweeping left and right as we walked past the black glass crane and down the hallway.

Liggett was in the lead and stopped his sweep at a room on the right. *"Here they are. Put your hands where I can see them."*

There they were, seated on the floor in a corner behind the bed, blinking in the beam of the flashlights. Scott flipped on a light switch. There was DeeDee, hands in the air, and Abigail, sweet little Abigail, with her hands up. She saw me and jumped up, running past the agents, those hands now held up to me.

"Kitteee, Kitteee, you found me!"

I took her up in my arms. "We sure did, Sweetheart. Are you okay?"

"Yes, but I don't like her." She pointed at DeeDee, now being brought to her feet by Special Agent Scott. He turned her around and cuffed her behind her back, saying "You're under arrest for kidnapping. You have the right to remain silent...."

Abigail said, "Why did he say kid napping. Who was asleep?"

They agreed to drop Abigail and me at my place, with my promise to contact her foster parents and Grace O'Quinn. I borrowed a cell phone on the way and called Gran to give her the great news. She agreed to call Grace, who could then call the Eppersons, suggesting they were welcome to meet us at our place and we'd take it from there. It was getting late for little people, and Abigail had already gone to sleep on my lap in the front seat. DeeDee was unwisely protesting her innocence in the back seat with Special Agent Scott.

Scott hand-wrote an elaborate receipt for the bag of money without bothering to count it. Liggett witnessed, writing on the hood of the car. Abigail remained unconscious in my arms with her head draped over my shoulder. We made it up the elevator and to the condo without her stirring. When I knocked on my own door, having left my key before this long evening had begun; it was jerked open by Gran, with Reggie beaming behind her. I realized they had never met this precious burden sleeping in my arms.

Abigail was able to awaken and participate in a joyous reunion with her cat, and experience tears of delight from my grandmother when Gran embraced her for the first time. The Eppersons soon joined us and we celebrated with champagne. Wilma had graciously planned ahead and brought some of Abigail's things so that she could spend the night with us. We all agreed to sort it out the next day.

Geoffrey O'Quinn called and invited us all to a lunch celebration the next day at Boulevard Restaurant. He said that Grace was already sleeping peacefully and would talk with me tomorrow. He expressed his gratitude to me again with a catch in his voice. Before we said goodnight, we both made our plans contingent on delaying the police, who would want us first.

Gran helped her new little friend bathe and get ready for bed. The loveseat in her room converted into a single bed and Gran reprised her mothering role from my childhood.

# CHAPTER 37

Reggie and I were having coffee when Abigail and Jem, two buddies back together, padded into the kitchen. Abigail came straight to me and climbed on my lap; Jem rubbed against my leg.

"Good morning, sweet girl. Did you sleep well?"

"Oh, yes. I did. I rilly, rilly did."

"That's good. Now Sergeant Reggie will make you breakfast. He plans pancakes!"

"Goody, goody!" she clapped her hands.

"And I shall need help, Miss Abigail," said Reggie. "Come over here."

Abigail jumped down and ran around the kitchen island. Reggie helped her up on the kitchen step-stool and tied a too-long apron around her.

"Who are you?" said Abgail. "Are you a grandpa? Kitty called you Sergeant."

"Well, I have many names. How about calling me 'Sarge' for now?" He winked at me.

The two of them worked happily together, Reggie ruddy-faced and beaming, Abigail with a look of concentration as she measured ingredients, tongue sticking out the side of her mouth.

Special Agent Scott called before breakfast was completed. Gran had joined us and she and Abigail were chatting away like fast friends, Gran with a perpetual twinkle in her eye.

"Mr. Grant, we'd like to schedule an interview with you; and all the other principles, of course."

"What about the police?"

"We plan to do it jointly."

"Would it be possible to hold off until afternoon? Mr. O'Quinn wants us all to have lunch with him before they depart for LA. You have Marshall, the cabbie, and also Tolliver and Jacob."

"I think we can handle that. We'll want Ms. O'Quinn and the girl... Abigail isn't it?"

"Where and when?"

"FBI headquarters at two would be appropriate."

As soon as the connection was broken the phone rang again. This time it was Grace. "Gideon, I have to see you, and soon."

"My first priority. Is anything wrong?"

"What's wrong is that you're there and I'm here. Can you come?"

"With wings of eagles...or a taxi. I'll ask Reggie and Gran to bring Abigail to lunch."

"Hurry."

On the way to the Fairmont, I thought of the chance encounter that had brought me to this moment. It was a hand dealt by fate, or a plan by God to save a little girl, depending on one's perspective. I believed this morning's encounter, not by chance, would begin the direction of the rest of my life.

She was waiting for me as I came into the front entrance; a vision of loveliness in a blue cashmere sweater and tweed skirt, just as she was dressed the first time I saw her.

She rushed into my arms, almost knocking me down. We kissed with a passion far, far from the brotherly restraint I had used in the past. Other patrons passing by in the magnificent lobby smiled as us, perhaps wondering what story lay behind our meeting. I was consumed by the clean scent of her and dazzled again by her emerald eyes and her golden hair.

"You're my hero, my knight in shining armor," she whispered.

"I'm not, but it's good to hear. And I love you with all my heart. There, I hope I've waited long enough."

"Time now has no meaning."

We found a quiet corner couch away from the crowd, and sat as close together as public decorum allowed. She held my hand and told me her story; the trauma of their capture, the fear for Abigail's safety, the indignity of confinement. She knew we'd try to find them, but never heard from Dickerson what he hoped to accomplish. She had lost track of time.

Her narrative lasted for perhaps an hour; then she wanted to hear from me. She was delighted by the transponder idea. "It really worked," I said. "As a matter of fact, Gully may be checking my whereabouts at this very moment."

She laughed. "Maybe we'll just keep that, and I can learn how to use it. When you get the cast off, you could wear a collar."

It was great seeing her sparkle return after the way she was last night. "I must caution you not to mention the transponder to anyone. We decided not to tell the FBI and police because we were afraid they'd step all over everything. They wouldn't like it now, if they knew."

I finished telling her the rest of the events of the night before and of my conversation with Dickerson before the dramatic moment he shot himself.

"He struck me as weird, probably mentally unbalanced. He seemed batty to me, anyway…which brings me to another subject. Did Abigail know it was her father?"

"She must have, but they separated us."

"We have to tell Abigail what happened to her parents, somehow."

"I'll talk with other counselors at the office. We'll come up with a plan."

"Good. And another thing; it's not fair to the Eppersons that she continues to stay with us. We'd love it, but it's probably best if she goes back to them until the rest of this mess is untangled." I told her of the appointments with the FBI and police and made a quick call to Julia to tell her about them.

Her parents came down and found us in our corner. We rose as they approached. Her mother rushed straight to me and enveloped me in an embrace. "Gideon, thank you, thank you for bringing her back to me."

"I had help, but it was for me, also. I told you how I felt."

"Have you told her?"

"Yes."

She released me and Geoffrey O'Quinn stepped forward and clasped my hand in both of his saying, "I'll be forever grateful to you."

O'Quinn had hired a Lincoln Town Car to take us to the restaurant over on Mission Street near the Bay. We were a little early and were escorted to a private table set for nine. Gran and Reggie arrived next with Abigail. She came bounding into the room and went first to Grace to give her a hug, then bouncing to me for the same, exclaiming in turn, "Grace!" then "Kitty!" She surveyed the table, going to the side with three chairs. Pointing the center one, she said, "I'm gonna sit right here, and Grace you'll sit here and Kitty will sit here," placing us on either side of her. I apologized quietly to the Eppersons who had arrived as she was making the arrangements.

Wilma smiled. "It's okay. We understand, especially with what she's been through."

To Abigail's credit, she came around the table and gave them each a hug.

Dr. Luttrell and assistant Stephanie were absent and not mentioned.

We had a joyous and wonderful lunch, with champagne toasts and best wishes passed around. Abigail basked in the attention from the circle of adults, but was more subdued than I expected. Perhaps she correctly worried about the outcome of everything that had happened to her.

When we broke up to go our separate ways, Mina O'Quinn came to hug me and say goodbye. She kissed me on the cheek and said, "I assume we'll be seeing you again?"

"If it's up to me, for the rest of our lives."

We scattered like a covey of quail: Gran and Reggie back to the condo; Geoffrey and Mina to the hotel and airport; Clifford to go to work; Wilma to shepherd Abigail through her interview with the FBI; and Grace and I also to the FBI.

Grace volunteered to me that she would talk to Abigail about the FBI and the reasons she'd be going back to be with the Eppersons for now. She took Abigail aside and sat with her on her lap, talking quietly.

Abigail shook her head and wiped tears from her eyes. Grace hugged her and kept whispering to her and finally Abigail nodded her head.

Four of us shared a cab to FBI headquarters, where we were ushered to the same conference room near Scott's office. There we were separated for our interviews into smaller rooms. Abigail and Grace each were to go with female FBI agents. Not much was expected from Abigail's testimony so the police skipped that one. Wilma Epperson went with her. Detective Peak accompanied Grace, so San Francisco's finest would be involved. My deposition attracted a larger crowd: Special Agents Scott and Liggett, Lieutenant Haney, Julia Mangini, and a stenographer with one of those machines court reporters use.

It began as a formal session with Scott speaking the names of all present and the purpose of the session. I was asked to state my name and address, and we began.

It was to last all afternoon, with only a short break after two hours. I'd brought a small notebook that I'd used for my own investigation and they had my logbook. We ground through everything over the past weeks. Julia was there to give me advice, but nothing seemed to go in that direction. They began with the most recent events, particularly the second-hand statements of Dickerson before he shot himself. They'd interrogated Gully and Vince during the morning, so seemed satisfied that forensics and testimony proved he shot himself. Dickerson's words focused on the role of his parents, so we skipped to my notes on my encounter with them. Scott volunteered that FBI agents were talking with them again as we spoke.

That led to a discussion of DeeDee Marshall. It seemed to me that she was overly interested in what I knew, and her apartment seemed richer than her station in life. Dickerson used the word "we" when talking of his plans. His denial that he shot Richie carried little weight, but raised questions. Haney volunteered that Richie was killed with the same gun Dickerson used on himself, but the firing pin signatures didn't match the shell casings from the yacht. Marshall was being addressed, but Haney volunteered no other details.

Someplace out there were others, perhaps only temporary hires, who had helped with the abduction. Police were on the streets looking, Haney said.

My talk with Richie's ex-wife was of little interest, as was my discovery of the yacht. Blowing up the cigarette boat and its crew would have been easy, Haney speculated. "It 'ud be easy to plug the vents in the engine compartment, then trigger a spark with a cell-phone device," he said.

"Sounds like you've seen it before, or thought about doing it," I said. He just smiled. I was amazed that my deposition began to sound more like a brain-storming session. It was finally over, with the stipulation that they might want to talk to me again. I would probably be called to testify when anyone would be brought to trial.

"Two requests," I said. "I'd like my money back and the boats released so they can be reconditioned. How about it?"

Haney and Scott looked at each other. Scott said, "We'll work with the DA on both counts. I don't see the value of either as physical evidence in a courtroom."

When we were ushered out, I was surprised to find Grace sitting in a small waiting room downstairs. It was almost six o'clock and she should have been long gone.

Julia glanced at Grace and said, "I'll see you soon." I thanked Julia and she left.

"Grace, what are you doing here so late?"

"Waiting for you." She rose and came to me, putting her arms around me. The young FBI agent nodded and left, since we were outside the secure areas.

"You must be tired, my love."

"That's why I waited. I don't want to go home alone."

# CHAPTER 38

Throughout November and December, events on the case had proceeded in an orderly fashion, but with the expected sluggish pace of investigations. DeeDee Marshall had a trial date set in February. Julia came up one evening and filled me in on Marshall's interrogation by the police after getting the inside story from her new boyfriend Greg Peak. Gran and Reggie were invited to join us.

Julia began her narrative. "Greg got to be in a viewing room as Haney and some female FBI agents went at her. Other police and FBI, including Scott, were watching also.

"He said it was great theater. We're not supposed to know even this much, but he hit the highlights. They didn't tell her at first that Dickerson was dead. She said, 'I'm babysitting for a friend. I know nothing about any kidnapping, for crying out loud.' Once they got her talking, Haney, the 'bad cop' waded in with the news flash that her boyfriend Brad was dead."

"I bet that was something to see!"

"It was. Then he hit her with the news that Brad left a suicide note in which he laid out the whole scheme; held up a piece of paper saying 'sorry, sister, there ain't gonna be any tropic isle.' Greg said Haney read to her from the so-called note and said it was a thing of beauty."

"Wow," said Gran. "Then what?"

"She lawyered-up, but it was all over, especially when Haney claimed the fake suicide note said she'd killed Richie."

"Did they have any proof of that?"

"No, but it was enough. Police can lie, you know. Anyway, she pleabargained to twenty-to-life and will go before a judge for confirmation at that trial date."

"Not a bad result," said Reggie.

"Did she open up after the bargain?" I asked.

"Yes. Apparently she knew Bradley was back before you talked to her the first time. She wanted to find out what you knew. He'd been giving her money long before the Dickersons sailed away. She wouldn't admit to knowing what Brad had in mind, just that he'd 'fix things.'

"And by the way, Greg says the FBI are convinced the armored car thing was complete coincidence after they'd gathered all the evidence."

*December 31, 1999*: The senior Dickersons were scheduled before an upcoming grand jury after the FBI had unraveled all the financial and phone records of dealings with their son. Both boats were in the yard being refitted, and my bag of money had been returned. I surprised Vincent Jacob with a wad of cash and used the remainder for Gully, setting up a series of payments to avoid large tax penalties for him.

Gran and Reggie rescheduled their world travels, agreeing to wait until the New Year. My cast was removed to disclose a withered white limb, but it was coming around after some painful physical therapy. Maybe some elbow-bending on New Year's Eve would help.

My custody application for Abigail was approved after a coroner's inquest ruled her mother deceased. It was to take effect in January. The hearing brought together testimonials from my past and statements from Grace, the Eppersons, Gran and Reggie, and Julia. I had in hand the certified document from her paternal grandparents, giving up all rights. Life was good.

*Chelsey's* is not a very large restaurant, but my favorite, with wonderful food and service and a great location overlooking the Bay, perfect for a New Year's Eve celebration. My friend, the owner, agreed in November to let me hire it out for the evening for a private party. I insisted on a generous payment, more than she could expect from the public. It was worth it to me for what I had in mind.

Grace and I agreed to avoid openly living together over the past couple of months, but were together at every opportunity. Being with her was everything I dreamed it would be, to echo Tony Bennett's "Young and Warm and Wonderful." I was confident what her answer would be, and there could be little doubt on her part what my intentions were. Too many long conversations about life and the future had taken place for it to be otherwise.

Marta had her restaurant at its best: candlelight, flowers, and tasteful New Year's decorations. Ice buckets of champagne were much in evidence. She'd arranged all the tables into a large square with crisp white tablecloths. Geoffrey and Mina O'Quinn had honored us by giving up Hollywood to be with us. Grace's sister was in France, so could not attend. Gully surprised me by bringing a date. She was petite and muscular, a gymnastics coach with her own studio.

Julia Mangini and Greg Peak arrived intertwined. The Eppersons brought Abigail and their two children at my invitation. And, of course, Gran and Reggie were there. We planned for a long evening, starting at eight with a cocktail hour for everyone to circulate and get better acquainted. Gran was the life of the party in a long green gown, lavishing attention on everyone as she worked the room, large martini in hand.

At the end of the fantastic meal of standing rib roast and roast chicken for the children, it was time for me to face a grand moment. I stood and began as the conversation died.

"Ladies and Gentlemen, boy and girls, thank you for honoring us by being here. Nineteen-ninety-nine was a hectic year for me but the best year of my life. A chance encounter allowed me to fall in love twice, and in each case, love that I hope will last my lifetime."

Abigail was beaming at me and Grace was wiping away tears.

"As all of you know, Abigail is to become my ward and I hope my adopted daughter—"

Applause erupted. Abigail jumped up and hugged me.

"Thank you. And now to Grace. I ask myself over and over how I could be so lucky to walk into that office and come face to face with someone so wonderful. I knew it, I knew it, I knew it from that first moment. Since then, there were trials to face and obstacles to overcome. But now here we are."

I took her hand and she rose to face me. "Grace O'Quinn, I love you with all my heart and I want to spend the rest of my life with you." I knelt and looked up at her. "Will you marry me?"

"We'll see!" piped a small voice and there was general laughter.

I rose. "Abigail, shame on you!" I couldn't help my own amusement as I explained. "Abigail says that's the standard answer when a little kid asks for something. Well, this is not the time for that...I hope." More laughter.

Back down on my knees, I asked. "Would you like me to repeat the question?"

Smiling, she said, "I think I got it, but it wouldn't hurt to hear it again."

"Grace, I love you with all my heart. Will you marry me?"

"Yes, yes, yes!"

I rose and took her in my arms to more applause, including from all the restaurant staff, who had gathered at one end of the room.

"Oh, there's one more thing." I took the ring box from my coat pocket. "I hope this is suitable."

"Oh, wow! It's beautiful," she said.


We all watched the turn of the clock as we entered a new century and a new life for me, a life I could not dream of only months before. The dire predictions about computers and the New Year proved to be false. A few tweaks here and there were sufficient to avoid any problems from Year Two Thousand, Y2K.

# CHAPTER 39

*July, 2000*: Jemima perched on the front of the coach roof, aglow in the light of the rising sun, waiting to pounce on any living thing that arrived on deck. Hunting wasn't as good since I'd had safety netting installed all the way round the deck from lifelines to toe rail. Now and then a leaping baitfish would make her day. She considered it worth the effort, despite occasional spray from the rise and fall of bow meeting wave.

A head of curly dark hair appeared in the companionway, brown eyes peeping over the lower hatch-board. Then the owner of our vessel stood up and smiled at me, a smile that made my life worthwhile. Abigail jumped over the board, onto the deck and ran into my arms.

"Kittee!"

"Good morning Sweetheart. Are you ready for breakfast?"

"Ye-s-s. Can I have Spagetti-Os?"

"*May* I have Spagetti-Os. No, not for breakfast. If you want Os, how about Cheerios?"

"'Kay. Can…uh, may I wake up Grace?"

"No, she had a night watch, so she gets to sleep a couple more hours."

"I want her to play with me."

"Not before she gets her sleep. Then she will play with you, and you get to do your school work."

"When can we see Great-Gran so she can play with me?"

"Remember I told you that she and 'Sarge,' as you call him, will meet us in Fiji. It'll be a couple of weeks yet."

"When will we get to Mama's memorial place?"

"It should be today, Sweetheart."

"It's sad when I think about her. I wish I could see her."

"Yes, it is, Sweetie. All we can do now is always remember her and keep her in our hearts."

At two-thirty in the afternoon we arrived at the GPS coordinates corresponding to my plot of weeks ago when I encountered the abandoned yacht. There was simply no way to pinpoint the exact spot where the tragedy occurred, but it was close enough for our purposes. I furled all the sails and put out a stabilizing sea anchor to slow our drift. Grace had awakened earlier and fixed our lunch. Now the three of us gathered in the cockpit. I took Abigail on my lap to explain to her what we were about to do.

"Sweetheart, have you ever been to church? Did your mother talk to you about God?"

"We didn't go to church because Daddy didn't want us to, but Mama told me there was a God up above who lived in a place called Heaven."

"That's good. When we get back to California, we can see about going to church to learn more. For now, when I was little we learned to believe that when we die we will go to heaven to be with God. I hope and believe that's where your mother is right now and that we'll see her again someday."

"When we die?"

"Yes. Until then, we'll be together here and we'll keep remembering her. So right now, we plan to have a little memorial to her near the spot where she was last alive. I had a bronze plaque cast with her name, which we'll leave at this spot."

I unwrapped it for her to see and read it to her. "It says, 'Solene Grebo Dickerson's soul departed on this spot October, 1999. She is the beloved mother of Abigail, San Francisco, California.' Sit here and you can hold it on your lap. It's heavy. I'll read a few words from the Bible."

This was something I'd never done, but the occasion called for words to be read. Grace was looking at me with tears in her eyes; Abigail looked solemn, trying to understand. "I'm going to read a very famous psalm from the Bible. A psalm is like a poem, talking to God, who we also call Lord. I'll change the wording a little to make it easier to understand, but we can talk about it again. It's the twenty-third Psalm:

The Lord is my shepherd; He gives everything I need

He makes me lie down in green pastures; He leads me beside quiet waters.

He restores my soul.

He guides me in the proper way for me to live my life, for his name's sake.

Even if I walk through scary places, I won't be afraid.

For you are with me, God; your power and strength will comfort me.

You will prepare a table for me in the presence of my enemies.

You have anointed my head with oil and have filled my cup.

Surely your loving-kindness and mercy shall follow me all the days of my life; and I will live in the house of the Lord forever.

"Did you like it?"

She nodded solemnly and Grace was smiling through her tears.

"Okay, we'll say one more little prayer and you and Grace can drop the plaque over the side. I have a towel laid across the deck on the side there." We got them in position and I read modified words I'd found in a Lutheran book before we left:

"Let's bow our heads.

"In sure and certain hope of the resurrection of eternal life through our Lord Jesus Christ, we commend to almighty God our sister Solene and we commit her body to the deep. The Lord bless her and keep her. The Lord make his face shine on her and be gracious to her. The Lord look upon her with favor and give her peace. Amen."

I nodded my head and there was a splash as Grace helped Abigail release the plaque over the side. Then there was silence. They turned to me. I picked Abigail up in my arms, and Grace embraced us both for a long moment.

We retrieved the sea anchor, hoisted our sails, and set our course for the South Pacific and the rest of our lives together.

# EPILOGUE

*pril, 2014*: I sat in my office in the corner turret of our Victorian house. Windows on three sides presented spectacular views over the vineyards climbing the slopes that surrounded our home. We'd found this jewel of a vineyard in Sonoma County soon after our return from the South Pacific early in 2001. Grace was then expecting our first child together and our dreams were to live a life in the country.

The former owners had the same dream, but had invested heavily in non-productive assets: this beautiful house, a guest house, a stable, and other enhancements. Unfortunately, not enough attention was paid to the vineyards. It was perfect for us. I immediately hired the best vintner I could find, a Frenchman in his sixties. With his expertise and my willingness to invest, by the fifth year we were turning a profit.

Our main focus has been on our family. That first child, a son, was followed three years later by a daughter, a beautiful little duplicate of Grace.

As I had these thoughts, I saw a red Subaru Forrester come up the lane and wheel into the circular drive. I dashed downstairs and embraced my first daughter as she burst in the front door.

"Dad, you're squeezin' the life out of me!" she giggled

"I haven't seen you for a *month*. What do you expect?"

Abigail was finishing her first year at Stanford on a track and basketball scholarship and was home for the summer. Grace's home schooling and Abigail's dedication fast-tracked her into advanced courses. We were proud of her.

"Where're Mom and the kids?"

"What Moms do. Geoff's at soccer practice and Elizabeth's at her dance class. They'll all be home for lunch. I'll help you unload your stuff."

Gran and Reggie had finished their world travels and agreed to settle in the guest house as long as their health allowed. Their presence and devotion added richness to our lives.

As for me, life is good. Every day I awake giving thanks for having Grace beside me, and my beautiful family.

I often marvel at the little things that have monumental effect on our lives. A little change in wind direction out in the vastness of the Pacific, and a chance encounter gave me everything.

END

**R**oger Meadows is the author of *A CHANCE ENCOUNTER* and a prior suspense novel, *HANGMAN, A Deadly Game*. After college and a tour as an Army aviator, he began a career in industry, completing graduate school along the way. He conducted business throughout the world, dealing with many cultures.

He has written dozens of essays and short stories, and edited the works of other writers. He has participated in writers' groups in Spartanburg, Greenville, and Hilton Head, South Carolina; and Knoxville, Tennessee. He and his wife, Wanda, are members of the local chapter of Sisters in Crime.

Mr. Meadows enjoys reading, sailing, kayaking, travel, and wooden boat building. He and his wife live in the Upstate of South Carolina. They have three adult children and two grandchildren. He welcomes your comments to him at RDM730@aol.com.

Made in the USA
Charleston, SC
15 March 2015